MORALITY
Book One

Where Have All the Young Men Gone?

Casey Dorman

Avignon Press
Newport Beach

Cover western Libya, part of the Sahara. Photo by Luca Galuzzi (http:// Image: Leaving traces on soft sand dunes in Tadrart Acacus desert in www.galuzzi.it/). Subject to GNU free distribution license.

Dorman, Casey, Morality: Book One—Where Have All The Young Men Gone? Fiction—Terrorism—Politics—Satire

ISBN: 978-0615885537

Avignon Press
Newport Beach, California, USA

Books by Casey Dorman

Pink Carnation
I, Carlos
Chasing Tales
Unquity
Prisoner's Dilemma: The Deadliest Game
Fermentation: Short Stories and Poems About Aging
Appointment in Mykonos: A Brian O'Reilly Cruise Ship Mystery

To My Wife, Lai

Morality (Merriam-Webster Dictionary)
1. beliefs about what is right behavior and what is wrong behavior

2. the degree to which something is right and good : the moral goodness or badness of something

Prologue

Mogadishu, Somalia

A gusty dry wind swept dirty scraps of paper into the air, sending them cartwheeling like leaves down the filthy street until they were lost among the cigarette butts, animal waste and crumbled bits of asphalt, which constituted the remains of the ruined road. There were no signs of the usual press of beggars, whores, soldiers, street-peddlers and urchins who made up the teeming wasteland of Mogadishu by day. Word had spread among the masses of poor and desperate who lived in this section of the city that something special was about to happen here tonight—something dangerous.

On the deserted street, lit by a single streetlamp, its weak light filtered through overhanging tree limbs whose long shadows danced like primitive stick figures around the doorways of devastated buildings, a lone man emerged, his back as straight as a majestic Jackalberry, his pace slow and measured. Although he was only an inch above six feet tall, he gave the impression of greater stature.

His destination was the tiny patch of dirt that formed the intersection of this street with two others, angling in obliquely from the north and east like a three-sided star. As he passed the narrow alleys that snaked between the buildings on either side of him, curious faces peeked out, then followed a cautious twenty yards behind, their numbers gradually swelling into hundreds as they fell into step behind him until he stopped in the center of the square.

Robert N'gomo was a legend, and most of those in the crowd had never been sure whether the spiritual leader was a reality or a myth. Mothers held up their babies for a better view while young couples grasped each others' hands in eager anticipation. Young men with shiny, black automatic weapons took up positions of defense on the fringe of the crowd.

Robert N'gomo held up his hands to silence the murmurings. His eyes were bright, radiating hope, but when his gaze fell upon the men with guns it was as if a cloud had swept across his face. "We do not need guns. I want no one killed in my name," he said, his voice booming out over the masses in the square.

The young men at the edge of the crowd looked at each other, then one of them shrugged and muttered something to his companions and they turned to leave.

"No, stay! Just put your guns down. My message is for you, too—especially for you." Though his words were inviting, his tone was commanding.

Like obedient children, the men laid their guns down on the street and remained in place. The crowd murmured in fear.

N'gomo gazed across the tops of their heads. His expression was tired, and he heaved a long sigh before he continued. "For almost forty years people have been trying to kill me, but here I am in front of you tonight. I have walked across the continent of Africa, defying governments, tribal chiefs, and gang leaders. I have been imprisoned, tortured and sentenced to death. But I have never ceased to try to understand and love my persecutors and I always survived while those around me, those who chose to express their defiance with violence, are all dead. I ask you to follow my example."

"If we do not fight we will be slaughtered," a woman whose face was covered in a black shroud, shouted.

"If you live without violence your enemies will be powerless against you" he answered.

The crowd murmured. The speaker was not saying what they had hoped to hear. They wished for a leader who would help them rise up against their repressive masters and war lords.

From the edges of the crowd there were more shouts and then cries of alarm. "The militia is coming!" The young men with guns snatched them from the ground and swung them toward the streets leading into the square. In the distance, shadows moved between buildings, the growl of jeeps and pickup trucks could be heard, like the ominous roar of a pack of wild animals, above the voices in the crowd.

"We are doing nothing wrong," N'gomo reassured the crowd, his voice booming out above the others. "Put down your guns."

The men at the periphery had taken up positions behind the corners of buildings or behind cars parked on the street and they began to fire at the approaching soldiers. The soldiers returned fire, scattering the crowd, who ran screaming in the opposite direction. Some in the crowd pulled out weapons of their own and began firing back at the soldiers. Soon bullets were falling amidst the remnants of the crowd and the slower to disperse—a pregnant woman who lumbered toward the shelter of an open door and an old man who dragged one stroke-disabled leg—were being hit. Screams could be heard from the fallen victims. The pregnant woman writhed in agony on the dusty ground while the old man twitched wordlessly, then stopped moving. Everyone who was able to move ran from the square.

In the center of the square, Robert N'gomo gave up trying to speak to the crowd. No one was left to listen. Those who remained in the square were the young men with guns, firing furiously at the relentlessly approaching militia, who now were firing automatic weapons and rocket propelled grenades. The young men were dropping like flies. N'gomo shook his head and walked slowly across the square, bullets flying all around him but leaving him unscathed. Finally, as the militia entered the square, he disappeared behind a building.

Chapter 1

Although overcoming my habitual cynicism was an extraordinary occurrence, Derek Stewart's story had piqued my interest. As a professional writer, now tasked with generating feature stories for the only local rag that would hire me, I tended to express what was left of my literary talent by lashing out with reckless, though hopefully entertaining, abandon at whatever topic I was directed. Tom Edwards, my paper's editor, a man of infinite shallowness whose constipated narrow-mindedness was equaled only by his thick-witted arrogance, had assigned the story to me in order to keep me from writing a more serious feature which might provoke a backlash against his notoriously conservative paper.

Need I say that these recent years were not the best of times for a writer who had based his aspirations on the freedom of expression he had thought was a bulwark of American democracy? Freedom of the press was a concept that had gone by the wayside along with the suspension of most of the other freedoms I and everyone else my age had grown up to expect to enjoy. Unfortunately, I was one of only a few who continued to complain about it. My editors felt that Stewart's story was a safe one—in other words, one that I couldn't screw up even if I tried. And one more screw-up would be my last. The paper had made that perfectly clear to me.

Although Stewart's story, given the remarkable tale it had to tell, would make the front page, its selling point, if it had one, was going to be the human interest side of Stewart's tale, the side which could cause no harm to anyone and especially not to the newspaper that reported it. Or at least that's what my weak-spined editor thought when he gave me my assignment.

If you're wondering why I was working for a conservative tabloid like the Washington Times, the answer was that I needed the money. My alternative would have been to join the staff of one of those tiny upstart, radical publications, most of them no more than internet blogs and none of them surviving more than a few months before the Federal Immigration Investigation

Enforcement Bureau, the FIIEB, known colloquially as the "Feebs," Homeland Security's newly created domestic anti-terrorism agency, threw them in jail or, if they were not born in America, had them deported

Besides, I'm a biographer not a lowly journalist.

Unfortunately, I'm persona non grata in the book publishing world due to an incident in which I squandered the advance on a book I was contracted to write but never got around to writing and the subsequent, inebriated tongue-lashing I gave the publisher when he demanded I return his money. My argument was that I had done the publisher a favor by never completing a book that government censors would have edited into platitudinal mediocrity. The job with the Times was my last-ditch effort to keep bread on the table while I tried to convince the book publishing world that I wasn't the drunken, cynical has-been writer that they thought I was. Which brings me back to the story I was assigned to write on Derek Stewart.

I had done a piece on Stewart about five years earlier, when I was still flush enough from my last book sale to be working freelance. Derek Stewart was the celebrated last U.S. victim of the Vietnam war—the last American soldier to be wounded before the U.S. troop pullout two years before the North Vietnamese finally overran Saigon and the South Vietnamese government, its leaders scampering like rats from a sinking ship, their suitcases filled with cash, capitulated. What made the story interesting to me was the man's condition. Derek Stewart had been in a coma since April, 1973.

I remember that I'd expected something creepy when I'd arrived at St. Elizabeth's for that interview five years ago—a cadaverous body with a small factory's worth of hardware wired to it, the ghostly sound of breathing machines providing a constant background to the solemn ministrations of overweight nurses creeping back and forth in squeaky, rubber soled shoes as they checked to see if anyone remained at home within the silent patient's emaciated body. I hadn't really wanted to go to the hospital at all—I mean how many pithy quotations was I going to get from a guy in a coma? Besides, the first person, heartstringtugging, description of someone whose quality of life had become similar to that of a turnip, wasn't exactly fodder for my caustic writing style. But Billy Lamb, my photographer, who had visited the comatose soldier to snap some preliminary pictures, had informed me that I'd be surprised by Stewart's condition—surprised enough that I might want to talk about it in the story. So there I was, entering a room occupied by a man who, at that time, had been asleep for thirty-five years.

What had impressed me when I'd entered Stewart's room was the hushed silence. Then I'd seen Stewart and I had understood. His face had this beatific expression on it, as if he had his eyes closed and was listening to a wonderful and calming message that the rest of us were unable to hear. Even more remarkably, he didn't look at all like the nearly fifty-five-year old man he must have been. He looked as if he was still in his twenties.

"We have seen this in a few other long-term coma cases," explained the young East Asian neurologist, Doctor Anwar Bhottu, in that peculiar Eastern way of appearing both subservient and patronizing at the same time. He was a head shorter than myself and wider and softer, although there was something solid about him. His expression had been resolutely serious. At age 31, he had been rumored to be the next Chief of Service at the Bethesda Naval Hospital's famed neurological unit, where the most unusual and exotic service-related brain injury cases were transferred from Walter Reed and the other service hospitals. "It's as if living without any stress is a protection against visible aging," the doctor had continued. "In fact, most of his body is still just like a twenty to thirty year old's."

"But why doesn't he just waste away?" I had asked, looking around the antiseptically white room, the shiny machines with their dials flashing on screens etched with measurements of God knows what. I felt as if I were in a spacecraft looking at a passenger who was in suspended animation during an interstellar flight.

"He gets more exercise than either you or I do," the sober young doctor had told me. I had wondered if my middle-aged, neglected body was more revealing of my dissipated lifestyle than I'd thought it was. He'd glanced at the door and a large black man had nodded at him. "That's Josh Mannerly, one of Stewart's physical therapists—he has two—they've been with him for more than ten years. They exercise him night and day, every day. Of course it's passive exercise, so he isn't muscular, but he's not wasted away and his body is in excellent shape, considering his condition."

"What's the point?" I'd asked. "He's pretty much a vegetable isn't he?" I might as well have reached over and jerked out Stewart's feeding tube, given the way Mannerly had looked at me. I'd later found out that Mannerly was an ex-pro football player, who had been sidelined by bad knees. Mannerly still worked out every day and, although his knees prevented him from sprinting as fast as he'd used to, he was at least as strong as he'd been during the height of his playing years. And his hostile glare in my direction had been a warning that he might not be beyond using his strength to teach me to curb my tongue.

Dr. Bhottu had more politely managed to conceal his distaste at my comment. "We have to treat the patient as if he might still wake up. It's not unheard of."

"Really?" I'd done my homework and I'd known that almost no one woke up from a coma after more than a few years. There had been scattered reports, of course, such as the case of Terry Wallis, who'd emerged from his coma after 20 years, but that was the longest I'd been able to find.

"You mean like Terry Wallis?" I'd asked, letting him know that he wasn't talking to some uninformed country bumpkin.

The good doctor had nodded in assent, though he'd seemed unimpressed by my display of medical knowledge. "Stewart is in a similar condition to Wallis. It's what we call a *minimally conscious state*—not really a coma in the classic sense because there is some indication of awareness of his surroundings."

"That's why the hushed atmosphere?" I'd asked.

"Exactly. You've come during one of Stewart's sleeping times but there are other times when his eyes are open. He seems to respond non-randomly to sounds and movements around him. He shows pleasure when Josh changes his position."

Josh would have had to be a lot better looking and wearing a dress before I'd have shown pleasure at having him change my position. "Can he communicate?"

Bhottu had taken a deep breath and shaken his head. "We've had no luck getting him to communicate with us—not even eyeblinks or head nods. If I had to describe what's going on when we try to talk to him, I'd say he's just not paying attention to us."

The doctor's manner had been boring enough that I might not have paid attention either. "Because he can't?"

"I don't know. It's almost as if he's preoccupied with something else."

Doing his income taxes, writing the great American novel in his head? "So what makes you think he could change—wake up more completely?"

"Two things, really. First, Stewart's injury is to his brainstem. He has less cortical damage—damage to the thinking part of his brain—than almost any recorded case of this kind of coma. And second, Terry Wallis' case has shown us that the brain can reorganize itself—even after decades."

"Do you mean the 'rewiring' that they talked about with Wallis?" I had been showing off again.

Dr. Bhottu had given me a look like I was a smartass student who had just raised his hand in class to tell the teacher that 'fornicate' was just a polite word for 'fuck'". "We don't like to use that term," he'd said, disapproval lacing his well-mannered tone. "What appeared to happen with Wallis' brain was that the brain cells that were intact grew new axonal branches. The new branches didn't follow the old pathways, which were damaged and didn't have enough white matter left to support them. The clearest case was with regard to the connections between the two halves of Wallis' brain—the corpus collosum. Wallis' corpus collosum was severely damaged. What happened was that the cortical cells that were destined to connect the two halves of his brain by crossing the corpus callosum, took a different route and grew around the back of his brain. They achieved a similar functional outcome using a different anatomical pathway."

It had sounded like re-wiring to me. "And you think that could happen with Stewart?"

"We don't know."

Why did doctors always use the imperial "we"?

"Are you doing brain scans to detect if it's happening?"

Bhottu had nodded but hadn't said anything.

"And…?"

The young doctor had looked me in the eyes, his expression had hardened. "If you want to know, it will have to be off the record."

"Why?" Guarantees by reporters that comments would remain off the record were notoriously meaningless, but Bhottu hadn't known that.

Bhottu had looked at me and continued. "Terry Wallis' case became hopelessly distorted by reports to the media that were misinterpreted by both the press and the public. I don't want to start the same kind of pop-neurology frenzy with Stewart's case. It would serve no purpose and ruin my academic reputation."

A sensational story about miraculous brain rewiring might have hurt the doctor's career, but it could have done nothing but help mine. The public loved scientific speculation even more than real science. On the other hand, I had kept what vestiges of self-respect I still had by sticking to the truth in everything I wrote, usually to the displeasure of others. I'd agreed to keep what he told me out of the story.

"Stewart's brain has reorganized itself to a degree I would have thought impossible," Bhottu had begun. "The areas that have experienced the greatest growth of neural connections are those related to completely intact parts of the cortex—areas such as the parietal and temporal lobes, the hippocampus and parts of the pre-frontal cortex."

"What do those parts of the brain do?" I'd asked. He'd reached a level of technical detail at which I'd been clueless.

"They serve language, visualization, planning and memory."

"Everything needed to think," I said. "So what's going on?"

"It's as if instead of growing new axons that might allow him to wake up, or move his limbs, or even talk, Stewart's brain is concentrating solely on thinking—or maybe dreaming."

"And is his brain still reorganizing?"

"That's one of our problems and one of the reasons I haven't brought any of these findings out into the scientific literature. Until Wallis' case came along it hadn't occurred to anyone to do any serious brain imaging with a comatose patient such as Stewart. When he was first injured we didn't have the technology, and after that we assumed his brain was static, so we did an MRI every once in a while but not the kind of sophisticated studies that would show us reorganization if it was happening. After Wallis' case we started doing more in-depth studies and found what I told you. But the truth is, we have no proof that his brain wasn't like that before he ever was injured."

"So if he's thinking—and I'm saying *if*—is that something you can detect?"

"Oh he's thinking," Bhottu had said, his face still as solemn as ever, though, to my lay ears, he'd been conveying startling news. "He's an active dreamer. In fact, he seems to enter periods in which his EEG is much more like someone doing math or reading a book than being in a dream state."

Had I been right about his doing income taxes or writing a novel in his head? "You mean he's doing calculus in his head while he lies there asleep?" I'd had visions of Stewart waking up and shouting "the derivative of a constant function is zero!"

The young doctor had been unable to conceal a frown. "I doubt that he's actually performing mathematical proofs, but his mind is very active. What he's thinking about—if anything—we'll never know unless he wakes up."

"He looks as if he's awake now," I'd said. I had glanced back at Stewart's motionless form in the bed and, to my shock, had seen that his eyes were now open. He was staring straight up at the ceiling. The expression on his face had turned from blissful to pained.

Dr. Bhottu had moved closer to Stewart's bed, but Josh Mannerly had been at the patient's side almost immediately.

"I think he wants to be moved," Josh had said to the physician.

"Go ahead," Bhottu had replied.

Mannerly had pulled the sheets away from Stewart's body, and I'd been able to see that his legs were thin as saplings. In fact his whole body was thin, though not emaciated. He wore a diaper-like garment around his hips, and with his dark skin, he reminded me of pictures of Mahatma Gandhi. The physical therapist had begun to shift his legs, first gently bending them at the knees several times, then laying them back down in a different position than before. He repeated the procedure with Stewart's stick-like arms. As I carefully watched his face, Stewart's expression had changed from one of discomfort to one of contentment.

"I see what you mean," I'd said to the doctor. "There's no denying that he's aware of the change in position."

Bhottu had nodded. "I will try to get his attention."

The neurologist had bent over the patient's head and had stared into his eyes.

I'd thought I'd detected a slight smile cross Stewart's face.

"Can you hear me, Mr. Stewart? If you hear me please nod your head or blink your eyes." Bhottu asked.

Stewart made no response.

"I see what you mean," I'd said. "He looks preoccupied, as if he's too busy thinking about something else. But what could he be thinking about?"

"We'll never know unless he wakes up and tells us ," the doctor had answered.

And now, five years later, Derek Stewart had awakened.

Chapter 2

The neurology ward at the naval hospital hadn't changed in the five years since I'd last visited, except that the floor was crowded with reporters and I hadn't seen so many physicians in one place since the last time I'd visited a Mercedes Benz dealership. I recognized Dr. Anwar Bhottu, He was clearly the one giving most of the orders to the other staff in white coats, so I figured he must have gotten promoted since I had last been there. Over Dr. Bhottu's shoulder, I caught a glimpse of Josh Mannerly, the massive physical therapist whom I'd seen during my earlier visit. He hadn't changed much, except he looked even angrier and more threatening now than he had back then. He was talking to a petite Asian woman, who seemed as if she was trying to calm him down.

I pushed my way toward the front of the crowd of reporters and camera people. Being a cutthroat lot, they weren't eager to let me get to the head of the line, but they grudgingly moved aside when it looked as if they would have to mount physical opposition if they wanted to stop me. When I got to the front, I was stopped by a pair of stone-faced, crew-cut men in dark glasses and earphones whom I recognized by their blank expressions as Feebs. Derek Stewart was a war hero, but I hadn't thought he'd merit such high-level government attention.

I waved a hand to signal Dr. Bhottu. I thought I saw a flicker of recognition on his face, but then he went back to his conversation with his colleagues. After giving one last order to the group around him, the neurologist strode toward the flock of reporters pressed together in the hallway like chickens at feeding time.

"I can't have this kind of disturbance on the unit," Dr. Bhottu said, speaking in the precise, clipped English that reflected his native India while he cast a severe look in the direction of the reporters. Flash cubes were popping and most of the video cameras were running. Reporters being reporters, no one paid any heed to the doctor's admonition and a flurry of questions was directed toward him, asking about Stewart's condition.

"I'm scheduling a full news update downstairs in the press conference room in another hour," Dr. Bhottu announced. "All I can say now is that Mr. Stewart has awakened from his coma and is in a confused state. We're not sedating him because we aren't sure that it's safe, given the condition of his central nervous system, but we're trying to keep his environment quiet, dark and with a little stimulation as possible. That's why all of you have to leave right now."

"Is he able to speak?" I asked, hoping my question could be heard above the shouting from the gaggle of reporters behind me.

Dr. Bhottu looked relieved to see a face he recognized. "He has spoken but only a single sentence so far," he said. "Good to see you, again Mr. Evangelista," he added. I guess my tersely factual story about Stewart five years earlier had won me points with the doctor, despite it's disappointing effect on my editors.

"What was the sentence?" I asked, greedily holding onto the doctor's attention now that it was directed my way.

Bhottu face broke into an uncharacteristic smile. "He said 'It's good to be back.'"

"That's it?" I asked.

"I'm afraid so." The neurologist looked past me at the others. "No more questions for now." He looked at the two government men, who nodded in the direction of the patient's room. "I'll see all of you downstairs in an hour."

I watched as Dr. Bhottu spoke briefly with the two government stooges then led them into Derek Stewart's room. It was clear to me that the government was going to get first crack at interviewing the newly awakened war hero, although why the Feebs or the Secret Service or whoever they were, were conducting the interview was a mystery to me.

I didn't really have much idea what Derek Stewart could say that would be of interest to my paper's readers, but the story itself, involving the last hero from the Vietnam war waking up after four decades, was bound to be receive a lot of attention. In fact Stewart himself, as I'd written in my first article about him five years ago, was a fascinating human interest story by himself. As I slipped into an empty hospital room and waited out my options, I thought about who he was, having meticulously described his background in my earlier article.

Derek Stewart was African-American, in the truest sense of the word. His features were a mixture of Caucasian and Negroid—his nose being more aquiline than broad but his lips full and his cheekbones high, and especially in his wizened state, very prominent. Even with a minimum of flesh on his bony features, he was a remarkably handsome black man. On the Caucasian side his immediate ancestors hailed from Massachusetts, from a family whose American origins dated back to the early 1600s.

Stewart's ancestors hadn't arrived on the Mayflower, but they must have caught the next ship out. Like so many of the early settlers, at least the ones who were not killed off by disease, starvation, or the New England winters, his family eventually amassed immense wealth, derived from centuries of prudent investments and ruthless business dealings in land, shipping, and manufacturing, not to mention disenfranchising all of the native Americans who had greeted them with turkeys, cranberries and open arms upon their arrival.

Following another American tradition, after wringing as much wealth as was possible from the labor of their fellow, but less fortunate, new world settlers, the family, in the person of Derek's grandfather Edwin Stewart, a captain of industry and a New England Brahmin, had turned their sights toward the third world and founded an investment firm that put together money for construction projects in Africa and the middle East, making it one of this country's first global businesses.

Derek's grandmother, Marian Baker, was a highly intellectual, but mystical woman from a very liberal New England family, which had been Christian Scientists, the esoteric Boston-based religion, most known for eschewing modern medicine (his great grandmother was a cousin to the religion's founder, Mary Baker Eddy). She also had been a devotee of the Theosophist movement, a group of deluded but mostly wealthy, Americans and Europeans who were waiting expectantly for a spiritual savior to appear in human form amongst them. Despite their personal wealth, most of the followers of the movement fervently hoped for a leader, a "great teacher" to guide the world away from its materialistic worship of power and money.

In the late 1920's the sect's first candidate for this honor, Jiddhu Krishnamurthi, forswore his title (and considerable riches that would have gone with it), leaving the position, which was also dubbed the Maitreya Buddha, and was supposed to be a leader to rival Christ, open to a future annointee. Marian, like most of the other members of her group, was humored by her tycoon husband, who judged that it was better that she dabble in a futile social cause than take up his valuable time actually paying attention to how he made the family's money.

The couple's one son, Richard Stewart, had been spoiled by both his mother and his father; his father making it clear to Richard that he was to inherit the family businesses and fortune, and his mother, when she was young, harboring a hope that her son might be the new age spiritual leader prophesied by her Theosophist teachings, but, as he grew older, realizing that, because of hers and her husband's indulgence, he was turning into a sociopath. Marian Stewart gradually grew to reject her son, though she loved him and didn't blame him for his blatant narcissism and lack of conscience. At 19, he was smart, good-looking, lived the privileged life, attended Harvard, where he was admitted on the basis of his family's donations, and drank and caroused with his friends.

In 1953 the Stewarts traveled to Africa's Gold Coast, in order for Edwin to oversee his mining investments. The area was in turmoil with the country's president, Kwame Nkrumah, agitating for independence from England, but nevertheless, the Stewarts, believing as did most Americans and Europeans who were in the country at the time, that they were above the daily happenings among the people, except to the degree they were able to manipulate them with their money, invited their son, Richard, to visit them during his winter break from Harvard.

Always an exception among the White business and diplomatic crowd within which she was expected to move, Mrs. Stewart was, despite the political turmoil going on around her, highly involved with the local residents, studying their mystical religion, which involved what could best be described as ancestor worship. In her commerce with the local African population, she had repeatedly run across portraits of a beautiful young African girl. The mystic painters never made clear whether this image belonged to a real person or was an archetype symbolizing purity, virginity, and innocence. Even after her son's arrival, Marian Stewart dedicated herself to finding this young girl, to see if she really existed, hoping, as she had with her son at one time, that the young virgin might represent a new savior, in female form, to rescue the human race from its descent into hostility, war and neglect of its suffering members.

While his father plundered the local economy and his mother searched for her elusive, virgin savior, Richard, on his own in Accra, caroused with other privileged young Americans and Europeans, sons and daughters of diplomats and business people, who flaunted their wealth and treated the Africans with disdain. One night, the Stewarts discovered that their son, along with several friends, had brought home, against her will, a fifteen year–old African girl, who resembled the very young girl in the mystical portraits that were the object of his mothers quest, and had raped and beaten her. The Stewarts, both appalled and frightened that word would get out about what their son had done, took in the young girl, who had no immediate family of her own.

The Stewart's efforts to conceal their son's transgressions were for naught. The local natives had become aware of young Richard's offense and recruited their most powerful Juju men to cast a spell on him. Probably out of sheer coincidence, the young man contracted, and in a short while succumbed, to a fatal bout of malaria. Soon after, his parents discovered that the girl was pregnant. They took her with them back to Massachusetts where she gave birth to their grandson, but, tragically, died in childbirth. The son of this ill-gotten union was Derek, who was adopted by his grandparents, who concealed the fact that he was, in truth, their biological grandson. Instead they claimed that this dusky-skinned child was the son of their deceased teenage African housekeeper, who had been like a daughter to them. Only 35 years later, when both grandparents died and their inheritance was passed on to the comatose Derek, did they, through their will, reveal the story of his true relationship to them, though that very same will indicated that they had made it quite clear to Derek himself, at a very early age, that he was truly their grandson as well as the true identities of his mother and father.

Marian Stewart had been determined to raise Derek differently than she had raised her own sociopathic son. She studiously kept him away from his grandfather and his moneyed friends, and took him along with her on trips and to spiritual retreats where she introduced him to many of the great philosophical, spiritual, mystical and even political thinkers of the time, including Aldous Huxley, Alan Watts, Jiddhu Krishnamurthi, Martin Luther King, Bertrand Russell, Albert Schweitzer, Philip K. Dick, Robert Oppenheimer and even Bobby Kennedy.

The boy, Derek Stewart, with chocolate skin because of his half-African blood, was intellectually brilliant, athletic and a natural leader. He was enrolled in the prestigious Milton Academy where he distinguished himself academically and led his school in athletics, despite having a reputation as someone who eschewed competition. When tested for entrance into the school, his IQ had been assessed at a stratospheric 200, the upper limit of the testing instrument. His grandfather, much as he had done for Derek's father, had secured a place for him at Harvard, although Derek would have been easily admitted on his own merits. However, the ill-fated Vietnam war was already well underway at the time and, although he had doubts about the legitimacy of the war, after reading a speech by the assassinated Bobby Kennedy on the responsibility of the privileged to not leave the fighting up to the poor and uneducated, Derek forsook his entrance to Harvard and voluntarily joined the Army, much to the dismay of both of his grandparents. He hoped to be a medic, so he could save lives, rather than take them.

By the time Derek arrived at the front, the war was already drawing to a close. It was 1972 and he was only 18 years old. Nevertheless, over the next year of warfare Derek repeatedly distinguished himself in bloody combat situations being fought by the retreating U.S. army, giving his fellow soldiers first aid, even under withering enemy fire. In the spring of 1973, during the final hours of the U.S. evacuation, he and a group of fellow soldiers were ambushed and Derek received the head wound, which left him in the coma, out of which he had just emerged after 40 years, the last American soldier to be wounded in the Vietnam war.

Derek's grandparents died in the late 1980's, his grandmother never giving up hope that her "adopted" son, who was in reality her grandson, would wake up. When she and her husband died within a week of each other, their will revealed Derek's true parentage—and bestowed upon their somnambulant grandson billions of dollars, managed as a trust until the day he awoke or to be donated to charity, should that day never happen.

I know all of this background because of my earlier story, and because even at my nadir as a writer, I was still at heart a biographer. I had searched Derek Stewart's background as carefully as I would have any waking person about whom I was writing a story. In his case, of course, he was unable to provide any direct information about himself, and I was confined to researching public records, acquaintances of his deceased grandparents, etc. But now all that had changed. Derek Stewart was awake, and as soon as I could circumvent the government censors, I was going to give him his first interview with the press.

Chapter 3

I, just as well as anyone else, knew full well that government intrusion into private life was an ugly and constant fact of life these days, but that still didn't explain what the Secret Service or the Feebs or whatever Gestapo-like government agency those two guys who had been in Derek's room worked for, wanted with Derek Stewart. Fremont F. Ferris, our virtually anointed president for a third term, had often touted Stewart as a true American hero. Perhaps Ferris was hoping to get his grasping mitts on Stewart before the newly awakened folk figure said anything that might undermine the president's use of him as an icon to support his own ends. Those ends were mostly the promotion of his religio-patrio-babble brand of Christian conservatism as the last bastion of hope against a world-wide fundamentalist Islamic revolution, which was, according to both Ferris and most of the other leaders of the Western World, threatening to undermine not only world stability, but the very moral foundation of free societies.

Since Ferris himself was the greatest threat to freedom with which I was acquainted, I regarded that whole line of reasoning—or lack of same—as a sorry sack of horseshit. But I was apparently in the minority—or if I wasn't, there was no way for me to know that I wasn't, given that speaking out against the government was nearly always followed by imprisonment or complete disappearance. 'Where have all the gulags gone?' I often hummed to myself, knowing that they were alive and well and that many of my friends were in them.

In the hallowed tradition of all historic leaders who portrayed themselves as the guardians of their country's values, Ferris had long ago suspended most of the constitutional rights related to free speech, freedom of religion and the doctrine of habeas corpus. His march toward absolute power had begun with the famous "Patriot Act III," in which any public or private speech or gathering of people in support of *ideas* that could be used as a basis for overthrow of the government had been made a crime. Given the broad sweep of such a definition of seditious speech, the impact of the law was to make all criticism of the government or its leadership illegal. While such measures were initially described as temporary, to meet the exigencies of the War on Terror, there was no longer any talk of removing them and they had become as firmly stitched into the fabric of the national life as baseball and apple pie.

The country's war footing had not just led to the curtailment of free speech. Although stopping short of a declaration of a national religion, Ferris and his faithful congressional flock had managed to amend the constitution by inserting the phrase, "Christian union" into several of its paragraphs relating to the philosophical basis for uniting the various states and commonwealths and then had outlawed Islam as a religion on the grounds that it was both "foreign" to American traditions and that it favored overthrowing the U.S. government. Along with his counterparts in France, England, Spain, Germany, Italy, and most of the Eastern European nations, who themselves were fearful of the political power of the growing Muslim constituencies in their countries, President Ferris had forged international agreements that claimed that any Western country must subscribe to "Christian values," even though only France, Italy and Spain went so far as to establish Christianity as their official state religion.

But what did Christian values or the threat of Islamic terrorism have to do with Derek Stewart? Surely he would not be arrested for a violation of the "Terrorist Speech Act," as it was called, based on the first utterances to issue from his mouth in 40 years. These were the questions I was pondering from the dark corners of the vacant hospital room into which I'd withdrawn to avoid being spotted when I was flabbergasted to see the Reverend Merrill Goodson, the Alabama evangelist who had become the president's, and unofficially the nation's, spiritual leader, come striding down the hospital corridor, accompanied by his own retinue of FIIEB bodyguards. The rotund minister's slow and sanctimonious stride—more of a waddle, actually, given his pear-like narrow shoulders, short legs and fat behind—and his characteristic prayerful clasping of his hands at his chest, even when he was just strolling through a hospital ward, were unmistakable. I always thought he looked like a fat Bela Lugosi coming to greet an unsuspecting visitor to his Transylvanian castle, which is why I had once referred, in print, to Goodson as the *preying* minister. I quickly realized that the agents whom I thought had been assigned to watch Stewart, were, in fact, just holding the fort until the good Reverend arrived. The two waiting government men rushed up to the new arrivals to become part of the phalanx of Feebs who whisked the born-again presidential advisor into Stewart's room.

Unable to resist getting close enough to see what would transpire when the prestigious minister confronted the newly awakened Vietnam war hero, I donned a white coat, which had been left hanging across the back of a chair in the nurse's station, and I stole to the edge of the crowd of doctors peering into the room where the newly awakened Stewart, like Gulliver awakening in Lilliput, was about to meet the official greeter from the era of the spiritually awakened modern America.

Reverend Goodson in his distinctive "healing" pose, his left fist against his heart with his right arm outstretched, his fingers splayed wide, as if to ensnare his helpless target, headed straight for the reclining and unsuspecting patient. Stewart, his eyes open, paid no particular heed to the corpulent minister, who was descending upon him like a spider about to devour its hopelessly ensnared meal

Josh Mannerly stepped in front of his helpless charge and defiantly barred the reverend's path. The tiny Asian woman I'd noticed earlier and who was wearing an all-white outfit with a therapist patch on the sleeve similar to Mannerly's, came to her colleague's side and assumed what appeared to be a martial arts position. Slim as a rail, but giving the impression that she was all muscle, her shiny black hair streamed halfway down her back. Her expression was inscrutable.

"What is the meaning of this?" Goodson asked, bringing himself up short in his headlong rush toward the man in the hospital bed. A flash of irritation had temporarily dislodged the mindless smile of beneficence, which had been plastered on his face when he entered the room. All four of the FIIEB agents crowded around him, encasing him in a protective cocoon, two of them drawing weapons and aiming them at the two physical therapists.

"Mr. Stewart is extremely sensitive to touch," Dr. Bhottu intervened, putting up a hand to try to bring calm to the group. "Mr. Mannerly and Miss Nguyen have orders to keep anyone from touching their patient."

Reverend Goodson, who had looked as if he was about to go ballistic with uncharitable Christian rage, relaxed. "Stand down men," he said to the FIIEB agents, who reluctantly peeled themselves from around him and even more reluctantly holstered their guns but continued to eye the two physical therapists with suspicion.

"I felt called upon to put my hands on you and pray, my son" Goodson told Stewart, who was staring at the minister with what appeared to be amusement in his eyes. "But praying from a distance will have to suffice," he said, the irritation not entirely removed from his voice. "God's power is everywhere."

The good Reverend then lowered himself to his knees, with some difficulty because of his bulk, and clasped his hands in front of his face and began praying in his deep, Southern and theatrical, basso profundo. "Dear Lord Jesus Christ, thank you for returning this lost son to us at this time of great need. He will be a guiding light in our defense of Christian values against the forces of evil in this world. We thank you for giving him back to us and look forward to his testimony regarding your great power."

In response to the reverend's message, the patient's eyes narrowed in intensity and he sat bolt upright in his bed. "Martin… is that your voice? Are you talking to me?"

"I forgot to tell you he hallucinates," Dr. Bhottu interrupted. Stewart was still sitting upright, wrapped in his sheet and looking like a thin ghost, staring eagerly at the stark white wall in front of him.

"You mean he's not completely out of his coma?" Goodson asked, a worried look adding enough wrinkles to his brow that it began to resemble the fatty creases below his chin. He had finally gotten to his feet and shaken off the Feebs who had been clinging to his arms like orthopedic crutches,.

Dr. Bhottu shrugged. "It could be that there is some residual brain damage or it could simply be the effects of prolonged coma. We know he was dreaming during the entire time he was comatose. Perhaps the dreams are still going on, even though he's awake. As I said, he's not completely awake. Most coma's resolve slowly, and it's more accurate to say his coma has lessened rather than he's out of it completely."

"Can he hear me?"

"I think so."

The reverend looked around at the little knot of white coated people crowding into the room. "May we now have some privacy?" he asked in his booming orator's voice, the one he used for his Sunday morning television broadcasts in which he extolled the virtues of a Christian America and berated the "Godless" Muslim hordes in other parts of the world. He directed his gaze at both Josh Mannerly and the Asian woman.

Neither of the two physical therapists acknowledged the minister's request, except to move closer to the patient's bed.

Reverend Goodson swung around and directed an irritated look at Dr. Bhottu. "Could you ask your staff to leave us alone, please?" His tone was that of an order not a question.

"I'm afraid the patient himself has asked that both Mr. Mannerly and Miss Nguyen remain with him. It's the only request he has made," the neurologist answered. His own tone expressed a mild defiance.

"Then the rest of you can leave." Goodson said, the benign smile back on his face, though the look he directed at Dr. Bhottu was as cold as a stone.

Dr. Bhottu turned and looked at the crowd of doctors behind him. When he saw my face, his expression registered his surprise, but he didn't say anything. "You all can return to your other duties for now," he told the group around me. Then he turned back to Reverend Goodson and addressed him. "I'm afraid it's my medical duty to remain with my patient. As I said, he's not completely out of his coma, and it's not wise to have him try to converse with visitors without a physician monitoring his condition." The defiance in his tone was strong enough to force a grudging acceptance from Goodson.

With great reluctance I moved away from the door, along with the other, real doctors, who, muttering to each other, drifted toward the elevators, probably resigned to having to leave and head for the golf links early, while I used the opportunity afforded by their clubby exclusiveness to duck into the room adjacent to Stewart's and put my ear to the wall. I could hear voices inside the next room distinctly enough to decipher what was being said.

Reverend Goodson was being introduced to Derek Stewart by Dr. Bhottu. Stewart's response was weak and I could barely hear his voice.

"The president of the United States sends his regards to you and wishes you a quick recovery, now that you have returned to us from your long period of… from your coma," Goodson announced. I couldn't imagine what it would be like to wake up to discover that forty years had elapsed since your last memory. And now the poor schnook had a fat preacher standing over him, giving him greetings from the president

I could hear Stewart's weak "hello, president.…"

"We haven't brought Mr. Stewart up to date on the complete details of his condition—such as the duration of his comatose state," Dr. Bhottu interjected, his anxiety apparent in his voice. "We'd like to go slowly. It will take some mental adjustment on his part."

"Certainly," Goodson answered, though it was clear from his tone that he dismissed the neurologist's admonition. "We're just pleased that God has chosen to bring you back to us, soldier. We have a hero back, and your tiny miracle, Mr. Stewart, is going to bring us even closer together in our fight against the Godless peoples in the rest of the world."

"The war is not over? Stewart asked weakly. I could barely hear his voice, but I could sense the alarm in his question.

"I don't think we should get into this right now," Dr. Bhottu interjected.

"Your war ended." Goodson answered, brushing away the neurologist's warning. "You were the last casualty of that war, which is why you're a hero. But we're fighting a new war now, a war against fanatical anti-Christian forces who want to destroy modern civilization. Your rebirth, so to speak, is going to inspire us in our fight against such mortal enemies."

I heard a loud moan, which I presumed came from Stewart.

"I have to call and end to this," Dr. Bhottu said, his voice shrill.

"I'm not done," Reverend Goodson answered, just as shrilly.

Stewart moaned again, and I heard the physical therapist, Josh Mannerly's voice above the others. "No more questions. Didn't you hear the doctor?"

"This man can't address me like that!" Goodson said sternly.

Stewart moaned even louder.

"Everyone out!" Dr. Bhottu ordered, his voice deep and commanding. "This is my patient, and you are endangering his mental condition. Everyone clear the room."

Goodson's voice regained its melodious tenor—the tone he used when he was talking about God's goodness rather than preaching fire and brimstone toward sinners and non-Christians. "We certainly don't want to disturb your patient, doctor. I just wanted to be able to tell the president that I had given Mr. Stewart his greeting and that we were eager to re-enlist him in our country's noble effort to defend freedom and Christian values."

I could hear people moving around and the door to Stewart's room opening. I ducked behind a curtain so no one would see me when they walked past the door to the room in which I was hiding.

"I'd like to say a few words during your press conference downstairs," I heard Goodson say as he and his entourage walked down the hall. "You don't mind, do you doctor?"

"Say whatever you like," Dr. Bhottu answered. "I'm just going to give a medical update. If you want to turn the conference into a propaganda moment for the president, go ahead."

The group was right outside my room. I peeked from behind the curtain. Reverend Goodson was holding up one hand to bring the procession to a halt. "I resent your tone, Dr. Bhottu. I want to remind you that this is a government hospital, and you are replaceable as the physician in charge of Mr. Stewart's case. In fact, your name has come up as perhaps being a suspicious alien, though I of course dismissed the notion when it was brought to my attention. But Mr. Stewart's re-awakening has wider..." he seemed to be searching for words, "wider social implications than just the reversal of his medical condition and you need to accept that. Do I make myself clear?"

Dr. Bhottu stared at the minister for about five seconds before answering. "Perfectly clear, Reverend." The doctor turned and walked back toward Stewart's room.

Chapter 4

I was still desperate to talk to Derek Stewart myself, but his door was closed, and from what had just transpired, with threats being thrown around like confetti at a New Year's Eve party, I decided that this might not be the most propitious moment to request an interview. Instead, I shed the white coat, which I had appropriated, and took the stairs to the conference room on the ground floor. The room was packed with reporters, photographers, and TV cameramen, and I had to stand at the back. Within minutes after my arrival, Reverend Goodson, accompanied by two FIIEB agents, entered the room, provoking a surprised murmur from the crowd. He was immediately followed by Dr. Bhottu, who strode to center of the dais and took a seat. Reverend Goodson stood impatiently behind the doctor, as if he was only waiting for the preliminary medical update to be over so he could address the crowd.

Dr. Bhottu was seated behind a thicket of microphones. He cleared his throat and began to speak in his precise, accented English. "Mr. Stewart is currently in a somewhat disoriented condition, having awakened, after approximately 40 years, from a coma caused by a battlefield injury to his brainstem. In his current state, he waxes in and out of consciousness and has, at times, been responsive to his surroundings, including being able to speak in answer to questions put to him. His condition appears to be stable at the moment and we are hopeful that he will continue to become fully conscious, but that is impossible to judge at this time." He looked around the room. "I will answer questions."

"Can you tell us about brain changes that would account for his waking up?" someone asked.

"Mr. Stewart's condition for the past 40 years has been a peculiar one, from a medical point of view and one we technically describe as a *minimally conscious state*, to distinguish it from either normal waking or a deeper coma such as a *persistent vegetative state*. Unlike most patients who are minimally conscious for prolonged periods of time, his brain has given signs of being completely active except he has spent most of his time asleep and has had no control over his motor functions. We have seen no changes on either EEG or MRI to suggest any change in his brain that would account for his change of state. He has simply woken up—or more precisely, is in the process of waking up."

I noticed that the doctor made no mention of Stewart's brain having *rewired* itself during his period of coma.

"Is he now able to move?" someone asked.

"Yes, he is able to initiate movement on his own and has raised all four limbs, though he is currently too weak to be able to support himself. He has been able to hold a cup and drink unassisted, however."

"What has he said?" Several reporters shouted the question at once.

"He has said 'It is good to be back,' he has said his name and repeated the names of myself and two physical therapists who are with him. He has answered in the affirmative when asked if he wanted water. He has also spoken spontaneously, though his meaning has sometimes been hard to decipher."

"What's his prognosis?" another reporter asked.

"Most people with this type of coma caused by brainstem injuries either wake up quickly or progress to a more profound coma and even death, since some of the vital bodily functions are usually affected. There have been occasional reports of patients waking after many years, the most famous of them being the case of Mr. Terry Wallis. Mr. Wallis woke after twenty years and was able to converse without difficulty though he had a profound amnesia both for the period during which he was in his coma and for remembering any new experiences—something we call *anterograde amnesia*. Mr. Stewart appears to have amnesia for the period of his coma. He has responded as if he were still in 1973, the year in which he was wounded. However, he has quickly learned the names of myself and the other hospital staff who have attended him and has shown no signs of having the type of anterograde amnesia as did Mr. Wallis. Obviously the exact nature of his cognitive functioning will have to await further study." Dr. Bhottu looked around the room, then shoved his chair back from the microphone and got up and walked off the stage.

Reverend Merrill Goodson duck-waddled to the center of the stage and, instead of sitting, picked up the microphone and addressed the audience. "This is an occasion for celebration by all American people. Private Derek Stewart was the last American soldier to be wounded by enemy fire in the Vietnam war and is a genuine American hero. He has been asleep for four decades, and now, I'm sure due to the unrelenting prayers of a faithful Christian nation, he has awakened. I am sure that Dr. Bhottu will agree that it is a genuine medical miracle." He lowered his voice. "I had the opportunity to talk with Private Stewart a few moments ago." The reverend scanned the audience to be sure he had everyone's attention. "I could sense Private Stewart's response as he heard my prayers, and I am here to tell you that I felt a communion between the Holy Spirit and this brave hero." The minister's voice became subdued, but still immersed in emotion. "Such a moment puts me in awe of God's power. I must tell you all that. I conveyed greetings from President Ferris and I told Private Stewart about our current war with the heathen world of fundamentalist Islam." His voice began to rise. "He received my words about the challenge to Christianity with alarm, and I was afraid to say more for fear of jeopardizing his fragile health. Now, I eagerly await, along with all of you, for Mr. Stewart's full recovery. I look forward to him joining our fight to preserve Christianity in the face of those Godless forces in the world who are out to destroy us." The reverend bowed his head, as if in prayer. Every reporter in the room except me was wildly scribbling their notes of his speech.

I had to marvel at Goodson's facility in weaving Derek Stewart's total unresponsiveness to him into a compelling, if incoherent, account that fitted his own inspirational message. No one in the audience seemed to care that the reverend had not actually said that Stewart had said anything to him at all. They were used to Goodson's sermon-like press conferences and would probably write stories describing an actual conversation in which Derek Stewart had a heart-to-heart conversation with the reverend about the necessity of winning the war on terror. That was the kind of story that would play well with the public anyway and each reporter was well aware that his or her future access to information from the White House was dependent upon writing stories that were favorable to the president and his chief religious advisor.

For my part, I had no intention of writing the drivel that Goodson had spouted to the other reporters—not after I had personally overheard what had and had not transpired. I text-messaged a brief communiqué back to the office with the information Dr. Bhottu had provided and the news that the president had sent Reverend Goodson to bring his greetings to the newly wakened soldier. My description of the interaction between the minister and Stewart was completely at odds with the account given by Goodson, whose story I debated calling whimsical, fanciful, fictional and finally characterized as a blatant lie. I had no doubt that my editorial depiction of the conversation would be deleted, but true to my suicidal nature I couldn't resist including it in the article. If there was going to be a real story connected to Derek Stewart, I knew that I had to get into the soldier's hospital room and secure the first interview with him.

Chapter 5

"Where is that Goddamn, Goodson?" president Fremont F. Ferris fumed, pacing back and forth from one edge to the other of the thick carpet, the piles of which were inlaid with a stitched replica of the presidential Seal. Ferris was of average height, but his broad shoulders hinted at his younger years as an active hunter, fisherman, horseman and athlete. His finely chiseled features had become more fleshy with age. He still sported a full head of steel-gray hair. The audience for his tirade consisted of Senator Frederick "Army" Armbruster, the heavy-set, ex-West Point football player and Vietnam war veteran who was the president's long-time Alabama friend and colleague and Jervis Donovan, presidential aide and architect of the infamous "Anti-Jihad theory," the idea that changing leadership in a time of war was too dangerous to be allowed, even if the constitution demanded it. The upshot of such a theory was the repeal of the 22nd amendment of the U.S. constitution, allowing the president to be elected for more than two terms in order to maintain continuity in the war on terror—a war which, coincidentally, was purported to have no foreseeable conclusion. Both men were familiar with the president's short fuse and habitual impatience, aspects of his temperament which were carefully shielded from public view behind a persona of folksy, good-ol-boy informality but which had gotten perceptibly worse since the inception of a, theoretically at least, lifetime position as the nation's Commander-in-Chief.

"It's your fault, Jervy," the president said stabbing the air in the direction of his aide. "You were the one who had the bright idea to send Goodie off to talk to that …whatever his name is, who just woke up from a forty year sleep."

His aide had an almost stork like appearance, caused by the way his head jutted forward over an abnormally long neck and thin, hollow chest, but in contrast, his face was filled out with soft, pink-cheeked fullness, smoothly shaven, to match his perfectly bald head. He always wore a newly pressed shirt and pants and highly polished wing-tips. Donovan had a law degree

31

from Harvard and a Ph.D. in economics from Princeton. Ferris was suspicious of all highly educated people, such as Donovan, but the senior aide's cold-blooded ruthlessness, concealed beneath a thoughtful intellectual manner, had long ago won him the president's confidence.

Jervis Donovan wasn't a hateful person—in fact he rarely even harbored grudges—his highest ambition was to do his job well. He had risen to the top of the hierarchy of government advisors by having no philosophical agenda whatsoever—in fact he had no philosophical sentiments—he was neither a liberal nor a conservative. He was a supreme bureaucrat—asking nothing more than to serve those for whom he worked. He served his president and his government faithfully, if blindly, bringing brilliance and originality to the task of stripping away all threats to Fremont F. Ferris's hegemony.

"The man's name is Derek Stewart," Donovan said, his round, soft features remaining placidly unperturbed by the president's tone, which he was quite used to, having been Ferris's top political advisor for over twenty years. "He is the last American soldier wounded in Vietnam and if we can get him in our camp before anyone else gets to him, he'll be political gold."

"But why Goodie, dammit? What has any of this got to do with my Chief Religious Advisor who I happen to need here with me right now?" The president was just as thoroughly dependent upon his religious advisor as he was upon his political advisor. Ferris's deep religious feeling and his strong, unexamined Christian faith, were genuine and formed the axis of his presidential philosophy. He was absolutely convinced that being president was his "divine calling," and like many genuinely religious leaders who felt that they were the chosen tools for carrying out God's wishes, he believed that his own ambitions, decisions and whims carried the weight of divine decrees. The Reverend Goodson played a large role in shaping the president's thinking—almost as strong as Vice President Rogers, the mysterious second-in-command who had not been seen by anyone since shortly after the president's first inauguration.

Vice President Daryl Rogers had gone in hiding when the terrorists had bombed the New York Subway system. The theory was that if a terrorist attack killed or disabled the president then the vice president must remain safe. Given the constant nature of the terrorist threat, however, Rogers had made the decision not to emerge from his hiding. That had been nine years ago.

Everyone, including the president assumed that someone, perhaps the Secret Service or the FIIEB, or even the CIA knew where Rogers was, although with everyone sworn to secrecy, no one was sure. His lack of physical presence did nothing to dampen the vice president's influence, however. He communicated by email, using a secret code that only a handful of people close to the president, including Jervis Donovan, could decipher, and he was regularly consulted by telephone. In fact, even when he wasn't consulted he maintained an internet blog, which allowed him to comment on anything that he felt was of national importance, including his own superior's handling of affairs of state. The blog alone, which rivaled Reverend Goodson's television show in terms of influencing American opinion, made Rogers a force to be reckoned with—that and the fact that, despite his seclusion, he retained ties with most of the major international corporations who controlled the American economy and channeled millions of dollars into the coffers of the Republican Party, by dictating who got most of the lucrative non-competitive government contracts that were regularly doled out as part of the emergency actions of the war on terror.

President Ferris listened to his vice president, but right now it was his religious advisor who was on his mind.

"Goodson thinks that Stewart's awakening is a message from God telling the country that we're on the right path in our war against the Muslims," Donovan continued. "People are getting tired of constant war and we need a new hero to fire them up again."

"Tired of war?" The president said, a look of angry disbelief on his lined face. He still worked out every day and had managed to maintain his slim waist and muscular upper torso, but the strains of the presidency had ravaged his once handsome face. "Did you hear that Army?" he asked, turning toward Armbruster, "Don't these fucking people know that the future of the world hangs in the balance? Those damn heathens want to wipe us off the face of the earth because they know their religion can't stand up to American freedom and Christianity. Why can't our blasted people understand the depth of the evil we're up against? For Christ sake, I thought the damn FIIEB jailed all the liberal peaceniks among us. Who the hell is poisoning the people's minds now? "

"I don't know, Mr. president," Armbruster answered. "There are a heck of a lot of atheistic liberals still out there. They've just gone underground. But it's a fact the people don't understand why we can't win the war. We keep telling them we have the most powerful fighting force in the history of the planet and yet those ragheads running around in the desert seem to have us pinned down in a bunch of no-win situations."

Ferris's face displayed his irritation. "No one is supposed to know that. That's why we control the Goddamn press. For God's sake, didn't we decide that reporting any American defeats in this war was treasonous? I know we did. Daryl Rogers drummed up support for that position on his blog. He argued that since we all agreed that America has the strongest and bravest and best equipped fighting force ever assembled in the history of the world, it's inconceivable that we could lose any battles. Therefore, anyone who says we're not winning the war must be lying and trying to undermine our national determination—and according to the Patriot Act III, that's treasonous. Who's telling people we're bogged down?"

"Nobody has come right out and said we're losing, sir, Donovan answered. "They only know that this war is going on a long time and, though we keep reporting victories, we don't seem to have any progress to show for it."

"I don't think people want out, though," Armbruster added, casting an irritated sidelong glance at Donovan. "I think they want total victory."

"And that's what we're going to give them," the president said, narrowing his eyes and looking like the gritty, resolute leader that was pictured in all of his campaign ads. "America isn't going to turn tail for a bunch of heathens. But where the hell is Goodie? He's our strongest advocate with Pope Gregory. The rest of those Goddamn European countries hang on every word that candy-ass pope says. We need to get those fainthearted Euros on board for one last push against the Jihadists."

"Do you mean the you want to use the *Big Bang* option?" Donovan asked. His calm expression didn't change, although he was asking the president about a plan that involved sending nuclear warheads into virtually all the major capitals in the Islamic world. It was a plan he had developed himself, based on urging from the vice president. Donovan had changed the name that Rogers had given to the plan, which had been *The Final Solution*, reminding the vice president that comparisons would be made to a similarly named plan developed by the Nazis more than half a century earlier. Rogers had reluctantly gave up the name but had observed that the Nazi's, in his estimation, had gotten a lot of underserved bad press.

Ferris stopped pacing and looked from one man to the other. "I mean at least the *Little Big Bang option*—take out Beirut, Tehran and Damascus. Then we can hold off on Baghdad, Cairo, Amman and Riyadh until we see if the Jihadists throw in the towel. But I want the French and the Germans behind us. Fuck the Russians and Chinese. They're happy as pigs in shit to stand on the sidelines while the rest of us shoulder the burden. We just need Pope Gregory to give his blessing to the idea so we can bring the fucking Euros on board."

"Pope Gregory's already condemned the entire Muslim world with his Benedictine Re-Affirmation," Armbruster said.

"That's a bunch of intellectual bullshit—another fucking angels on the head of a pin argument. Re-affirming Pope Benedict's statement that Islam is an inherently violent religion doesn't cut it when we need to take action," the president answered, his face showing his disgust. "The pope has to make it clear that the heathen religions need to be wiped off the face of the earth. Goodson knows that, and he's the man who can tell it to the pope, one religious man to another. Where the hell is he though? The pope is only here for two days, and I need Goodie to spend at least a couple of hours with him."

"We don't need the pope's support on this," Donovan said, stroking his soft, receding chin as if he were thinking out loud. He always resembled an accountant adding up numbers when he pulled back into his own thoughts. "We know the Iranians have got a nuclear weapon of their own and it's aimed at Israel. The only thing stopping them from launching it is fear that we'll retaliate. But suppose we secretly let president Farhoud Kharazzi in Iran know that we won't retaliate if they go after Israel? If we can make him believe us, he might be fool enough to do it. Then we can hit them with our nukes and nobody in the whole Western world is going to object." He waited expectantly for the president's reaction. Donovan had come up with the plan weeks before and checked it out with the vice president, who had heartily approved, although he had suggested that it might be appropriate to resurrect the *final solution* nomenclature, noting that this time, it might be more apt. Donovan had waited for just the right time to broach it to the president.

"You mean we encourage the Iranians to drop a nuclear bomb on Israel?" Armbruster interrupted, his mouth remaining open in shock.

The irritated expression left president's face, replaced by a slowly spreading smile. "Don't sound so shocked, Army. Jervy's on to something; let's think about it."

"Of course," Armbruster agreed, nodding his head vigorously. The Senator may have been one of the president's most trusted friends, but he knew that any substantial disagreement with Ferris would signal the abrupt end of that relationship. " I was just thinking that only two days ago I got back from Tel Aviv after having reassured the Israelis that they didn't need to take out the Iranian nuclear facilities because our nuclear threat would keep the Iranians at bay," he said sheepishly.

"Don't worry Army. You told them exactly the right thing. But we've got to do something. Anyway, those fucking Jews are a pain in everybody's ass. Once their country's been brought to its knees—which won't be a bad thing by the way, considering how damn arrogant they are—we can move in and take them under our protection. They may get nuked once, but we can make sure it never happens a second time. Goodson and Pope Gregory agree that we want to re-establish Jerusalem as a Christian city anyway. The Jews messed up their claim to it when they killed Jesus. It's time we rebuilt the place in God's image."

"You mean after the radiation in the area cools down," Donovan reminded him.

"Everything takes time," The president answered, beginning his pacing again. "Goddamn that Goodie. Where the hell is he?"

"Don't worry," Donovan answered. "He'll be here. His visit with that soldier is important. We don't want to underestimate the backlash we're gonna get when we use the nuclear option. We need a new American hero to be on our side. We've won three elections in a row, but there's always the next one to worry about. This Derek Stewart could be invaluable to us."

The president's expression darkened and the weariness of his ten years in office showed. "All this constant electioneering is getting me down, Jervy. Can't we just suspend elections indefinitely?" Ferris had returned to one of his favorite topics. In his opinion his administration spent so much time and effort manipulating public opinion that asking the voters to acknowledge that they wanted him to continue leading them was a complete waste of time.

"As I've said before, there's no precedent for that, sir. When we got rid of the prohibition against more than two terms we were just removing a constitutional amendment that was less than 100 years old. We've never suspended elections, even in the midst of world wars. Besides, after we use the Little Bang Option, the war will be over."

Ferris' expression changed to a sneer as his impatience reared its ugly head. "For Christ sake, Jervy, get your head out of your ass. Do you think knocking out a few key cities is going to stop al Mout li Kafir from attacking us?"

Donovan looked perplexed. *Al Mout li Kafir*, which translated as *death to infidels*, was the Islamic fundamentalist terrorist group that had mounted the attack on the New York subway system and had surpassed Al Qaeda as the dominant leader of the Islamic fight against the West. Their leader, Moustafa al Adim was the spiritual and tactical leader responsible for most of the attacks against Western countries. "Yes, I do," Donovan answered.

"Get real Jervy. Moustafa al Adim loves the role of martyr. He'll keep sending suicide bombers until he hasn't got anyone left—and the last one will be al Adim himself, if we don't get him first. We may only be getting the death throes of the Muslim extremist movement, but it will be unpleasant and messy. There'll still be plenty of threat to warrant suspending elections."

When Ferris talked like this, Donovan remembered that the president wasn't the witless Southern boob that he sometimes appeared to be. Still, the advisor looked skeptical. "I don't know. You'll get a lot of opposition if you try to get rid of the elections."

"I think Jervy could have a point, sir," Armbruster said, cautiously. In fact he knew that Donovan was completely correct, but he wasn't going to disagree with the president so blatantly. "Elections and democracy are strongly associated in the American mind."

"It ought to be freedom and democracy, Goddamn it," the president answered. "Elections are just a detail and if our freedom is threatened, elections don't amount to a hill of beans in the big picture."

Donovan and Armbruster exchanged doubtful looks.

"We'll see," the president said, gazing out the window into the distance. "You know those seventeenth century monarchs enjoyed some real advantages. It's hard as hell running a democracy when you have to worry about convincing the great unwashed to vote for you every four years. Maybe it'll take one last big terrorist attack on our soil to convince people that if they want to preserve their freedom they need a leader with absolute power."

"I hope not," Armbruster said, a look of alarm widening his eyes amidst the layers of fat on his round, usually jovial face. "such an attack would be devastating,"

"A catastrophe," Donovan added, but his eyes were alert to the president's meaning.

"It would be terrible of course, Army," the president answered, barely able to conceal a sly smile. "But we can't control all the events of the future. We can just pray. God works in mysterious ways, remember? " He whirled around and stared at the door to the oval office. "Where is that Goodson? I need him here now!"

Chapter 6

General Robert Ologabawa awoke with a start. He was a light sleeper, especially when he was in the field, as he had been for the last six months, waging this latest incursion into the territory held by the Sudanese army. He remained nearly immobile, moving his head imperceptibly as he swung his gaze slowly around the perimeters of the narrow confines of his field tent. He listened for the sound that must have awakened him, stilling his own breathing to a whisper, but around him all was silence. Even the raucous late night laughter from his troops, some of whom still had a supply of Canadian whiskey left over from the abandoned U.N. Field Office they had ransacked, had died down. He stared at the glowing face of his watch. It was 3:30 a.m.; too early to get up if he was going to lead his troops on a long march today. He closed his eyes, willing himself to fall back asleep.

"Open your eyes slowly and don't say anything." The voice was deep and melodious, but carried an unmistakable force.

Ologabawa froze. How had the enemy reached his tent? Where were his guards? He opened his eyelids slowly. Above him, like four enormous Jackalberry trees, towered four giant men, their faces obscured in the dark.

"We are here to talk to you," spoke the same deep voice, from somewhere behind the other four.

"May I sit up?" His automatic pistol was sitting on top of the small box containing his toiletry articles, an arm's length away.

"Surely. We have removed your weapon, of course," the voice said. There was a gentle quality, as if the speaker sensed the disappointment Olagabawa would feel when he realized he had no means of defense.

The general sat up. His upper body was of normal height. It was his long legs that gave him stature, identifying him as a nearly seven-foot tall Dinka warrior. If he had stood, he would have towered over even the "giants" who now looked down on him. "I'd prefer to see who I'm talking to."

One of the four men surrounding him knelt down and placed a small electric lamp on the floor. It's light was dim, but the faces of the men became clear. Ologabawa was shocked. They were all Asante—fierce warriors from Ghana, their arms and faces covered with tattoos and their hair in tight braids, similar to the style of the legendary Masai. Even in the dim light the sheer bulk of each man was frightening. They appeared to carry no weapons.

"We are unarmed, but not defenseless," came the voice from behind the men. A figure stepped forward. Ologabawa recognized the man at once. Robert N'gomo's grizzled sixty-year old face looked down on the general with a steady gaze.

"What do you want?" Ologabawa was trying to display as much dignity as he could, sitting in his sleeping bag wearing only his underwear, but he was also in awe of the man who was addressing him. He had only seen pictures of N'gomo, but he had heard the legends.

"I have spoken to General Shamoun, the head of the Sudanese Army. I wish you both to stop fighting. The two of you have killed thousands of innocent people here in Darfur. General Shamoun is interested in a truce."

"But the government of Sudan is dominated by the Arabs. Even if they stop trying to exterminate the tribes in Darfur, they will not give them representation in the government. What good is a truce if we gain nothing?" Ologabawa kept his breathing normal and spoke in measured tones, but he was in shock that N'gomo had talked to his enemy or that he had gotten him to consider a truce. Although he knew N'gomo was capable of miraculous deeds and could gain the ear of any leader across the entire African continent, General Shamoun had never before agreed to consider an end to the fighting.

"Mustafa Al Adim has contacted president Koury. He made an offer to settle the dispute between your *Justice and Equality Movement* and the government in Khartoum if he can have both yours and General Shamoun's soldiers put under his command. He wants to begin a movement to invade other East African countries and impose his fundamentalist regime on them.

General Shamoun dislikes this prospect. He thought you might feel the same"

"Shamoun and I are in agreement." Ologabawa was not a Muslim, and his religion was flavored with the indigenous beliefs of his parents and grandparents and the Dinka tribe from which his family had originated. He refused to abide by rigid Islamic prescriptions. He knew that Shamoun, although a Muslim himself, was as vehemently opposed to the fundamentalist Muslim forces that were gaining favor in many of the northern African countries as he was. The reason for Shamoun's cooperation was now clearer to him.

"I don't care what religion you Sudanese choose, but I don't want a Sudanese army turning its neighbors' lands into killing fields," N'gomo continued. "I told General Shamoun I would contact you to arrange a meeting."

Ologabawa stiffened. Was he being lured into a trap? Was this all just a ploy to get him to meet with Shamoun and allow himself to be killed or captured? "I cannot trust General Shamoun ... and I trust president Koury less."

"Koury does not want to give in to Moustafa al Adim and his murderous al Mout li Kafir. He has promised that if I can arrange a truce between you and General Shamoun, he will honor it."

How do I know they are not planning to kill me?" There was no fear in the general's voice, only curiosity.

"You have my word.. The meeting will be just between you and Shamoun. My Asante men will stand guard."

Ologabawa looked at the four giant men who stood above him. "They don't carry weapons."

"They don't need to."

General Ologabawa thought about what he was being asked. He had nothing personal against General Shamoun. He only fought him because president Koury had prohibited any of the Southern and Southwestern Sudanese tribes, especially the Dinka, who had led the nearly thirty year rebellion which had concluded with the secession of South Sudan from the larger country, from being represented in the government.

That had been ten years ago. Ologabawa, who had been a rising young star and a colonel in the regular Sudanese Army, had revolted, and he and others of his tribes and their allies had built a resistance army of their own, which eventually became the military arm of Khalil Ibrahim's *Justice and Equality Movement*, the JEM. Although Olagabawa was a Dinka, his army and the supporters of the JEM were an eclectic mix of various tribes, including even disaffected Bedouins and Arabs. General Shamoun had been ordered to bring them to their knees with military force. Ologabawa's answer had been to wage the bloodiest war on the African continent. Building upon the Arab's fear of the fearsome, tall Dinkas, he encouraged his troops to be ruthless in their terrorist attacks and their torture and killing of the soldiers of the Sudanese Army. So far, despite ten years of the bloodiest fighting in the history of East Africa and the death of countless innocent civilians, his military operations had gotten him no political concessions.

But what if the meeting and the truce were all a trap? He gazed up at the face of Robert N'gomo. The man's actions had stopped numerous bloody African wars. His honesty and character were never doubted by anyone on either side of any dispute. If a truce was ever to come, it would come through a figure such as N'gomo.

"I will do it," Ologabawa said. "Take me to General Shamoun."

Chapter 7

The nurses had re-populated their station on the fourth floor of the Naval hospital and were back to being efficient and impersonal, every one of them so busy bending their heads over medical charts, that I figured that each chart must have a Bloomingdale's catalog hidden inside. The Feebs, whom I had at first thought were protecting Derek Stewart from reporters, had left with the rest of Reverend Goodson's entourage. I still had possession of my purloined doctor's coat and no one took any notice as I swaggered with the brio of a physician down the hallway and into Stewart's darkened room. As I was about to congratulate myself on my good luck and brilliant display of chutzpah, I was grabbed by the shoulder and brought up short.

"What the hell are you doing in here?" Joshua Mannerly asked, his fingers digging into the flesh of my shoulder. In the darkened room, I hadn't seen him standing just inside the doorway. Now his face was menacingly close to mine and I could see him just fine.

"I'm here to interview Mr. Stewart," I answered, trying my best to curtail the impulse to scream from the pain he was inflicting on my shoulder.

"Mr. Stewart is not having any interviews. I'm going to call security and have them escort your ass out of here." He still hadn't loosened his grip on my shoulder, which was beginning to throb. "Tina, call security."

I hadn't noticed that Miss Nguyen, the other physical therapist was also in the room, seated stoically, like a small female Buddha, on the other side of Stewart's bed. The two therapists seemed to have taken on the role of self-appointed guards. I would have to do some fast talking to avoid getting thrown out.

"Can't we just all get along?" I asked Josh. "I'm not here to cause any harm. I just want to exchange a few words with Mr. Stewart, now that he's awake. He's better off giving his first interview to me than to some government lackey who'll try to twist his words around." My words sounded lame even to my own ears.

"Why would someone do that?" asked a weak, but steady voice from over Mannerly's shoulder. With a shock I realized that Derek Stewart had just spoken to me.

"They want you to endorse their war," I said, trying to look past Mannerly's threatening face at the supine figure in the shadows behind him.

"Come forward," Stewart said. It was clearly a request and not a command, though, even in his weakened state, Stewart was able to project a peculiar forcefulness.

"Do you mind?" I said to Mannerly, doing my best to wiggle my shoulder free of his grip, though it felt as if I might never regain normal function in the whole left side of my body. Reluctantly, he let go of my shoulder. I walked forward, rubbing my arm to try to get the circulation going again. When I reached Stewart's bed and looked down into his face I was surprised by how young he looked—and how tired. Tina Nguyen had come around the bed, and she and Josh Mannerly were each standing at my shoulders, ready to intervene if I made any suspicious moves. I suspected the slight Miss Nguyen could do as much damage to me as the well-muscled Mannerly.

"Josh and Tina, you can sit down. I know Mr. Luke Evangelista." This time there was a definite sense of command in Stewart's voice.

"You know me?"

"You are familiar to me."

"I visited you when you were in a coma, but that was five years ago. How could you remember?"

He heaved a tired sigh. "Your presence brings with it a sense of déjà vu."

"I came before to write a story about you."

"I know." He paused and his breathing was labored, as if he was tiring. "Tell me about the war. I thought it would have ended by now." There was a sound of sorrow in his voice.

"The war in which you were involved continued for two more years after you were wounded, but America was no longer involved. After two years Saigon fell. The North Vietnamese—the Viet Cong—won the war and unified the country under a

Communist regime. That was almost forty years ago. They are now our allies. Your therapist, Tina was probably either a refugee that fled the Communist takeover when she was a child or she may be the daughter of such a person."

"I was born in Saigon under the Communist rule and I and came here as a baby," Tina Nguyen offered. In contrast to her assertiveness when she had thought I was threatening her patient, she now appeared shy and looked at the floor when she spoke.

"So the winners and the losers of that war are now friends?" Stewart asked.

"Strong allies. Vietnam has forsaken Communism, except in name only, as have Russia and China. Everyone is a capitalist. The split between East and West is now a different one."

"Tell me about it," His voice sounded far away, as if he had begun to retreat back into himself. I began to worry that our conversation was exhausting him.

"The Western countries—the Europeans and the Americans—are now at war with the Middle Eastern countries—those in which Islam is the dominant religion. It is becoming a battle between Christianity and Islam."

He closed his eyes. I thought he had fallen asleep. I tried to imagine what it would be like to have gone to sleep near the end of the Vietnam war and woken up in the midst of the War on Terror. Even to some of us who'd been awake during the whole experience, the current situation made little sense.

His eyes fluttered open, slightly unfocused. I wondered if he had had a mild seizure. "What you have told me is disheartening. I need to think about it."

That he was disheartened meant he must have understood what I'd told him. My own reaction to the current situation had been a profound depression that was now beginning its second decade. He looked so exhausted I hesitated to go on, but I still had an interview to conduct. I was a reporter, after all and I needed something for my paper. "What did you think when you woke up? Did you think you were still in 1973?"

He heaved a long sigh, as if he was aware that I was now pursuing my own agenda. "I can answer only one or two questions. I am tired. When I woke up I had no idea where I was or when it was. I was returning from another world."

"What world?"

"I dreamt almost constantly. At first my dreams were incoherent but I gradually learned to control their content. I began dreaming stories based on my memories. At first I controlled the stories, but eventually I gave up control and just participated in them."

"Participated?" Though he appeared lucid, I wasn't sure his mind hadn't lost its grip.

"The people in my dreams expressed their own personalities, not only the parts that I remembered. They were people from my past who seemed to be in a play in which they interacted with me and with each other. Eventually things settled into a single story that continued without interruption. Whether it lasted for years or only a few minutes I can't say, but in my mind it spanned decades."

One continuous dream for forty years? It seemed impossible. And anyway, how would he know? I had had dreams myself that were clearly produced in response to a finite stimulus, such as a voice calling to me to wake up, yet they often felt as if they had spanned the entire night's sleep.

"What was that story about?"

"The search for truth." He closed his eyes. I noticed that his eyelids were red, as though the time he had spent awake was exhausting him. When he reopened his eyes, it was only to look at me and mutter, "I must sleep now."

His enigmatic answer left me more puzzled than informed, but I didn't want to cause a medical crisis or drive Stewart back into his coma. I wanted to talk to him again, but for now I had enough to file a story. It would be based on the very first interview with a man who had been asleep for 40 years.

Chapter 8

Mahmoud Fahkry looked out of the window of his downtown Beirut office. The crowds in the streets below, their tightly packed numbers roiling like the surface of an angry sea, were a familiar sight, but this time their hand lettered cardboard signs and their chants carried a different message. They were not demonstrating in support of Hezbollah, the Shiite party that was responsible for electing Fahkry to his powerful position as Speaker of the Parliament, a position within the Lebanese government always reserved for a Shiite. Such a demonstration would not have worried the Speaker in the way that this one did. But these were not Hezbollah supporters, though they were shouting for the same thing for which his party had clamored for years. The people on the street below were predominantly Sunni Muslims and the signs they held proclaimed "al Mout li Kafir!"—"Death to infidels"—the name of the organization headed by the former Saudi, Mustafa Al Adim.

The popularity of al Mout li Kafir engendered an ominous feeling in Fahkry, one that he couldn't displace. His own party, Hezbollah, had been formed to rid his country of the Israeli intruders, and the party continued its fight because there was still land to be returned and because the Israelis continued to act as if they had the right to invade their neighbors any time they felt like it. They labeled every incursion onto Lebanese soil as an act of defense—no matter how absurd the claim—and received Western support on every occasion. But Fahkry knew that Hezbollah could live with Israel if the Zionists changed their ways. And, so long as the Americans didn't themselves put their troops on Lebanese soil, Hezbollah had no argument with them—other than their uncritical backing of every Israeli move.

Moustafa al Adim and his al Mout li Kafir organization were different. They would be satisfied with nothing less than the elimination of Israel, and their chief activity appeared to be to antagonize the United States and other Western countries. Since moving into Lebanon, they had launched no less than four terror attacks on European countries and had made it known that it was only a matter of time before they again attacked the United States on its own soil. If the price to be paid for such an attack was the nuclear annihilation of Beirut, al Mout li Kafir didn't appear to mind. Martyrdom—even when it was someone else's—was glorious.

How could any thinking Lebanese entertain such thoughts, Kahfry wondered. But the undulating crowds, shouting beneath his window, were proof that many Lebanese supported al Mout li Kafir.

It didn't help that the Western countries, led by the militant American president, Fremont F. Ferris and the dual religious leaders, Reverend Goodson and Pope Gregory, had denounced the Muslim religion, or that troops from the Western coalition now occupied Iraq, Afghanistan and continued to have bases in Qatar, Kuwait and Bahrain, not to mention, Saudi Arabia. There were plenty of Muslim leaders who were ready to mount a full scale terrorist war to rid their countries of the occupying West. Bombings and ambushes against the American army were an everyday occurrence. No one but the Westerners referred to such acts as terrorism.

In Kahfry's mind, such defense against a Western occupation was legitimate. But launching attacks outside of the Middle East was going too far. Only al Adim had reached into the heartland of the West and attacked both America and Europe on their own soil. Khafry knew he had to satisfy the demands of the militants in the streets below, but he didn't want to sacrifice his country to do it.

Kahfry lifted the receiver on his telephone. Farhoud Kharazzi, the president of Iran, was a shameless demagogue who would do almost anything to remain in power, and he too, was burdened by the growing presence of al Mout li Kafir in his own country. Kharazzi's anti-Western rhetoric, which fanned the flames of his country's citizens hatred of Israel and the United States, was coming back to haunt him. He couldn't bluster forever without his constituency demanding action. Now his people had begun listening to al Mout li Kafir.

"Mr. president," Kahfry addressed the Iranian leader, "my sources indicate that your own religious leader, Ayatollah Khatami has urged your people to listen to Moustafa al Adim. Can that be true?" Even as he spoke, he kept an eye on the surging movements of the chanting crowd on the street below. Their presence lent a sense of urgency to his call.

Kharazzi's voice over the telephone was shrill. "Khatami is old and senile. He listens to Al Adim and forgets the man is a Sunni. I think that the Syrian president, Ahmed Aptha has been poisoning Khatami's mind. Syria would like nothing better than to have us attack Israel while the Syrians sit on the sideline and watch.

"But you yourself have been calling for an attack on Israel."

"I have always said the Jews must go. What am I to do, sit on my hands while Moustafa al Adim takes over leadership of my people, while my own Ayatollah calls me a coward for not ridding our region of the filthy Jews?"

"But the Americans will answer with nuclear weapons if you fire on Israel."

"Khatami favors a non-nuclear attack. He believes we can defeat the Israelis using conventional means."

"Then you are right, Khatami is senile. The Israelis are too strong to defeat with our armies."

"The Israelis are whimpering dogs who beg at the feet of the Americans," Kharazai said, his voice achieving a new level of shrillness. "They have grown soft and cannot stand up to our Iranian army."

"Save that talk for your speeches to your own people," Khafry answered. He had always thought that Kharazzi made the mistake of believing his own rhetoric. "Whether the Israelis do it by themselves or with the help of the Americans, you are going to be destroyed if you try to fight them head-on."

"Al Adim has told the Ayatollah he can bring in Al Mout li Kafir forces through your country and even from Iraq to join in the fight. We Muslims will be united in our fight against the dirty Jews."

Kahfry watched the crowd below. He saw that many of the men had rifles. "Perhaps a l Adim can do that. His al Mout li Kafir is strong in Lebanon—almost as strong as Hezbollah. But you will not be strong enough. If Israel is seriously threatened, either they or the Americans will launch a nuclear attack."

"Then we will launch a nuclear attack first. We will wipe out the Jew-dogs!" Kharazzi's voice was now a high-pitched scream.

The man is a complete fool, Khafry thought to himself. "Pull yourself together Mr. president. The Americans will drop bombs on us all. They won't care if it was Iran or Syria or Lebanon or al Mout li Kafir who attacked Israel. It will be their excuse for wiping us all out."

"So what can I do?" Kharazzi asked, his voice more subdued. "If I don't do something, the Ayatollah and Moustafa al Adim will win over my people, and I will be out of office. I have to attack someone."

"I need to feel the Americans out," Kahfy answered. "See if they are as interested in avoiding a larger conflict as we are. If you can guarantee them that you won't use your nuclear weapons, maybe they will not interfere. You can launch some skirmishes— send a few air strikes across the Israeli border—sponsor some terrorist attacks within Israel. Maybe your people will be satisfied."

"Can you trust what the Americans tell you?"

"Can any politician be trusted? The Americans create their foreign policy on the basis of whether it will win them an election. The American people are weary of their leaders' costly adventures. Perhaps for once they will resist joining in a Middle Eastern war."

"Good luck, my friend. I must do something about those Jews."

The man's an idiot, Khafry thought to himself. "I will see what I can do."

"Ma'a salama."

"Allah ysalmak."

Chapter 9

General Ologabawa's heart was beating rapidly. It was the proximity to Khartoum that was causing his heart to race. He had not set eyes on the capital in ten years. He was, after all, a wanted man, and if the Sudanese Army chose to, they could descend on his small contingent of revolutionary soldiers and destroy them. How did he know that that would not happen? He didn't. It was only his faith in Robert N'gomo that had persuaded him to come this far. Nevertheless, he had insisted on coming on foot, along one of the many concealed pathways that followed the circuitous meanderings of the dry wadis that crisscrossed the arid semi-desert surrounding the capital.

Ahead, N'gomo walked at a relentless pace, never slowing, never going faster, stopping only once each hour for a tiny sip of water and a bite of smoked meat, which he ate continuously throughout the day. As N'gomo walked, his face was a portrait in stone. He could have been walking to his own execution for all of the emotion he displayed.

"We are on the outskirts of Khartoum," Ologabawa said to N'gomo. "Is it safe to keep pressing forward like this?"

"General Shamoun has guaranteed me your safety. You have nothing to fear."

"There are others besides Shamoun who operate around Khartoum."

N'gomo nodded without missing a step. "You mean al Mout li Kafir. Yes, Mustafa al Adim's militia can go where it pleases in this part of Sudan, but Shamoun has made his desire for your safety known to al Adim's men. Shamoun has no desire to provoke an even bloodier war than is already going on."

Ologabawa was about to ask about N'gomo's own safety and whether that, also was guaranteed, when the grass on either side of the path erupted with figures dressed in green camouflage, their AK-47 automatic rifles pointed directly at him and his men, who, in a reflexive gesture they all made as one, crowded around the general and raised their weapons. They were halted by a sharp command from N'gomo.

"Lower your weapons. Show them we come in peace," N'gomo shouted.

Ologabawa's men looked at him for direction. He nodded and motioned for his men to lower their guns. Whoever their ambushers were, they could have already killed his party if that was their aim.

"Are you from General Shamoun?" Robert N'gomo asked. There was no hint of fear in his voice.

A short, very dark middle-aged man stepped forward. He wore the uniform of a colonel in the Sudanese Army. "The General awaits you in the city. We will lead you to him." Without waiting for their response, the colonel turned and motioned for his men to take the lead and they began walking forward along the same path Ologabawa's men had been following.

Ologabawa walked alongside of N'gomo, towering over the older man. "How do we know we can trust this man?"

"What are our alternatives?" N'gomo asked His fate was in the hands of the little colonel he was following toward the capital.

As the party of soldiers emerged from a stand of overhanging trees, a break in the grass ahead indicated the site of a dirt road... one that looked well traveled. The colonel pointed forward, then led them from the path onto the rutted tracks of the road. "My armored vehicles are ahead," he said.

Ologabawa was uncertain how he felt about getting into vehicles that were owned by the Sudanese Army. When he saw the three armored Humvees ahead, he slowed his pace and looked over at his second in command, Colonel Bendori. The colonel's expression was uncertain. He looked back at his commander for a signal. The general knew that Bendori was ready to fight the little colonel and his small brigade of soldiers, which far outnumbered Ologabawa's own contingent, even if it meant certain death.

"We must trust these men. It is the only way to have a chance to achieve peace," N'gomo said, moving up quietly next to the general. "They will take us to General Shamoun."

Ologabawa and his men, along with N'gomo and the little colonel and a handful of Sudanese soldiers, boarded the Humvees. In a cloud of dust the three vehicles took off at full-speed down the dirt road. When they reached the paved highway, they lurched onto the asphalt without slowing their speed, fishtailing onto the main road and then straightening out as they headed toward the center of Khartoum.

At the center of the city, the three armored vehicles drove through the gates of the Central Armory, the main stockpile of weapons for the Sudanese army as well as the headquarters of its high command. They skidded to a stop in front of the armory's command post. From the doorway of the offices, which were guarded by two heavily armed soldiers on either side of the door, strode General Shamoun, dressed in his parade best, carrying a gold-handled, slender ebony riding crop, which he switched back and forth in the air as he walked.

The General was only five-feet five, which made him seem as if he were some kind of midget or dwarf compared to the Dinkas, who had been his adversaries for the last twenty years in the fight for South Sudanese independence, a fight he and his government had lost when the free world united behind the South Sudanese and an election gave them their own country. The memories of that defeat clouded his countenance as he did his best to overcome his size disadvantage by assuming a Napoleonic air—wearing uniforms that were weighted down with epaulets, medals, buttons and other trappings that signaled that, despite his diminutive size, his status was elevated well above those around him. Beside him was a figure familiar to Ologabawa. Dressed in his most formal ministerial finery, though not equal to the plumage worn by General Shamoun, Benjamin Said was president Koury's right hand man and his Minister of Defense.

Ologabawa turned to Robert N'gomo. "I thought this meeting was to be between only myself and General Shamoun."

N'gomo looked toward General Shamoun. "What is the meaning of Mr. Said's presence?"

"Mr. Said represents president Koury. If we come to an agreement, that meets Mr. Said's standards, he can guarantee the president will honor it," Shamoun answered.

General Ologabawa nodded in assent, though the look of suspicion did not leave his face.

Shamoun nodded back. "Welcome Mr. N'gomo and General Ologabawa," he said, transferring his riding crop to his left hand and extending his right hand to either of them. "Welcome to these talks of peace."

Ologabawa knew that Shamoun could have surrounded the Humvees and placed all of the occupants under arrest if he had chosen to—but he hadn't. General Ologabawa shook the other general's hand.

Shamoun motioned for them to enter the building. Ologabawa and the Defense Minister, Said, hesitated, eyeing each other warily, but Robert N'gomo strode through the door. The others followed. Ologabawa's men stayed outside, looking uncomfortably at the government soldiers who were loitering alongside the building. "Your men will be quite alright out here. My men will bring them water and food," Shamoun said.

Inside, they all took seats at a round conference table in a room that looked as if it also served as General Shamoun's office. On the wall was a large picture of president Koury. On the desk were pictures of a woman and two children, which General Ologabawa assumed were Shamoun's family. A private in uniform served them all glasses of chilled tea. When the private left, there were only the four of them in the room, seated around the table.

Surprising the other three, Robert N'gomo began the conversation. "You have been fighting for twenty years and General Ologabawa's forces have retained their control of the west while president Koury has kept control of the north and the rest of the country as well as the government. The war has cost millions of lives, both in soldiers and civilians. It is time you laid down your arms."

"Why isn't president Koury here?" Ologabawa asked.

"The president knows he will be unable to wage war if his Army disagrees with him," Said answered. "Anyway, he has authorized me to negotiate in his name."

Ologabawa looked around the table. "I am here because I trust Robert N'gomo and, like you, General Shamoun, I am weary of war. My people have suffered with little to show for our effort. Our entire country has gone backward as a result of this internal battle. If we agree to cease fighting, I must be sure that our western region and its tribes share in the wealth afforded by selling the oil that is in the territory we currently control. In the past the money all went into the pockets of the bureaucrats in Khartoum."

Shamoun nodded. "Of course. We will make arrangements that guarantee an equal sharing of the profits from the oil. I would expect you to ask for no less."

"And amnesty for my soldiers," Ologabawa added.

Again Shamoun nodded. "Of course."

"And a place in the government. Not just parliamentary seats, but a cabinet position as well," Ologabawa eyed Said when he spoke.

Said nodded in acquiescence. "Ministerial level. The president has already conceded as much."

"And what do you want in return?" Ologabawa asked. "And what does president Koury want?" He continued to direct his penetrating gaze toward Said.

The Minister of Defense straightened himself in his chair. "A truce would be to all of our advantage. We must present a united front, or we will be unable to resist the incursion of Mustafa al Adim and his al Mout li Kafir into our country. The terrorists want to use Sudan as a base to launch their attacks on our neighboring African countries. If they succeed, our land will run with blood. The Westerners will attack us with horrible weapons, and our neighbors will band together to drive us into the soil."

General Ologabawa narrowed his eyes. "Are you telling us that Mustafa al Adim will stay out of Sudan if our armies are united."

Said raised his head in pride. "We will be a mighty nation when we are united. We are not Somalia or Afghanistan, subject to occupation by whatever terrorist group wants to set up training camps on our soil."

"We are not Pakistan either or Lebanon," Ologabawa answered. "They are both powerful countries, and al Mout li Kafir has proven that it is no respecter of governments or armies. They will come to our country even if our armies are united. Sudan has many Muslims who are sympathetic to their cause."

Said's expression suddenly became uncomfortable. "Our president has secured an agreement with Mustafa al Adim."

The two generals both looked at the minister with suspicion.

"What kind of agreement?" Shamoun asked. "I was told of no agreement with al Mout li Kafir."

Said avoided the general's gaze. "Al Adim has only one demand."

"What is it?" Shamoun demanded.

Said continued to look away as he spoke. "He demands we turn over Mr. N'gomo to him."

General Ologabawa stiffened. "There will be no truce. We do not trade the life of Mr. N'gomo for the cooperation of a mass murderer."

General Shamoun nodded. "Mr. N'gomo has brought us together. No one else could have done that. He is not of our country, but all Africa needs him."

Said's embarrassment was gone. He looked both generals in the eyes. "Then there is no point in your talking to each other. We shall return to war."

Ologabawa stood up. "So be it."

Robert N'gomo held up his hand. "Wait."

Ologabawa sat back down. Everyone at the table looked at N'gomo.

"What is one life compared to thousands, even millions? You have been killing each other for many years. If al Mout li Kafir establishes a base in your country, even more millions will die. This demand comes as no surprise to me. I suspected that it would be a condition of al Mout li Kafir's cooperation when I brought you together. I am willing to make the sacrifice."

"They will kill you," General Shamoun said, a pained expression on his face.

"We were all given a pledge of protection for this meeting," General Ologabawa said, looking angrily at Shamoun.

Shamoun looked away from the other general's stare. "Mr. N'gomo asked for no protection," he muttered.

"I will not allow him to be taken," Ologabawa stated. His tone was like ice.

"Will the truce go ahead, and will al Mout li Kafir honor its pledge to stay out of Sudan if I am handed over to them?" N'gomo asked, turning to Said. He did not sound afraid.

"president Koury and Mustafa al Adim have agreed," Said said, his voice barely loud enough for the others to hear.

"It's out of the question," Ologabawa said, a note of near hysteria in his voice.

"It is a fair price to pay for peace. I am comfortable with the agreement," N'gomo said.

"They will kill you. They will parade you in front of television cameras and make you denounce the West and then they will kill you," Ologabawa said, his voice pleading.

"I have been tortured many times. I will only say what is in my heart," N'gomo answered calmly. "If my death can save thousands who would die in your war, I do not mind. Besides," he looked at each of them, "someone greater than myself is coming behind me."

"What are you talking about?" Ologabawa asked.

All three of the others stared at N'gomo, waiting for his explanation. They had heard him talk of such things before, but never understood what he had meant.

"You will know him when he appears. He has been sleeping for many years."

"He is African?" Ologabawa asked.

"He descends from the Asante, the great fathers of Africa."

"He is one of your people?" N'gomo was Asante himself.

"One who has been away for many years, but he will return. That is all I can say."

The other three all looked at each other. "I still refuse to go along with this deal," Ologabawa said.

"Please do it for me," N'gomo said, looking directly at the general. "I knew that this would be the price I would pay when I embarked on this task. It is a small price to pay for peace. It is what I wanted all along, General Ologabawa."

"Are you going to allow someone to be taken prisoner when he is under your protection?" Ologabawa asked Shamoun accusingly.

Shamoun did not look the other general directly in the eyes. "It is up to Mr. N'gomo."

"My decision is made," Robert N'gomo said.

Ologabawa was silent. He looked at each of their faces, then fastened on the face of Robert N'gomo. What he saw was a sublime look of peace and contentment. He realized he had no choice. "I will agree. We will sign a truce today. I am afraid, though that my conscience will haunt me forever for what I have done."

"Your conscience can be clear," N'gomo said. "You have chosen to save lives rather than to waste them. I am a happy man today and you too should be."

Chapter 10

My story had not even made the front page of my own paper, which had instead printed a brief AP news release and directed readers to the feature section where my interview with Derek Stewart, padded by material from my earlier background story about him, could be found in its meager entirety. It was admittedly pale in comparison to the embellished accounts in the other papers, written by reporters who dutifully described Stewart's enthusiastic, though completely fictitious, response to the Reverend Merrill Goodson's message concerning the nobility of our country's war against the Muslims. My report was true, but even I had to admit it was less stirring than the false reports of the others. Truth may sometimes be stranger than fiction, but it is rarely as entertaining.

Tom Edwards, my editor, as well as those above him who wielded even more power than did he and who were principally concerned with circulation and pleasing the Washington administration, were furious with me. Edwards accused me of writing a deliberately bland story because of my well-known animosity against President Ferris and Reverend Goodson. I accused him and his superiors of not wanting to print the truth and told them what they could do with both their paper and my job—references to shady areas of their anatomy included.

I was, of course, fired.

I should note here, lest you become misled, that I regard myself as a moral coward. On the other hand, I have an ingrained resistance to authority, no doubt left over from some childhood incident or failure on my parents' part. That resistance is every bit as strong a determinant of my behavior as my fear. As a result, I find myself living cautiously until the moment when someone with the power to do me serious harm arouses my indignation, at which point I cannot resist challenging him or her, sometimes in the most blatant manner. This perverse defiance has sometimes been confused with courage. But since it is as completely involuntary as if I had reacted by turning into a whimpering lump of jelly, I take no credit for it. However, as in the present case, I do suffer its consequences. Truthfully, I am not terribly dismayed by them, since I long ago abandoned any hope that my irrational habit of thumbing my nose at authority would come to anything short of catastrophic results.

Though unemployed, or perhaps because of it and the fact that I now had unlimited time on my hands, I found myself unable to abandon my interest in Derek Stewart. What interested me, to a degree that even I had to admit was a puzzle, was his assessment of the world into which he had re-awakened. For some reason, what Derek Stewart thought of the Orwellian world to which I had become accustomed but in which he now found himself , was of enormous importance to me. It was as though his opinion would constitute some sort of objective judgment on how far America had strayed from the version of the country into which I had been born and out of which Stewart had so precipitously been removed. At any rate, I decided it was worth one more attempt at surreptitiously re-entering the hospital and conducting another interview with Stewart—before I had to pay attention to necessities and begin looking for another job.

I was mildly surprised that the security around Stewart's room was still as intense as it had been on my previous visit, until I learned that the reason for such dedication was that Stewart himself was going to be meeting the press that very afternoon. My paper would have made sure that I was barred from a press conference, and they may even have alerted someone in Washington of my subversive intentions. I had next to no chance of sneaking into the press room at the hospital. On the other hand, no one expected me to walk into Stewart's room, and of course they wouldn't have expected me to be dressed, again, as a doctor.

No one except Derek Stewart, who didn't seem at all surprised to see me.

"Mr. Luke Evangelista, I am glad you have returned." Stewart's voice, although deep and confident, was casual and inviting, as if he and I were old friends. He sounded refreshed and resolute. At his side were the ever-vigilant and faithful giant Joshua Mannerly and the diminutive, but no doubt deadly, Tina

Nguyen. This time they did not step forward to bar my path to his bedside, although they both eyed me with suspicion and would probably have torn me to shreds and stuffed me into the trashcan labeled *disposables* if I made any untoward move.

Stewart looked alert, although his face still showed fatigue. He was looking directly at me today and smiling. His face was unlined. Only his eyes showed his age—they had a look of wisdom, tempered by a hint of humor. "I was afraid you might not come. Josh read me the various newspaper accounts of my recovery yesterday and yours was the only accurate narrative of the events or of my own words. I have a high value of the truth, Mr. Evangelista. Josh informed me that it would probably cost you your job for being so honest. But he must have been mistaken, for here you are today."

"Josh was not mistaken. My newspaper and I have come to a mutual agreement that we can no longer work together. I am here on my own."

"How will you write your story, if you no longer work for the paper?"

"Perhaps I won't. I guess I'm here to satisfy my curiosity." I had a momentary fear that Stewart would send me away. What purpose could it serve him to give an interview to an unemployed reporter?

"I'm pleased to hear that," Stewart answered. "The search for truth is not to be undervalued." He paused while he let his gaze run over me. I felt as if I was being weighed and judged, like a prize steer at a county fair. "I understand that you are a biographer," Derek said.

"I have written biographies in the past—when we had more freedom in this country to describe things as they really are."

"Would you like to be my biographer?" He asked the question quietly, as if he was sharing an intimate secret with me.

I was floored by his offer, but then I thought about the reality of my situation. "No publisher will publish anything I write as your biographer—especially since my newspaper is spreading the story that I'm out to undermine the credibility of the administration. For all I know I will be arrested as soon as I leave the hospital today."

"You needn't worry about a publisher," he said cheerily. "I have found out—from a family lawyer I didn't know I had—that I am extremely wealthy. I can employ you myself and even publish your book when it is finished." He gave me a wink. "And I don't think the government will arrest the biographer of the person they are hoping will be their newest hero, do you?"

He was right. I felt as if a silver spoon had just been inserted in my mouth.

"Offer accepted," I said, not wanting to give him time to re-think any of what he had proposed. "Can I begin interviewing you now?"

"I am tired and I have to meet the press in two hours. But I can answer a few questions. After that, you can talk to my lawyer, Mr. Erskine, and he will draw up a contract, which will include your salary. Josh and Tina are also now employed by me, rather than by the hospital."

I was impressed. Stewart moved quickly for someone who had only woken up yesterday and he certainly had a penchant for rewarding those who were loyal to him. "You seem more alert today," I said.

"Dr. Bhottu has told me that I am fully recovered from my coma."

"No more dreams?"

"My dreams are now confined to the periods when I am truly asleep."

"What do you plan to do, now that you are awake?"

A look of fatigue crossed his handsome young-looking face. "There is much I need to learn about the world into which I have awakened. Even as I experience the present, I am at a loss to appreciate it because of my absence for the last 40 years. Much of what I see and hear makes little sense to me. I have asked Mr. Erskine to find me a tutor."

"A tutor?"

"I am as a newborn child in this modern world, am I not?" There was that same hint of a twinkle in his eyes.

"Josh has read you the newspapers, have you watched any television?"

"I have watched some, but I am confused. It appears difficult to find a genuine news program. I do not remember Chet Huntley or David Brinkley or Walter Cronkite giving their opinions so often on their newscasts."

"I'm afraid unbiased news reporting has disappeared. We are an opinionated world these days."

"The remarkable Tina Nguyen is teaching me to use a computer. She is very adept at it herself and an excellent teacher. But the information I have found on the computer is even more biased than that on the television, although it is in greater depth and one can sample different points of view more easily."

"You must have been amazed when you learned of personal computers."

"He learned to use a computer and navigate the internet in less than a hour," Tina Nguyen volunteered a note of awe in her voice. She continued to speak in a shy quiet voice.

"You're a quick learner." I too was awed. I still fumbled with anything more complicated than word processing and, like nearly everyone else of my generation, I was a babe in the electronic woods compared to the children and teens of the present day when it came to the likes of tablets and iPods. Now Derek Stewart, who was nearly sixty, had learned to use the modern computer in less time than it had taken me to learn to use my cell phone.

"Dr. Bhottu mentioned that your brain had reorganized itself in some way. It sounds as if it might have done so to your advantage."

"I had many years to focus on my own thoughts. I learned a good deal about disciplining my mind."

As he spoke I realized that, though he had retained the appearance of a man in his twenties of thirties, albeit a tired one, he spoke with a certain air of wisdom and experience. I wondered from whence it had come. I mean, how much wisdom can one gain by sleeping through his adult life?

"When I spoke with you before, you were telling me about an extended dream you had, populated with characters from your past."

His eyes crinkled in a smile, as if he was pleased that I had remembered his conversation from the day before. Then his smile faded and his eyes narrowed in a thoughtful expression. "As a child I met many wise people. I believe I took what I knew of their words and personalities and extended them, so that what they said in my dreams was what I imagined they would have said, if I had actually been talking to them." He looked away from me, as if he might have drifted off into a world of his own thoughts.

"Who were these people?" I asked.

He turned back to me, looking as if indeed, he was returning from a moment of reverie. "Krishnamurthi, Albert Schweitzer, Bertrand Russell, Sartre, Bobby Kennedy, Martin Luther King, a few others, including my parents, of course—or I should say my grandparents—and my mother."

I was not as shocked by the panoply of luminaries he named as I might be, but the mention of his mother confused me. "I understood that you never met your mother."

He nodded, acknowledging that my understanding was correct. "My grandmother returned to Ghana after my birth and collected stories about my mother from the people who had known her. My mother and her cousin were descendants of Asante royalty and their offspring were destined for greatness. That was the legend."

"Their offspring? Does that include you?"

"Me and my distant cousin—my mother's cousin's son. I intend to see if he is still alive."

"I doubt that his life has been as remarkable as yours."

He smiled. "I'm sure it has been more active."

I changed the topic. "You spent forty years talking to Sartre, Russell, all those others, in your mind. That must have left quite an impression on you."

"My mother's people believed that one's ancestors, particularly those who were great and powerful, lived on in the minds of their people. Her religion consisted of honoring the great ones' memory by consulting with them as they existed in the minds of the living. In her tribe certain people studied the words of the great ones and committed them to memory. They became the oracles through which the great ones could be consulted."

"And you see yourself in that role—as an oracle?"

He smiled. "I am only telling you about the legends of my mother's people."

"You are going to be asked your opinion on many things."

He sighed. He looked as if he was having a hard time keeping his eyelids open. "I know little about this modern world."

Though he was undoubtedly correct, the wisdom in his words made me think that his opinion was already worth more than most people I knew. "Your words will carry much weight. You're a war hero. Reverend Goodson says you were awakened by God so you could be enlisted in our war against the Muslim hordes."

He groaned. "I gathered as much from the newspaper articles. I'm afraid I will disappoint many people." He closed his eyes. He looked as if he had fallen asleep.

I was unsure whether to ask another question. I moved closer but Josh Mannerly moved in front of me.

"Let him rest," Josh growled at me.

I stepped back. "No problem. We're all on the same side, Josh. I work for Mr. Stewart now."

"I've worked for him for more than 15 years. I don't want him hurt."

I looked him in the eyes. "Neither do I."

Chapter 11

The press room was even more crowded than it had been the previous day, resembling the raucous floor of the stock exchange more than the conference room of a military hospital. Derek had insisted that I be allowed to attend his press conference, and I was given a privileged position in front of the dais on which he and Dr. Bhottu were to speak. My former employer, the Washington Times, had sent Tom Edwards to fill in until they found a replacement for me, and I couldn't resist catching his eye to give him a snide leer. His irritation was gratifying.

Dr. Bhottu entered the room and with his usual brand of diffident but commanding aplomb, gave a brief update on Derek's condition. He explained that his patient was fully recovered from his coma, but that he was still physically weak from years of inactivity . He had taken a few steps but that was all, and even the exertion involved in sitting up for more than several minutes at a time would exhaust him.

Looking as fatigued as Dr. Bhottu's description had suggested he was, Derek was wheeled into the room. He gave no speech, but offered to answer questions until he became too tired to do so any longer. The press was unsure where to begin and the first question was obviously meant to be an easy one for him to answer.

"Are you aware that you are the last soldier form the Vietnam war to be wounded by enemy fire, and how does it feel to know that?" The reporter who asked was from one of the cable TV shows, which, in my opinion, turned every news story into a human interest feature—always probing for syrupy expressions of feeling, and skipping through the information part of the news as if it were a series of pitfalls to be avoided at all costs.

No one was prepared for Derek's answer, spoken in a weary, almost melancholy, tone. "I was not wounded by enemy fire." He looked out over the stunned audience as if he was ready for their next question.

I was as shocked by Derek's answer as was anyone in the room, especially since I had read the official record of the incident and it clearly stated that he had been shot while saving his comrades from a Viet Cong attack during their dash toward helicopters waiting to airlift them out of Saigon.

"Are you saying you were wounded by friendly fire?" the same reporter asked.

"I was shot by a fellow soldier after I stepped in front of a Vietnamese woman he was intending to kill." Derek's expression was impassive, but his eyes looked adrift in sadness.

There was moment of hushed silence. No one knew what to ask next.

"Do you mean you were shot on purpose?" someone finally asked, his tone unable to conceal his dread as he waited for the answer.

Derek stared unemotionally back at the reporter. "Only the man who shot me knows the answer to that question."

"Will you ask for an investigation?" someone else asked.

"That war is over," Derek answered. "I understand we have moved on to the next one already."

The room was silent. "You mean you aren't going to have charges brought against the man who shot you?" someone finally asked.

"I hope he has learned something. I have nothing more to learn from the incident."

"Then you hold no grudge against him?"

Derek managed a fleeting smile. "No."

The reporters remained unsure how to react to Derek's revelation, but they had revived enough to bombard him with questions.

"Reverend Goodson says you were revived by God to help us in our fight against the Islamic Jihadists. Can you comment on that?" The questioner was a reporter from *The True Evangelist*, the monthly magazine that served as the mouthpiece for Reverend Goodson's ministry.

Derek looked over the crowd of reporters before he answered. "Reverend Goodson is more certain of the reason I woke up than am I."

The reporter looked disconcerted but other reporters took over the questioning before he could follow his question with another.

"What do you intend to do with your life, now that you are awake?" my old editor, Tom Edwards asked.

"Seek the truth."

"The truth about what?" Edwards asked.

"About the world into which I have awakened."

More questions were shouted from the other reporters, but Derek appeared suddenly very exhausted. He looked over at Dr. Bhottu, who raised a hand and announced an end to the press conference. Josh Mannerly wheeled Derek off the stage while the reporters flew out of the room to file their stories.

Derek's report of being shot by a fellow soldier would certainly gain some headlines and might even lead to an investigation, though I doubted anyone wanted to dig up any dirt about the army, even the old Vietnam-era army, given the current patriotic mood of the country. Anyway, Derek had indicated that he did not intend to pursue the subject. The questions from Reverend Goodson's reporter had fallen flat but I doubted that that would be the end of the administration's attempt to use Derek to pump up enthusiasm about the war. And what would the American public think? Had they just lost a hero or gained one? I didn't know the answer, but I was sure about one thing. I had a job and it looked as if it was going to be one of the most interesting ones of my career.

Chapter 12

Fifteen years ago, as a simple German Catholic Priest, Heinz Berthold would have been awe-struck by his surroundings. Now, in his new role as Pope Gregory, he was less awe-struck than disappointed in the worn and somewhat shabby appearance of the White House. The president's residence paled in comparison to his own at the Vatican. He felt a sense of satisfaction. After all, he was the leader of a world-wide religion, while the United States president, powerful as he might be, led only a single nation. The feeling of satisfaction was quickly replaced by one of irritation. He knew that President Ferris was waiting for the Reverend Goodson before admitting the pope into his office. Ferris seemed to think that he needed his own religious advisor in order to stand on equal footing with the Catholic leader.

The thought that anyone, much less the president of the United States would think that the pope and Reverend Merrill Goodson were equals was an insult to the Pontiff. Goodson was an unlettered simpleton who had gained his power by pandering to the American thirst for simple answers and braggadocio. He preached that America held a favorite place in God's eyes, much as had Israel in the Old Testament and that the Holy Scriptures were transparently clear to anyone—ignoring centuries of dialogue by theologians and philosophers about their meaning. His own sermons and speeches were sprinkled with misquotations from the scriptures and juxtapositions of snippets of biblical text, which were gerrymandered together to prove a point that was otherwise completely unsupported by an informed reading of the holy manuscript.

The only saving grace to be gained by Reverend Goodson's position of power within the Ferris administration was that the Reverend agreed with Pope Gregory when it came to the seriousness of the Islamic threat. Goodson's fear was that the Muslim hordes would terrorize his country and gain control of valuable resources, principally the oil in the Middle East and Africa, eventually challenging American world domination. Pope

Gregory's fear was that the Islamic revolution would sweep the world, particularly the vulnerable African nations, and replace Catholicism as the religion of the poor and dispossessed. Both men of God feared that the other would become the spiritual leader of the Western world in its fight against Islam.

The door opened and President Ferris strode into the Green Room. "I apologize for keeping you waiting, your Holiness," Ferris said, a look of concern in his eyes but a broad smile on his face as he extended his hand.

Pope Gregory, whose aides had immediately jumped to their feet and come to his side, did not stand. The pope was built like a fireplug, and he felt he looked more dignified when he was sitting, with his papal vestments concealing his height. He was more darkly complected than most Germans and underneath his papal hat, his hair was still jet black. He held out a hand for the president to kiss his papal ring. Ferris mistook the gesture and grabbed the outstretched hand and began pumping it.

"Why don't you come inside my office. Reverend Goodson is already here—I'm afraid he was a little late—and we can talk. Your people can wait here, if you don't mind…unless you want one of them to translate for you." The president had a habit of treating foreign dignitaries who struggled with English as if they might be retarded. He prided himself on speaking no languages other than English—or *American*, as he called it.

"I do not require translation," the pontiff replied, stiffly, in perfect English, "but I would like Cardinal Bertolini to accompany me to take notes. I prefer a record of all of my conversations."

"I don't blame you a bit, Pope," the president said, gesturing toward the open door to this office, "it's always good to have a record of what gets said. Saves a lot of misunderstandings in the future."

The pope rose and walked slowly into the Oval Office. Pope Gregory was no older than President Ferris himself, but he walked at a slow and stately pace in order to emphasize the superiority of his position. He was pope for life, after all, and Ferris could be ousted from office by a mere whim of the

American electorate. Before the pontiff had a chance to sit, Reverend Goodson rose from his chair and crossed the room to meet him. The reverend had one hand on his heart and the other outstretched as if he was about to bestow his blessing upon the pope. Gregory couldn't conceal his horror at the man's lack of decorum.

"Great to see you again, your Holiness," Goodson said, lowering his outstretched hand when he saw that the pope had no intention of extending his own for a handshake. "I apologize for holding up our meeting. I had to catch the press conference for a man I think can be very useful to us in our fight—fella who just woke up from a 40 year coma."

The pope took a seat. Cardinal Bertolini took the seat just behind the Pontiff's right shoulder, the Cardinal's pad and pen at the ready.

"I have heard about this man," the pope said. "A very interesting case, medically, but I am not sure what he has to do with our fight against Islam."

"I think his waking up was a sign, your Holiness. We need a shot in the arm, so to speak, to get the people behind us and God woke up Derek Stewart—a modern-day Lazarus, ready to go out and preach the Lord's gospel."

The pope's expression was chilly. "I do not require an additional messenger, especially one who represents nothing but a novel medical phenomenon, such as your Mr. Stewart. The European nations are already behind me."

Goodson looked irritated, but instead of answering the pope he turned to the president. "Maybe you'd better explain to his Holiness that we're going to need all the messengers we can muster."

"What is he talking about?" Pope Gregory asked, looking from one to the other of them.

The president looked glum. He shook his head sadly. "Politics is a lot rougher than you religious folks think, Pope. This whole thing with the Muslims may go nuclear pretty soon."

The pope's expression changed from disdain to alarm. "What are you talking about?"

"We've got some pretty good intelligence that says the Iranians may send a nuclear missile over to Tel Aviv. They and the Syrians are teaming up to put an end to Israel once and for all."

The pope looked aghast. "Can't you do something to stop it?"

The president rubbed his chin. He had the expression of a simpleton on his face, but his eyes shifted cagily back and forth between Goodson and Pope Gregory. "Maybe we can… maybe we can't. A preemptive nuclear strike by our side would be universally criticized. We might even lose the support of some of those European countries you were speaking about—France and Germany, for instance."

The pope narrowed his eyes. "So you are asking me to plead your case in front of the Germans and the French? To give my blessing to an American preemptive attack?" His tone indicated that the idea was unthinkable.

"No such thing, Pope," Reverend Goodson interrupted. "We're not talking about a preemptive attack at all."

The pope's expression showed his confusion. "Then what are you talking about?"

"We're talking about letting the Iranians take out Tel Aviv with their nuclear weapon," the president answered, the look of simplicity no longer on his face. His eyes were narrowed as he talked. "We're talking about letting them launch their attack on Israel. Then we'll counterattack. We'll nuke Tehran, Damascus and Beirut and we'll demand an Arab withdrawal from Israel or we'll just keep on nuking more of their cities. We'll wipe out the leadership of those Muslim countries and we'll put a NATO force in Israel—the parts that aren't radioactive, anyway." He hesitated and looked over at Reverend Goodson. "We'll declare Jerusalem—or what's left of it—a Judeo-Christian city and clear out the Muslims if there's any of them left alive. The Jews can rebuild their Temple in peace—under Christian authority."

"And prophesy will be fulfilled," Reverend Goodson chimed in, his round face beaming with excitement.

The Americans are crazy, the pope thought to himself. It wasn't the first time he'd had such a thought. "I don't mean to challenge your judgment, but has Vice President Rogers been apprised of this plan?" Since the vice president was on the Board of Directors of all the international companies who, in fact, controlled the leaders of most of the European nations, his opinion was of even greater importance to those leaders than was that of President Ferris.

"It was the vice-president's idea," Donovan said.

Suddenly the pope could see possibilities in the idea. "A modern crusade!" he exclaimed, his excitement rising. The American plan would restore Jerusalem to his authority he thought to himself. The Church would once again have dominance in the place that was the center of its religion. But he was getting carried away. "Millions will be killed," he said, solemnly, casting his eyes to the floor, his face a picture of gravity.

"The dead will be mostly Muslims who would kill us if they had the chance," the president answered. "We'll lose a boatload of Jews, too, but it can't be helped. They'll thank us in the long run."

"And what about al Mout li Kafir?" Pope Gregory asked.

"They will mount reprisals, we can be sure of that. But how many new converts are they going to get once the other Arab states see what we do to anyone who seriously challenges us? The Saudis, Egypt, the shaky Iraqi government who is known to be soft on terrorists within their borders—all of them will think twice about aligning themselves with Mustafa al Adim and his thugs. We expect there will be a crackdown on any al Mout li Kafir operating within other Arab nations."

"No Arabs are going to be happy about losing Jerusalem." Pope Gregory said, his skepticism returning. "Jerusalem is a holy city for Islam as well as for Christians and Jews They're not going to give it to us, even if it's been leveled by a war." The Americans were making things sound too easy.

"The fucking Arabs have got Mecca, for Christ sake, how much of the Middle East do they want?" the president exploded, then caught himself. "Sorry, I didn't mean to swear, your Holiness. But Jerusalem is a holy city for Jews and Christians. We don't need the damn Muslims there, too. They'll just have to live with us being there and with them being left out."

"What do you want me to do?" Pope Gregory asked. He had no intention of just carrying out American orders, but he suspected that was what these unlettered clowns were asking of him.

"We want you to carry our message to the European leaders, particularly, Segorne in France and Holtz in Germany as well as DeCrespi in Italy, of course. Let them know in advance that you heard from us that an attack on Israel may not be avoidable and that our plan, should such an attack happen, is to counterattack with full force—nuclear—and the end result will be to drive the Muslims out of Jerusalem. Let them know the religious, not just the political importance of this. They know, as well as we do, that we're in an ideological war with the Muslims, and this is our chance to deal them a telling blow. We just all need to stand together."

"They will want to talk to you personally, Mr. president." The European leaders regarded the pope as their spiritual leader, not their military strategist.

"Sure, sure, they can talk to me. I just want them to know that you and Goodson, here regard what we're going to do as necessary if we're going to finally put an end to all of this Muslim nonsense. Those people are savages and their religion is a savage one. That's the point you made in your Benedictine Re-affirmation, and we're just taking your point to its logical conclusion."

"We're trying to re-establish the morality of Christianity in this world," Reverend Goodson said in a solemn tone.

The pope nodded. He understood and agreed. He also understood that should the plan fail or world opinion not be supportive, it would be the Americans, with their Western gunslinger style and militant, fundamentalist Christianity who would be held to blame. He could always step back and preach moderation, if need be. It was a win-win situation for him. He was sure the heads of state in most of the European countries would see things the same way.

Chapter 13

It was the first time I'd entered Derek Stewart's room without having to steal a white doctor's coat to gain entrance. This time I was dressed in my working clothes—those I wore when I worked for myself and not for some establishment newsmonger—a pair of jeans and a wool Pendleton shirt and sneakers.

I was shocked to see Stewart standing beside his bed.

"Good morning Mr. Evangelista. You look surprised." Derek's deep voice sounded brisk and energetic.

"Dr. Bhottu made it sound as if it would be some time before you could stand." As soon as I said the words, I noticed that Dr. Bhottu himself was also in the room, just inside the door.

"Mr. Stewart continually defies medical predictions," the Indian doctor answered in his soft, crisp English. "Mr. Mannerly and Miss Nguyen must have done a better job of maintaining his muscle strength than I had thought."

I also noticed that both Josh and Tina were in the room. Although neither was within a few feet of Derek, they both looked as if they were poised to catch him should he not be able to sustain his erect position.

"Josh and Tina must give me room to try my wings," Derek said, turning and looking at the wheelchair, which sat about eight feet from where he stood. "I am going to walk to the wheelchair and sit down." With that he gingerly stretched out a foot in the direction of the chair. Both Josh Mannerly and Tina Nguyen sprang forward to come to his aid.

"I do not need your help, thank you," Derek said, gently, waving a hand in the air to shoo the two physical therapists away. He edged forward with two more unsteady steps, then seemed to gain strength and, straightening himself to his full height, strode purposefully the rest of the way to the wheelchair. When he sat down his chest was heaving with the effort.

"That is amazing," Dr. Bhottu exclaimed, the confused expression on his face echoing his words. "You are making medical history."

Derek had regained his normal breathing and he looked surprisingly relaxed, sitting upright in the wheelchair. "Speaking of history, it is about time for my tutor to arrive," he said.

At that moment, an attractive fortyish-looking woman, dressed in a pair of dark wool slacks, which I noticed, fit tightly enough to show off her shapely hips and long, slender legs, and wearing a white, equally figure-complimenting cashmere sweater while carrying a large, business-like black leather briefcase entered the room. She had a narrow face accentuated by high cheekbones and a wide, straight mouth, which seemed to be set in a grim expression. Large, dark-rimmed glasses gave her an academic appearance. "Mr. Stewart?" she asked, looking around at each of us. Her long, straight, brunette hair swished from side to side as she surveyed the room. She managed to flash a brief, polite smile.

"Professor Milne, I presume," Derek answered from his chair. To my surprise, he stood up, as if it was no effort, and extended his hand.

"I'm Doctor Karin Milne, your tutor. Mr. Erskine told me to report here today to begin our lessons." She spoke with the matter-of-fact directness of a teacher addressing a pupil.

Derek sat back down. "Doctor Milne is a professor of history at Georgetown and presently on sabbatical. She is an expert on the mid to late twentieth century, most of which I did not experience. She has written several books and published many papers in distinguished professional journals and comes highly recommended. It is her job to inscribe the events of the last forty years on the tabula rasa of my brain." He introduced each of us to her.

The business-like Professor Milne looked surprised when Derek announced my name. "Mr. Evangelista has written some notable books himself," she said, looking at me with an interest that hadn't been there before. "I even have one of his books with me for you to read. His biography of President Ferris, written at the end of his first term gained Mr. Evangelista much notoriety as well as disfavor with the current administration."

"How did you get a copy?" I asked. The publisher had been banned from continuing printing halfway through the first run. I had thought all the extant copies had been confiscated.

"It's my personal copy," she answered, not appearing self-conscious about her admission.

"Why did you choose Mr. Evangelista's book?" Derek asked, a look of curiosity on his face.

"Despite his shrill tone," she began, casting a disapproving glance my way, "I believe it is the most honest appraisal of President Ferris's background and his first term in office."

I tried not to blush. I was also wondering how far Professor Milne's adulation of my work extended, though it seemed to be mixed with disapproval. She was a beautiful, if somewhat intimidating woman. My ruminations were addressed almost immediately.

"I've been disappointed that Mr. Evangelista has given up his serious writing career for the opportunity to deliver pointless attacks on the establishment through the public media," she continued, directing a deprecating frown in my direction. "Aren't you now a reporter for one of the newspapers?"

"Thank you for your unsolicited assessment of my career," I answered. "You'll be pleased to learn I've given up my position with my newspaper, at their insistence. In other words, they fired me. I'll be able to serve as Derek's Boswell with no mixed loyalties."

The look she directed toward me was dripping with skepticism. "A real scholar, which you have shown you have the capability of being, would never have prostituted his talents to the public media, nor engaged in the administration-baiting for which some of your previous writing was known."

"Thanks for the view from the ivory tower professor. Some of us succumb to the need to put food on our tables. I don't know your work, but it's been my impression that even scholarly accounts of the current political situation have had to be laundered so as not to be critical of the administration."

The professor stiffened. "I don't slant my scholarly writing one way or the other. I simply do not write in a provocative mode as you do."

Derek's gaze flicked between the professor and myself and, rather than appearing alarmed at the verbal jousting that seemed to characterize his new family, he appeared to be suppressing a smile. "It looks as if we will be a congenial group. Now we must begin work. I need to learn as much as I can as fast as possible, professor. In two weeks, I am to be interviewed on national television."

"I'm afraid you won't be able to learn much in two weeks," Karin Milne responded, sternly, as if she wanted to lay down her ground rules for learning history right from the start.

"Who is interviewing you on TV?" I asked, fearing that it might again be Reverend Goodson or one of his group.

"Someone named Norman Wycroft. Mr. Erskine indicated that Mr. Wycroft has a very wide audience and is an excellent interviewer."

Norman Wycroft did, indeed have a wide audience and at one stage of his career he was an excellent interviewer. In recent years, however, he had, just like everyone else who wanted to keep their position in the media, succumbed to the kind of right-wing, jingoistic populism that had infected the country. His interviews were either harsh attacks on anyone who challenged the Ferris administration or shameless tributes to those who expressed platitudinal homage to God and country and represented the official government position on anything from the need for military strength to the danger of allowing personal freedom to undermine the war on terror.

"Mr. Erskine is either naïve or sadistic," I said. "Norman Wycroft will crucify you if you don't parrot the party line."

For a fleeting moment, Derek appeared amused. "Being crucified would put me in very good company." He looked directly at Karin Milne. "But we must get busy, professor, or I will disappoint everyone by my display of ignorance."

I wanted to say more, but I stopped myself. Derek had already defied medical odds, and he appeared confident that he would be able to handle the interview with Wycroft. Who was I to say he couldn't? "Do you mind if I stay and listen?" I asked, looking first at Karin then Derek.

Derek gave me a broad smile. "You are my biographer. You mustn't miss anything."

Karin Milne turned down her pretty mouth in a frown, directed toward me. But beneath the thin veneer of her obvious distaste, was she really happy that I was staying? I could hope, couldn't I?

Chapter 14

Mohammed Sahadi was only twenty-two years old but he had been responsible for carrying out a sufficient number of deadly terror attacks to gain him a place within Mustafa al Adim's inner circle. But this morning Mohammed was confused. Why had the leader of al Mout li Kafir asked him to return to Lebanon, when he had been about to complete his mission of blowing up the residence of France's president? Why was he being asked to participate in the interrogation of Robert N'gomo, a man about whom he knew nothing, and to put his mission in France on hold? Mohammed was not an interrogator. Neither was he a torturer. He was an assassin and an expert at making bombs. He had been since he was 15 years old.

Mohammed had been 13 years old when the last and bloodiest war between Lebanon and Israel had broken out. In his village in southern Lebanon, Hezbollah reigned supreme, running the local government and supporting the economy with donations derived from surreptitious support of the political organization's activities form Iran. His father was not active in Hezbollah, but he supported his neighbors, nearly all of whom were guerilla fighters. Mohammed's mother and father ran a small shop where they eked out a modest living repairing shoes. They taught Mohammed and his brother that Hezbollah was the party that would look out for their interests and defend them from the Zionists in Israel who wanted to steal their land, as they had stolen the land of the Palestinians.

When the war broke out, everyone in Mohammed's village celebrated. The Israelis were unable to stop the daily barrage of missiles launched from the hills behind his village. The threat of attack by Israeli land forces was countered by the Hezbollah militia, who ringed his village, built makeshift caves and hillside hideouts to conceal themselves and bragged that they would slaughter the Israeli soldiers when they walked, unaware, into what appeared to be a deserted town.

Mohammed and his family hid in the basement of their shop and waited for the battle. They had been told that there was no need for them to leave, so long as they did not make their presence known. The Israelis would enter the village and be attacked from all sides by the Hezbollah militia, hidden beneath the ground in the surrounding hills.

That was how it was supposed to go, but the reality had been terribly different. The Israelis came as planned, fanning out across the village, looking for hidden soldiers, rounding up the villagers who had been left behind. After a half day without resistance, the Israelis decided to use the village as an encampment. Every house and every shop became a barracks for the exhausted Israeli footsoldiers. When they entered Mohammed's father's shop, the family's hiding place was quickly discovered, and Mohammed and his brother and parents were confined to the shop and told to remain there, host to a handful of Israeli soldiers who kept their rifles trained on the family while they took turns sleeping and eating. There was a cursory interrogation regarding where the Hezbollah fighters had gone, but feigned ignorance was enough to satisfy the Israelis.

At sundown the bombardment from the hillside began. Mohammed knew that the Hezbollah leaders were aware that there were still villagers present among the Israeli troops, but someone had made the decision that a few Lebanese lives lost was a small price to pay for the prize of wiping out an entire Israeli division. The village was leveled. Mohammed was the only member of his family to survive. He watched his parents' shop explode around him from a direct hit by a Hezbollah rocket. Every Israeli soldier within the shop died, but so did Mohammed's father and mother and brother—his five year old brother who had never done any harm to anyone.

Mohammed did not lose his hate for the Israelis. If they had not invaded his village, his family would still be alive. But he also knew that it was the Hezbollah leaders from his village, men who knew his father and whom his father had trusted to keep his family safe, who were also responsible for his family's death. When the Israeli army retreated back across the border and the Hezbollah fighters returned to the village to bury their dead and begin the process of rebuilding, Mohammed knew he wanted nothing to do with the men who claimed to be heroes. A year later, when al Mout li Kafir began to circulate in secret among the people of his village, Mohammed listened to their criticism of the Hezbollah tactic of sacrificing Muslims to kill Jews. Mustafa al Adim, the Al Mout li Kafir leader preached that self-sacrifice—suicide missions—were holy, but killing fellow Muslims while keeping oneself safe, even if the purpose was to kill the enemy, was murder.

Mohammed left his village. There was nothing left for him there anyway. With a small contingent of fellow Lebanese, he traveled to Afghanistan where he volunteered to fight for al Mout li Kafir. There he met Moustafa al Adim for the first time in person. The leader of the infamous terrorist group, which had replaced Al Qaeda as the most feared army of bombers and assassins on the planet, was an inspirational and fiery commander.

Al Adim was the privileged son of a Saudi business magnate. He had rejected his father's ties with Western commerce and the Saudi government but not his access to his family's money. Almost single-handedly, the young Saudi had raised an army and an international network of fundamentalist operatives, none of them hesitant to lose their lives to wipe out the heathen Christians and Jews and dislodge all Western influences from their holy lands.

Mohammed identified with Moustafa al Adim's anger. But Mohammed, even at fourteen, was too wary and too disillusioned to be taken in by the terrorist chief's heated speeches. Mohammed knew only that he could use the Saudi firebrand's international network to wreak his personal vengeance on the Western powers that had allowed his family and his country to be destroyed.

Too slight and too young to be an effective foot soldier, Mohammed's quick intelligence and nimble fingers made him a natural as a bomb maker. For the next seven years he traveled throughout Europe connecting with small cells of al Mout li Kafir operatives and making their bombs for them. He was responsible for the deaths of nearly two hundred people.

And now he was back in Lebanon. On this bright and dry morning, he was standing at the side of Mustafa al Adim, who had moved his headquarters to Lebanon's Bekaa Valley, also occupied by Hezbollah, but an area so teeming with terrorist and freedom fighter training camps, that al Adim could coordinate his world-wide Jihad with impunity.

Mohammed had not witnessed an interrogation since his days in training in Afghanistan when he was fourteen years old. Now Mustafa al Adim had brought him back from France in order to participate in the torture and questioning of Robert N'gomo.

"He is a weak and ineffectual dreamer," Mustafa explained. The wild-eyed, forty-year old leader of al Mout li Kafir, paced, as he always did, when he talked, as if he was addressing a crowd even if only one other person was present. In this case the other person was Mohammed Sahadi, listening stoically, no expression showing on his young face. He had listened to al Adim before. He was familiar with the latter's theatrics. Although older than Mohammed by nearly twenty years, the al Mout li Kafir leader was almost as slim as the young Lebanese. His mannerisms contained just a hint of femininity, despite their violent portent. Mohammed had always wondered if al Adim wasn't trying to overcome his self-consciousness about his manhood by projecting such a fearful image. But the anger that fueled Mustafa al Adim's ravings was genuine.

"N'gomo has no belief in God—not Allah, not the Hebrew Jehovah, not even Jesus Christ or Buddha," al Adim went on. "He raises his hand against no one, yet he commands people and they do as he says. I do not understand him, but if we are to achieve our ends in Africa, we must destroy him." Al Adim stared hard at Mohammed, his eyes blazing with zeal.

"How can he be a threat if he is weak—if he will not fight?" Mohammed asked. He was not afraid to challenge Mustafa al Adim. Everyone else was afraid of the fiery leader or else they treated him as if he was a prophet. Mohammed didn't believe in prophets. He wasn't even sure he believed in Allah. But he knew he hated Israel and the European nations and America, all of whom had allowed Israel to invade Lebanon and kill Lebanese civilians at will. And Mustafa al Adim was the only man he knew who hated as much as he did. But he had trusted terrorist leaders before. He had trusted Hezbollah. Mustafa al Adim could command Mohammed's loyalty only if he continued to warrant Mohammed's trust. If he did not, Mohammed would walk away from al Mout li Kafir—or turn on them. He did not mind dying to appease his hatred.

"I do not understand it myself," Al Adim answered. "N'gomo is a persuasive speaker. He says what the weak and dispossessed want to hear—that they have the strength to resist their governments, to resist their barbaric militias who slaughter them by the thousands, to resist even our call to arms. His message is the opposite of ours and that is why he needs to be silenced."

'Then why haven't you killed him? Why are you questioning him? What can he know that is worth keeping him alive?"

Al Adim became even more agitated. They were talking in a small room in a stucco building that served as both the prison where Robert N'gomo was being kept and as an interview room for the prisoners. Al Adim wore his signature white galabiyya and checkered kafiyyeh with his face exposed. His lower face was covered by a dark beard. Mohammed, in contrast, wore a pair of baggy cotton pants and hiking boots. On his upper body he wore a sweatshirt with *Boston College* printed across the front. His face was clean-shaven. He was used to dressing as a young European immigrant. He had been in Europe long enough to feel odd and old-fashioned when he wore traditional Arab clothing, though he felt faintly guilty for feeling that way, but not guilty enough to alter his attire, not even in the presence of Mustafa al Adim, who despised everything Western.

"I had hoped to force him to disavow his calls to resist us," al Adim said, his face contorting in anger. "He will not do it. He has been tortured too many times before. Nothing we do seems to frighten him."

"Then why is he still alive?"

"He knows something we need to know. I want you to be present when he tells us."

"But how can you make him tell us anything if he has no fear of torture?" Mohammed thought that al Adim wasn't making sense. He often feared that the Al Mout li Kafir leader was, at bottom, crazy.

"He does not need to be forced to tell us. He makes no secret of what he knows."

"What is it, then?"

Al Adim went to the door. "I will have him brought in and you can hear it for yourself."

Mohammed took a seat while Mustafa al Adim went out of the tiny room and could be heard shouting orders to the guards in the prison. Presently, al Adim returned, followed by two armed guards who were dragging a large black man, a man who was in his sixties, stripped to the waist, his upper body marked from whippings and his face swollen and bruised from repeated beatings, one eye swollen shut. When the man grimaced in pain, Mohammed could see that several of his teeth were broken or missing. The guards jammed their prisoner down into a chair, and Mustafa al Adim stood at his side, staring menacingly down on the broken man in the chair.

"Have you changed your mind about telling your followers that they should join in our Jihad against the West?" al Adim asked, his voice subdued, despite the look of anger on his face.

N'gomo struggled to look up at his interrogator, but he had difficulty raising his head and the eyelid on his left eye only twitched feebly when he tried to open it. "Your battle, if it is fair, can be won without violence. If you must resort to violence, it is because reason and justice are not on your side." In contrast to his appearance, the prisoner's voice was deep and forceful. Mohammed could hear no trace of fear in the man's tone.

Mustafa al Adim looked at Mohammed Sahadi and raised his hands in a gesture of helplessness, as if to say, "you see?" He turned back to the prisoner. "If that is your view, then you will tell your supporters nothing, for unless you cooperate with us you will not be alive to speak to anyone." Al Adim paused to move back in front of N'gomo's face, even though it was not clear whether or not the prisoner could see him, or anything else any longer. "I want to know about the man you say is to follow you… the man from the West."

"He has nothing to fear from you, for he will speak the truth and truth always wins out over lies and hatred."

"Where is this man now?"

"He is in America."

"An American? They are all imperialist swine. No one listens to them any more. They have lied to every nation of the world."

"He is descended from Africans. He is my cousin. He is not associated with American lies."

Al Adim bristled. "Every American is associated with lies. The world understands that the Americans justify everything they do because they think they are privileged and strong. They think that Jesus will protect them."

"This man does not share the blame for American errors of the last decades. He has been asleep."

"Asleep—for decades? You must be mad." Al Adim's face showed his anger. He drew back his hand to hit N'gomo across the face.

"I have heard of such a person," Mohammed Sahadi said.

Al Adim spun around. "What do you mean, you have heard of him?"

"An American—an American descended from Africa— he just woke up from a 40 year coma. I read about it when I was in Europe. I saw him on television."

Al Adim turned back to N'gomo. "Was that your cousin—the one Mohammed saw on TV?"

"I do not know. I have never met him. But he has been asleep for decades. He is my age. His mother's cousin was my mother."

"And why is your cousin so special?" Al Adim demanded.

"He will speak the truth. He will lead people away from war."

"Lead the Americans away from war?" Al Adim laughed loudly. "The Americans don't want to hear the truth, and they will not be led away from war. Your cousin is in the wrong country, if that's his message."

"Your people will listen to him also. His message is not just for America."

"He will not speak to my people. I will see to that. Your cousin and you share something, N'gomo. You will both be dead soon—you sooner than him." Al Adim grabbed the prisoner by the arm and jerked him out of the chair. "Guards, take this infidel away. Lock him up again."

"He is a crazy person," Mohammed Sahadi spat out distastefully, after Robert N'gomo had been taken from the room. His anger concealed his fear—a fear he had forgotten that he could still feel. He was afraid because he didn't understand how the prisoner who had just been in front of him could speak with such authority. He had never seen someone who had such conviction but appeared to lack the hatred that fed both Mohammed's and Moustafa al Adim's passion. Yet, even without anger, Robert N'gomo showed no fear at all.

"He may be crazy, but people listen to him. He has stopped wars. The Sudanese war in Darfur will come to a halt because of that man. And you have verified with your own lips that the man of which he speaks is in America."

"There is a man in America who was in a coma for 40 years and just woke up. Whether it is the man of whom N'gomo speaks, I do not know." The story had caught his attention because of its bizarre nature, but he had not followed it to any depth.

"Well that's why I brought you here. You've heard N'gomo. He says his cousin will talk to our people as well as the Americans. We can't let that happen. I want you to travel to America and kill that person."

"America?" The thought excited Mohammed. America was the enemy, but it was also the land of everyone's dreams. He felt his anxiety rising.

"America is where this person is," Adim continued. "I want you to get close enough to find out if that is the person that N'gomo is talking about. If he is, then I want you to kill him. I don't need to tell you how to do that, do I?"

"No." Mohammed was very good at killing, perhaps better than Mustafa al Adim himself. "What will you do with N'gomo?"

"He is of no use to us. We will kill him. His only use is to let the African nations know that their symbol of peace no longer lives."

Mohammed remembered the soft voice and the total lack of fear in the man who had been so badly beaten. "Is it necessary to kill him? He is no longer a threat when he is in prison here." He was surprised, almost shocked, that he was feeling such a sentiment, and he was at a loss to explain his emotional reaction even to himself.

Mustafa al Adim's face hardened. He grasped Mohammed by the arm, squeezing it until it began to hurt. "Do not become soft, Mohammed. Perhaps you have spent too much time in Europe. You no longer dress as we do, and now you want to let our enemy live. If you become soft, you are no longer of use to us."

Mohammed jerked his arm away from al Adim's grasp. "I can still kill." He stared hard at Mustafa al Adim. There was no fear in his eyes. "And I will not be threatened… by anyone."

Al Adim stared back, his face hardened in anger. Then his expression relaxed. "Of course you can kill. That is why I have chosen you for this mission. You alone, can make it happen."

Mohammed nodded, then turned and stepped through the door into the shimmering desert heat.

Chapter 15

Neither Professor Milne nor myself was prepared for the super-human speed at which Derek devoured books, scanned computer screens and retained voluminous amounts of historical information, taxing our combined ability to feed him a coherent story of the events of the late twentieth century. Unlike a computer, of which Derek's information processing speed reminded us, the newly awakened learner's interests did not follow a linear pathway through the past 40 years. Instead, he bounced from topic to topic, event to event and geographical location to geographical location, weaving a web of connections which made sense only to him. Just when I was satisfied that I had deciphered the theme around which he was examining recent history—the growth of religious fanaticism, or race relations within developed nations, or the increasing economic disparity between the countries of Asia and Africa and the rest of the world—he abruptly changed topics and his inquiries darted off in another direction—scientific breakthroughs in genetics, for instance or the role of fossil fuels in geopolitics over the last half century—usually well before Karin or I was able to change gears and well before we could assemble enough material to satisfy his all-consuming curiosity. His ability to acquire and integrate new information had surpassed the level of any human capability with which either of us was familiar.

"Karin was correct in her appraisal of your book on President Ferris," Derek greeted me with his low, embracing voice, when I returned to his room the day after his first session with the professor and myself. "I read your book last evening. Though your writing style was more caustic than I would have liked, I sensed your attempt to be even-handed in your assessment of Mr. Ferris, and your conclusions turned out to be scathing, but largely supported by the facts." He stared at me with an intensity that would have made me uncomfortable, except that it also radiated warmth, as if he would accept me regardless of whether I measured up to any standard.

"Largely? Did you think some of my conclusions were unfair?" I asked. I was feeling surprisingly dependent upon his opinions about my work.

"You know the answer better than I."

His answer was enigmatic—something I was getting used to. I was less surprised by Derek's assessment of my book than by the fact that he'd read it. I had not left his hospital room until eight in the evening, and I'd thought he was too tired to continue with his studies after that. I was exhausted myself. My book, which he'd apparently read after I'd left, was nearly 800 pages long. Unless we were planning to import the Library of Congress into his hospital room, it was clear that we would have to move the location of Derek's sessions with Karin because my book had been the last piece of reading she had brought for him, and she'd intended for it to last several weeks, if not longer. She would have to work round the clock procuring new sources of information just to keep ahead of her pupil.

Our problem was solved when Derek announced to Karin and myself that, through the help of the obliging Mr. Erskine, Derek's attorney, we were all, including Josh and Tina, moving to a large Victorian in Georgetown that, it turned out, was owned by the family trust and was fortuitously vacant.

"Works for me," Josh said, a note of challenge to the rest of us in his voice. "I get here at 5 a.m. and don't leave until nearly midnight anyway. It would make my job easier if I could live at the same place I worked."

"I agree," Tina chimed in shyly. "I live with my family and they live many miles from the hospital. My brother forbids me to live alone because I am unmarried, but he cannot object to this arrangement."

"It's out of the question for me," Professor Milne announced, her tone leaving no room for objection. "I have my own house, my friends. I simply can't turn my back on my entire life just for this job." She looked at Josh and Tina defiantly, but toward Derek her expression was more embarrassed.

"I have to agree with the professor," I volunteered, looking hopefully at Karin to see if I'd gained any points by taking her side. The truth was, I had no intention of giving up my freedom by becoming a roommate of four other people. With a sudden stab of anxiety I wondered if I was reacting to the prospect of my voluminous drinking habits, which were concealed by my hermetic lifestyle, becoming public knowledge. "Moving in with my work was never in my plans," I said.

"I certainly don't want to force anyone to go along with my plan," Derek answered, a placid smile on his face. "But I will require nearly round-the-clock tutoring, at least until my appearance on the Norman Wycroft show, and I would like to have a steady stream of new material at my disposal while I am learning about the last forty years."

"I suppose I could stay over when I needed to," Karin said, her reluctance evident in her voice. "But I don't intend to move in nor give up my own apartment."

"Of course not," Derek said. He looked expectantly in my direction.

Karen's agreement to join with the others put a new complexion on things. Maybe joining the others just meant I wouldn't have to drink alone. "I don't want to be the party-pooper," I said. "But I'm not giving up my own place, and after the Wycroft show I'm moving back."

"Good," Derek said, smiling broadly at all of us. "Then we move at the end of the day today."

***

Derek's townhouse was a throwback to a bygone era when the financial moguls who controlled the burgeoning Georgetown waterfront economy built homes big enough for their extended families and their live-in servants. Derek's house was built in 1800, but all the fixtures were new. The ground floor was taken up by a foyer with highly polished, but aged, wide pine flooring and an old-fashioned rack on which one could hang one's coat and hat, a moderate-sized living room, complete with the largest oriental rug I'd ever laid eyes upon and a small parlor dotted with antique chairs and a small, intimate sofa. Just off the parlor was a wet bar and pantry for serving guests in the large dining room, behind which was the kitchen. On the second floor was another sitting room which we had made into an office, where we set up computers, and which was adjacent to a walnut-lined library, the shelves of which were soon loaded with books and journals Karin had had sent over from her university library. Above that floor were three more on which were located the six bedrooms of the house, each with its private bathroom. Each of us was assigned his or her own bedroom, and I was happy to find that Karin and I shared the same floor.

Even during our busy intellectually-oriented workdays, one-half hour out of every two hours was still devoted to Derek's physical reconditioning. Josh and Tina traded off or sometimes worked in tandem, although their function quickly shifted to dictating instructions and providing advice, since Derek's physical strength seemed to be progressing at the same miraculous rate as his acquisition of knowledge. Fortunately, both of the physical therapists were also excellent cooks, so as their therapeutic duties diminished, they also took turns preparing meals for the four of us. We alternated between down-south soul food, heavy on the chicken and ribs, and vegetarian-oriented Vietnamese cuisine, heavy on the noodles and sprouts. The food was having a salutary effect upon Derek. He had gained enough pounds to bring his weight into the normal range, although he was still slim. But with his constant exercise and Josh's insistence that he include weight training in his regimen, he was becoming lean and well-muscled—much as he had probably looked before he was wounded.

Karin taught, or rather directed Derek's studies, and I kept notes of the whole process, trying my best to record Derek's accomplishments with accuracy and not wander off into new-age speculations about how he was accomplishing his feats of intellectual and physical dexterity. I also managed, much to my delight, to spend nearly as many hours as I had ambitiously imagined with Karin, though not, unfortunately, pursuing the intriguing topic of getting to know each other.

Both of us realized we had stumbled into a situation that was more than remarkable. Besides the fact that no one, to either of our knowledge, had ever woken from a 40 year coma before, Derek himself appeared to be a bona fide genius, which, no doubt, he had been before his head wound, and had, through whatever neural growth process had gone on in his brain while he was asleep for all of those years, sharpened his mind even further—in fact so far beyond the limits of what either of us had ever encountered that we suspected he had exceeded the intellectual limits attained by any other human being. Both of us had had previous commerce with intellectual giants, she through her acquaintance with Nobel laureates in her own and related fields, and me through my interviews with some of the era's leading thinkers. No one in either of our experiences had even approximated Derek's sheer mental power.

Although we shared a mutual admiration for Derek's accomplishments, the relationship I had hoped would develop between Karin and myself had fallen far short of the titillating heights my imagination had conjured when I had agreed to spend my days and nights living under the same roof as the beautiful professor. As an intellectual, neither the sharpness of her mind nor the breadth of her knowledge disappointed me, since the latter attribute far exceeded my own meager store of highly biased facts about the world. But she was intellectually cautious, especially when it came to attaching values to her meticulously constructed conclusions about the meaning of historical events. In other words, she was not highly opinionated the way I was. Despite the fact that I made a superficial attempt to rein in my characteristic cynicism, not to mention my arrogant sense of always being right, my shoot-from-the-hip opinions drew her distaste, a fact which she made little effort to conceal. Each of my rants against the powers of darkness, which I felt ruled our country, were met with a stern admonition to "grow up." Not the most auspicious basis for kindling a romance.

The evening before Derek's appearance on the Norman Wycroft show, the whole "family" held a last-minute conference. Karin was the subject matter expert, but Josh, Tina and I had been watching re-runs of Wycroft's shows to try to predict what the cagey interviewer might ask Derek. In the process of doing our homework, I had discovered that both Josh and Tina were far from being all brawn and no brain. Both were highly informed and naturally intelligent. It only took the better part of a week for the two of them to learn to trust me. Highly protective of Derek Stewart would barely scratch the surface as a description of their relationship with him.

"Wycroft asks his questions as if he as in the pay of Ferris and Goodson," I volunteered. Josh and Tina nodded in agreement.

Karin frowned. "Let's try not to let our paranoia get the best of us," she said, to no one in particular.

"Suppose Luke is right," Derek surprised me by saying. He looked around the room, as if he was hoping to coax something precious from each of us. "What would that mean in terms of the kinds of questions Wycroft will ask?"

"Luke exaggerates, as usual," Karin answered, while directing a dour look my way, "but Wycroft will stick to certain themes, and ignore others because of his support for Ferris' administration."

"Such as?' Derek asked.

"I suspect he's still hoping to paint you as a gift from the past that, if he can manipulate you during the interview, will prove to be on the side of Ferris and his gang," I said.

"What kind of gift would he like me to be, then?" Derek asked, sounding only curious and not at all sarcastic.

"A Christian and a war-hero and a spokesperson for the Western countries' War on Terror," Josh answered solemnly.

"I am none of those things," Derek said, as if he was politely declining an offer, rather than correcting someone's drastic mistake.

"He may suspect that," I said, "although Reverend Goodson's account of his talk with you made it sound as if you were in his camp. Wycroft knows that Goodson can't be trusted and he'll probably be more subtle in his approach."

"Subtle—how?"

It was Tina's turn to speak up. She was the expert on Wycroft's strategies for pulling the answers he wanted out of his guests. Perhaps it was due to her own history of having to be alert to the underlying current of conversations after having been an ethnic minority and a refugee in this country. Or maybe the Asian mind really was more attuned to subtleties than was ours. She spoke shyly and avoided looking any of us directly in the eyes. "Mr. Wycroft will describe horrible terrorist attacks, such as the destruction of the World Trade Center or the bombing of the New York subway system and ask how that makes you feel, as an American, learning about such attacks on your homeland." She raised her head to look directly at Derek. "He will cite the most violent statements of Mustafa al Adim and other Muslim leaders and ask you how you feel about a religion that espouses such hatred toward others." She lowered here gaze. We were all impressed. She had managed to capture Norman Wycroft's strategy to perfection.

"Those are legitimate questions," Derek answered. "In truth, I am appalled by the terrorist attacks on the United States and the virulent statements of the Muslim Jihadists."

"So you don't mind being put in President Ferris's camp?" I asked, startled by his response.

Derek looked at me with what could best be describe as sympathy, as if he were concerned about me, that I could come to such a conclusion. "American bombs and guns have killed more innocent civilians than did either of those terror attacks. It is not more moral for men in uniforms to kill civilians using high explosive bombs delivered by drone airplanes or missiles, than for men without uniforms to kill civilians using car bombs or explosive strapped to their backs. The immorality lies in the killing."

Despite my relief at hearing Derek's sentiment, I felt a growing sense of panic. "You can't say that on television," I said, looking anxiously at the others to see if they agreed. Everyone's head was nodding.

"Perhaps I will not be asked," Derek answered, simply.

Karin and I stared at each other. We were both thinking the same thing. Derek's appearance on the Norman Wycroft show was going to be a disaster.

Chapter 16

Jeremy Swift sat in the basement of his mansion in the Achrafieh, the ultra-wealthy section of Beirut that contained most of the European embassies as well as the priciest shopping and liveliest nightlife of the city. He was dressed urbanely, in a pair of cream colored, linen slacks and white, silk shirt, open at the collar. Tufts of dark hair, speckled with gray peeked out of the neck of his shirt. His face was narrow and handsome. He had long ago given up his beard, when it began to show the graying signs of his middle age, although his trim physique was that of a man of younger years than his mid-fifties. He stared at the electronic gear on the table in front of him, waiting, while he smoked a Gitanes, enjoying the fact that the French cigarette, no longer made in France, was still available in Lebanon. The light on the receiver began to blink. He lifted it and put it to his ear while with his other hand he punched the record button on the tape recorder.

"Mr. Donovan, it is so good to speak to you again." Swift recognized the voice of Mahmoud Fahkry, the Speaker of the Parliament and leader of the Shia faction in the Lebanese parliament. "I appreciate you discussing this delicate issue with me," Fahkry said.

"I cannot speak officially," Jervis Donovan said, his tone over the telephone calm and reserved, "but I assure you everything I say to you has the knowledge and agreement of the president."

Swift put out his cigarette and immediately lit another. Neither the American presidential administration nor Speaker Fahkry knew that the CIA listened to their conversations. Both parties had been assured that they spoke over a secure line, their conversation thoroughly scrambled for any outside listener, should there be one. The device used to scramble their messages had been installed by the CIA.

Swift's villa, affordable and even necessary because of his cover as an independent oil broker, had ample room to house the most sophisticated listening post in the Middle East. He had been at his post for almost five years. For all of those years, Fremont F. Ferris had been president, but like every career officer in the CIA, except the DCI himself, Jeremy, had no partisan leanings. He planned to remain in his job long after the current president had left office.

"You must understand that my information is tentative and impossible to verify," Fahkry began. "If I had something more definite to report, I would convey it directly to your president. What I have to say is completely unofficial."

"That has been made clear all along." Donovan answered, a hint of impatience in his voice.

"You know that I am a friend of the United States, and I regard your country as my friend also."

"My government feels feel the same about you," Donovan answered.

"As I have told you before, I have no control over Lebanon's neighbors. There are men in positions in Iran and Syria who are not as temperate as we are in Lebanon. The continued belligerence from Israel is bringing the situation to a head."

"The Jews continually fan the flames of conflict."

"I wish they could be stopped. I am sure your president is doing all he can do." Fahkry stopped and there was the sound of him lighting a cigar. "I also am continually trying to calm my neighbors."

"The president has told me he appreciates your efforts, Mr. Speaker. He knows there are limits to what you can accomplish." Donavan's voice had lost its edge of impatience. He was coaxing the Lebanese politician down whatever road the conversation was taking.

"My colleagues in Iran and Syria are concerned that al Mout li Kafir is gaining popularity with the masses. Mustafa al Adim accuses our governments of being old and soft, unable to stand up to Israel because of our fear of America."

Donovan said nothing. He was allowing Fakhry to take the lead.

"Ayatollah Khatami in Iran is pressing president Kharazzi to take action against Israel in order to reassert Shia dominance and take away the momentum al Mout li Kafir has gained in our region." He paused. "Ahmad Aphta is willing to go along with Kharazzi if he attacks Israel."

"And what about Hezbollah?" Donovan asked a hardness evident in his voice.

"Hezbollah, too is competing with al Mout li Kafir for the support of the people. If there is a war with Israel, Hezbollah cannot stand on the side lines."

"Iran has nuclear weapons."

"Kharazzi has said he would use them only as a last resort."

"Such a last resort may come sooner rather than later. Israel has nuclear weapons of its own. They are likely to use them unless they are too incapacitated to do so." Donovan's voice was cool and unemotional, as if he was simply informing the Lebanese Speaker of the facts.

Khafry hesitated. Could the American possibly be suggesting that Iran use its nuclear weapons against Israel? Such a suggestion seemed impossible. "Suppose such powerful weapons were used against Israel," he ventured cautiously. "A single nuclear weapon could wipe out half of its population. Even if such an attack did not cost the Israelis the war the West would be horrified, would they not?"

There was a long pause on the American end of the line. Finally Donovan responded. "And you are asking what America would do if such devastating attack should actually happen?"

Fakhry was afraid to put the question so bluntly. "I am only hypothesizing."

"The president has imagined such a scenario. It is too bad the Israelis make such prickly neighbors. We recognize that they are an irritant, and Israel's continued occupation of Palestinian lands is a thorn in the side of the Arabs that must be removed, but we cannot stand by and allow them to be driven into the sea." Donovan paused again. "On the other hand, President Ferris does not want a wider war. If Israel were attacked, no matter by what the type of weapons, America's first response would not be to launch an attack ourselves and further inflame the situation. America would attempt to intervene peacefully—to mediate between Israel and its neighbors."

Fakhry let out a breath he had been holding throughout Donovan's statement. "It would not be in our interests to push America into a corner. If American mediation included convincing the Israelis to leave the Palestinian territories, our concerns would be met."

"Then I think your friends have little to fear. It is time the Israelis learned a lesson about the price of arrogance."

"You understand I am only voicing a hypothetical situation. I have no direct knowledge of a plan to attack Israel," Fahkry said.

"And I am not making any official promises, Mr. Speaker. I only tell you what I believe to be true based upon my reading of the president's state of mind."

"Of course," Fahkry said. "I appreciate your candor."

"And I appreciate your trust," Donovan answered. "Goodbye Mr. Speaker."

"Good bye," Fakhry said.

Jeremy Swift sat for more than a minute. He could hardly believe what he had just heard. The president's closest advisor had virtually promised Lebanon's Speaker of the Parliament that the United States would not retaliate if Iran attacked Israel with nuclear weapons. In fact, Swift could come up with no other interpretation of what he had heard except that the United States was encouraging the Arabs and Iran to teach Israel a lesson— with nuclear bombs.

Jeremy Swift considered himself a patriot. He had given the better years of his life in the service of his country, and for most of those years he had served in the most dangerous trouble spots in the world. There had been times when he disagreed with the policies of his country, even policies he was asked to carry out in his role as a CIA operative, but he had never considered opposing an action of his government—until now.

Swift had served in Jerusalem for eight years. He was well aware of the belligerence of the Israelis, and he was equally aware of the constant threat under which every Israeli lived and under which every Israeli leader had to formulate a policy that would insure the safety of his country and his fellow citizens. Swift had also come to love the Israeli nation and its people. He was not going to stand by and watch them be destroyed.

Chapter 17

Mohammed Sahadi couldn't help but feel a twinge of excitement about his assignment. He was going to America! That his mission involved killing a man he had never met, nor even heard of until recently, made no difference to him. He had rarely met any of his targets. This time would be different, because he was explicitly instructed to gain access to Derek Stewart, the recently awakened coma patient and verify that he was, indeed, the man to whom Robert N'gomo referred. Since N'gomo's description was vague and the African had never actually met the person whose coming he prophesied so fervently, it was only a guess that Stewart was that person. Mohammed couldn't really see why Mustafa al Adim was even concerned about a man no one had even heard of, who had never established himself as a Western leader, and who might exist only as a figment of Robert N'gomo's mind, but Mohammed was not used to questioning his orders. He would find Stewart and report what he observed to Mustafa al Adim. If the orders were to kill Stewart, he would do so.

Even as he packed his clothing for the trip to America, Mohammed could not help thinking about Robert N'gomo. He had never tortured anyone himself, but he had witnessed torture before. The prospect of death and the pain of torture could break any man. At least that was what Mohammed had always thought before he had seen N'gomo. The African man's face still haunted Mohammed. N'gomo had shown no fear—nor even anger—at this captors. Mohammed had thought he had looked sadly, even with pity at the men who had beaten him and who promised to kill him.

It bothered Mohammed that Mustafa al Adim was targeting people who posed no threat to the movement. How could one man, preaching non-violence among poverty-stricken African villages and slums harm al Mout li Kafir? Even al Adim admitted that N'gomo had only urged passive resistance to the movement's call to arms. N'gomo was opposed to any use of violence, even in self-defense. Mohammed had to admit that he, himself, had moments when he became weary with the anger and the killing and wished that a leader such as Robert N'gomo would champion an alternative. But then he remembered the war that had killed his family and the American attacks on Iraq and Afghanistan. In Europe he had experienced the hatred of the French, Germans and Belgians toward men of his skin color— Middle Easterners who were forbidden to follow their religion or wear their traditional clothing. His anger quickly returned. But he still could not imagine Robert N'gomo as an enemy.

"You are ready to leave," Mustafa al Adim, said, entering Mohammed's tiny room. Al Adim's expression was, as usual grim, but a strange light shone in his eyes. He was even more excited than usual. "If Stewart is the man of which N'gomo has spoken, he must be silenced."

"How will I know if he is the man?"

"You have heard N'gomo. The person he has prophesied about will say the same things, but to a wider audience."

"I do not understand. If a man preaches nonviolence to our enemy, what harm is there in that for us?"

Al Adim's face showed his irritation. "You have not paid attention Mohammed. The Americans will not listen to this man. The last American who espoused nonviolence was killed. Half the nation celebrated when he died. His name was Martin Luther King. Although he has now become an American hero, his stance toward violence has been forgotten."

Mohammed nodded. He had a vague recollection of the story. American history was not something with which he was highly familiar. "But if no one will listen, why kill him?"

Al Adim shook his head angrily. "You still don't understand. Americans may not listen to this man, but Africans will. He is N'gomo's cousin—an African. According to N'gomo he will return to Africa and become their leader, raising them up so that they become a force in the world equal to the East and the West. And his message will be one of nonviolence—even to the Muslims who are in Africa."

"Wasn't that N'gomo's mission? Why would an American be any more successful than N'gomo himself?"

"Don't underestimate N'gomo's success. We no longer have a presence in Sudan because of him. The Muslims and the southern tribes have declared a truce because of him and they have agreed to keep us out of their country. That is why N'gomo is here."

"What are you going to do with him?" Mohammed still harbored a hope that N'gomo would not be killed.

Mustafa al Adim"s usually angry countenance brightened. "We are going to put him on television for the rest of the world to see."

"But he will not say anything you want people to hear. He has not given in to your torture at all. Won't it be dangerous letting him address the world?"

Al Adim shrugged. "We shall see." A cruel smile played about the corners of his mouth. "Come let me show you something." He took Mohammed by the sleeve and opened the door, then led the young man down a hallway. "You have never seen the room where we tape our statements for television. This will be a treat." He pushed open a door and they were hit by bright lights. A video camera was set up on a tripod and aimed at a white cloth backdrop.

"You will see why I am not afraid of what N'gomo will say," al Adim said, the cruel smirk still on his face. "Bring in the prisoner!"

A side door opened, and three men dressed in black with their faces concealed by ski-masks marched into the room. Each man had a long, Arab battle sword at his side. Behind them came another man, carrying an object covered in a black shroud.

Mohammed's breath caught in his throat. He suddenly knew what was under the shroud.

"Show us the prisoner!" Mustafa al Adim commanded.

The last man whipped the shroud away. On a large silver platter was the battered, severed head of Robert N'gomo.

Chapter 18

Norman Wycroft was seventy years old, but his consciousness of his age didn't lessen his vanity regarding his physical appearance. The veteran television interviewer had a scalp implant and his artificial hair was jet black and slicked back in the style of a fifties rock and roll singer. He always wore a coat, and each of his jackets was constructed with extra padding in the shoulders to conceal the frailness which had overtaken him with the years. He had undergone two face lifts in the last ten years, giving his matinee idol good looks a brittle quality, as if his features might splinter into a thousand pieces at any time.

I knew Norman Wycroft only by reputation. He would have been the subject of a lively biography, but he jealously guarded the rights to any story about his life. His early career, beginning as a TV weatherman, then as an infomercial host, progressing to emceeing game shows and reality TV, marriages to three Hollywood starlets, each younger than him by dozens of years, and a thirty year battle with drugs and alcohol, would have offered a stark contrast to his last fifteen years in which he had risen to the pinnacle of talk television with his nightly interview show. The turnaround in his career had come when he had garnered an interview with then governor of Alabama, Fremont F. Ferris, just at the moment the latter's presidential aspirations were on the rise. Ferris's announcement of his intention to run for the presidency, while being interviewed by Wycroft on the latter's television program, had set a precedent. Other would-be candidates soon booked themselves on Wycroft's show to announce their candidacies and Norman Wycroft suddenly was hosting the evening television show that everyone in the nation was watching.

If Norman Wycroft owed Fremont F. Ferris something for providing his television show the credibility to launch it as a national phenomenon, Wycroft had paid the president back in spades. Reverend Merrill Goodson and Senator Frederick Armbruster, the two men other than the shadowy Jervis Donovan, who were closest to the president and who spoke for the administration's agenda, were regulars on Wycroft's program. In fact, with the election of Ferris to a third term, every guest, other than those movie and television personalities who were enjoying their fifteen minutes in the public spotlight, was either a staunch supporter of the president's War on Terror and his Christian world agenda, or if a detractor, was soundly roasted by Wycroft, one of the most wily and insidious interviewers to have gained access to the airwaves.

Derek Stewart was not likely to fall into the ranks of Fremont Ferris supporters. On the other hand, Derek's views were so unknown that Wycroft would have no way of knowing what kind of fowl he had on his hands. Neither did Karin, Josh, Tina or myself, for that matter. We had all been shocked by Derek's scathing assessment of the War on Terror—although none of us disagreed with him. He had arrived at his conclusions much faster than any of us, and Karin and I decided that that was because he had not had the experience of being indoctrinated over the years as we had, with the truth of the situation only slowly dawning on us as we read between the lines of the official government pronouncements. Derek consumed the entire history of world events over the last thirty-seven years in less than two weeks, and the stark realities of the modern absurdist world must have leapt out at him like headlines from the pages of the history books.

We held our breath.

Derek looked marvelously young and fit for his 59 years—more like a 25 year old—after the application of television makeup. Norman Wycroft must have been considering putting himself into a coma after eyeing Derek and realizing there was only an eleven-year difference in their ages. Perhaps it was generational jealousy that prompted Wycroft to go for the jugular with his first question.

"You've said that you're not a war hero because your wound was from friendly fire, but wouldn't you agree that all young men who put their life on the line, as you did in Vietnam and as hundreds of thousands of Americans are doing right now in the Middle East, are heroes?"

"A hero exists in the eye of the beholder," Derek answered, smiling politely at his host. "A hero to one man is a villain to another."

Wycroft's expression showed a momentary doubt. "But all of these soldiers are incredibly brave, are they not."

"Undoubtedly."

Wycroft's doubt lessened. One for our side, he thought, although he was not completely sure that that was true. "And you too, going to war for your county in Vietnam were a brave hero. The president has expressed his admiration for you. I think he would like you to speak out on behalf of all of those brave young men who are defending America right now."

Derek leaned forward, as if he was waiting for Wycroft to make his point.

Wycroft squirmed in his chair. His guest wasn't falling for his usual maneuvers, which were designed to draw out the kind of responses that Wycroft knew would garner headlines. "You missed out on a lot of American history while you were in your coma. What thoughts have you had since you've awakened?"

"I am still learning about the world in which I have found myself."

"But you must have some initial impressions."

"If I had read Orwell's 1984 only after I woke up, I would not know it was a work of fiction."

Wycroft started to smile, then he looked at Derek's face and realized his interviewee was serious. Wycroft's smile turned into a frown. "That's a devastating assessment. Perhaps you are not aware of the War on Terror and the need for highly increased internal security procedures to protect us from Muslim Jihadists."

"I have learned a great deal about the current war. My impression is that it consumes most of the public consciousness in this country. I can only regret that so much news coverage and public discussion is devoted to war." Derek's voice had taken on an additional quality, as if he was projecting it beyond Norman Wycroft and to the public on the other side of the television camera.

Wycroft looked dumbfounded. "What else should we be talking about?"

"Unchecked poverty and disease in most of the world's population, thousands of nuclear weapons still poised at the ready, a world getting warmer every year. Since I have awakened I have not heard a serious discussion about any of these issues."

Wycroft's face showed his irritation. He had lost his usual cool demeanor. "America is under siege. You may not be aware of it, but there is a battle going on for the soul of this planet."

"It seems to me that it is more about narrow religious beliefs and oil." In contrast to Wycroft's stridency, Derek's low voice was matter-of-fact, as if he was reminding his interviewer of an overlooked, but telltale detail.

I glanced at Karin. "Oops," I said.

Wycroft's face showed red even through his heavy makeup. "You obviously haven't been properly apprised of the current world situation, Mr. Stewart. I wonder if you have any idea how ruthless our enemies are?" He stared at Derek with a broad scowl on his face, as is he had just delivered a scathing indictment of his guest, rather than asked a question.

Derek nodded solemnly. "Any man who deliberately kills another is ruthless."

"But there is a difference between those who kill because they want to exterminate anyone who doesn't share their beliefs and those who kill to defend themselves and their freedom, wouldn't you agree?"

Derek sat perfectly still and regarded the television interviewer with curiosity. He appeared as if he was not going to answer Wycroft's question, but then he began to speak. "I would like to tell you a story, " he said, looking into the camera. His voice had taken on a low, melodious, mesmerizing quality. "Many years ago, in my mother's country, a tribe laid claim to a fertile piece of land. The people of the tribe planted it, raised their livestock, and their families thrived for many generations. They became the richest tribe in the region, and although they were a generous people and bestowed charitable gifts upon their less fortunate neighbors, some of the other tribes were jealous. The leaders of the wealthy tribe grew fearful that their neighbors might try to take away what they felt they had earned. They sent their people into the lands of their neighbors to search for weapons that could be used against them. The other tribes became angry at these intrusions onto their property, and some of them secretly came into the tribe's territory and killed their cattle and destroyed their crops. This made the leaders of the tribe even more fearful, and they took up arms and invaded the lands of the most warlike of their neighbors, whom they suspected were plotting to attack them. They killed many of the young warriors from these other tribes, claiming that they did so only in self-defense, and they occupied those other tribes' lands so they could not gather themselves up again and pose a threat for a second time. The surviving warriors from these neighboring tribes, now dispossessed, mounted attacks against the people who now occupied their property, killing everyone who belonged to the occupying tribe, whether they were warriors or farmers or family members. These marauding warriors became known for their ruthlessness and single-minded call for vengeance. The wealthy tribe who now occupied their land mounted a campaign to hunt them down and kill them to the last man." Derek continued to look at the camera. "In my mother's land, the story of these two tribes has been told for generations. The story always ends with the same question posed to each listener—which side was killing in self-defense? Which side was justified in its actions?"

Wycroft had listened with rapt attention. In spite of himself the expression on his face was eager. "And what is the answer?"

Derek gazed at the older man as if he was instructing a pupil. "Neither side killed in self defense. Neither side was justified. Either side could have chosen a different path at any point in the story." He spoke in a calm tone, the voice of dispassionate reason, but his expression was infinitely compassionate, as if he knew his audience was not fully capable of understanding—though he held them in no blame.

Wycroft looked disappointed. "But that story has nothing to do with us. We were attacked first!" he exclaimed. "We have only protected ourselves from those who want to destroy us."

Derek's gaze searched Wycroft's face, as if he was making sure that the older man could not come to a better conclusion. "Have we?" he asked gently. "And have we never had any alternative but to attack them back?"

"We aren't living in a fairy tale. These people want to kill us!"

"And we have no choice but to kill them and to send our troops into their lands?" He sounded as if he was chiding Wycroft.

"You sound like you're on the side of the Muslim Terrorists."

"I am on the side of truth." The pronouncement was made as if it was a declaration of fact.

Wycroft was steaming. His eyes narrowed in hatred as he sat watching Derek across from him. Finally a small smile began to play around the corners of his mouth. "We have a video clip for you to observe, Mr. Stewart. I'd like to hear your opinion of your noble Muslim friends after you watch it." Wycroft nodded to someone off camera.

Karin, Josh and Tina and I watched the television monitor. On the set, Derek was also watching. The picture was in black and white. A voice was speaking in Arabic. After a moment there was a voice-over translation into English. The banner at the bottom of the tape indicated it was a message from Moustafa al Adim, the leader of al Mout li Kafir.

"After a lengthy pursuit, the forces of Al Mout li Kafir finally captured the notorious Ghanaian infidel and leader of anti-Muslim activities, Robert N'gomo. Mr. N'gomo was offered an opportunity to recant his views, which involved primitive ancestor worship and resistance to Sharia law, and to convert to Islam. He continued to resist and now he has paid the price." On the screen, three hooded men dressed in black and carrying swords at their sides entered a room. They were followed by a fourth man carrying an object covered in a black cloth. When they were lined up against the wall, the fourth man pulled off the cloth, revealing a severed head on a platter. It was a Black man, his face battered and one eye swollen shut. The other eye stared straight ahead, lifelessly, into the camera. "Mr. N'gomo will preach his heathen beliefs no more, " the voice said.

The camera was back on Norman Wycroft and Derek. Even under his dark skin, Derek's face looked ashen.

"You see who we are up against? Robert N'gomo was one of the great indigenous leaders of Africa. He championed nonviolence and resistance to the Muslim takeover that is sweeping the continent. That is how the Muslims deal with anyone who defies them. Do you still compare their ruthlessness to ours?"

"It is a terrible event. A great man has died," Derek said, his face solemn. There were tears in the corners of his eyes. "I must leave," he said, getting up.

Wycroft's face showed his shock. "You can't leave. I'm not finished with the interview."

"Goodbye," Derek said. He looked off camera at our little group and held out a hand. Josh and Tina were immediately by his side. "Take me home," he said.

Chapter 19

I had half expected crowds of militant protestors to be surrounding our townhouse, but when we arrived home after our exit from Norman Wycroft's show, the streets outside were empty. Perhaps our attempt to keep the location of Derek's whereabouts a secret had been successful. We all went into the parlor and Derek drank coffee while, to my relief, Josh opened a bottle of Scotch and passed it around.

"Robert N'gomo was my cousin," Derek finally said, breaking the silence that had descended like a heavy shroud upon our little family.

"How do you know?" I asked.

"My mother's cousin. Her name was Tsanabe N'gomo, and she gave birth to a boy named Robert less than a year before I was born. During my recent studies I came across the name of Robert N'gomo, a man who has wandered Africa speaking out for peace for the last forty years. I traced the man's origins. He is the son of my mother's cousin."

"I'm sorry," I said. The others in the room echoed my words with silent nods.

"Do you think he knew about you?" Karin asked.

"His mother would have told him the same thing my mother told my grandmother and Tsanabe N'gomo would have known about her cousin's pregnancy, but after so many years of not hearing from me, I suppose he dismissed my existence. My mother never lived to maintain contact with her cousin. I don't know if my grandmother ever tried to contact her."

"Wycroft had no idea you and N'gomo were related," I said.

"No." Derek sat in silence. The rest of us looked at each other and mutely sipped on our drinks.

"You will be an unpopular person after the answers you gave to Wycroft tonight," Josh said, breaking the silence.

"I spoke the truth."

"Your point of view is not popular with the American people," Tina observed.

"I am sorry to hear that."

"Americans have been brainwashed to see the world through a biased set of lenses," I said.

"It is difficult to see the world as it really is." He looked at each of us. "Thank you for your assistance and your support. I am tired. I think I will retire now." Slowly he rose from his chair and walked across the room. Josh started to get up to offer his help, but Derek waved him away. "I am strong enough, physically. It is my spirit that has been dealt a blow tonight."

"Did you know about his relationship with Robert N'gomo?" I asked Karin after Josh and Tina had both excused themselves from the room. I had replenished my empty whiskey glass, and I was feeling a little more bold about talking to her.

"I knew of N'gomo. You probably did, too. But Derek never mentioned that they were related."

"He said nothing to me either. Yet he's sure that they were cousins." I filled my glass for a third time and topped off Karin's. "The shit is going to hit the fan tomorrow. The press will be all over Derek."

"We didn't do a very good job of protecting him," Karin said, looking at me with sadness in her eyes. I thought she looked more beautiful than ever. My whiskey was adding to her beauty. Or maybe it was because her habitual look of disapproval toward me was absent.

"You have the same reaction to Derek that I do," I said, testing the momentary lapse in the veil of displeasure that she typically directed toward me. "It feels as if he is innocent and needs to be protected from the evils of this world." I took another sip from my whiskey. "But he doesn't see himself that way and he may be right. Sometimes I also feel he has a level of wisdom that the rest of us haven't achieved. It is as if he knows exactly what he's doing, including when he said the things he said to Wycroft tonight."

She nodded, her demeanor still pensive. "Can someone be innocent and wise at the same time?"

I sipped my drink slowly, not wanting to get so sloshed that I blew this first chance for us to have a genuine conversation. "That's too deep a question for a mere writer to answer. You're the professor. What do you think?"

She looked across the room. A fire, which Josh had lit when we'd first arrived back from the television studio, was still smoldering in the fireplace, putting out a weak orange glow in the dimly lit parlor. In the ancient townhouse it felt as if we were in the midst of a Currier and Ives painting. "My parents were innocent, but they were foolish. I never knew my father, but from what my mother said, he was a lot like her. She was brilliant, but she wasted her talent on hopeless causes." She was staring into the fireplace.

"What do you mean?" I asked cautiously, sensing that she had let down her guard, but aware that it could be erected again in a heartbeat.

"Both of my parents were into the student protests of the sixties—and the drugs as well. Neither of them finished college. They met in a commune—where my mother had me—and my father left before I was born. He left for Canada or something. My mom took jobs waitressing, but she was on and off drugs. I was raised in a house filled with hippies and druggies until my grandparents took me when I was about twelve. My mom died from an overdose when I was fourteen."

"How about your dad? Is he still alive?"

"He was never part of my life. I don't know if he's alive or dead. I don't even know if he ever knew he had a daughter. As far as I'm concerned he doesn't exist."

"You've made it a long way, coming from such inauspicious beginnings."

Her features hardened. "I have avoided making the mistakes my parents made." She raised her eyes and held my gaze. "And I will continue to do so. Life is not a children's game in which we can do or say whatever we want without consequences." She looked at me accusingly.

"Why do I think you are talking about me as much as about your parents?"

"You have the same irresponsible attitude toward your life that they did."

"I try to seek the truth and reveal it, sometimes, I admit, regardless of the consequences. To not do that seems irresponsible to me."

"You can seek the truth without having to proclaim your version of it to the masses," she answered, her tone dismissive.

"And what good does it do for me to know the truth if everyone around me continues to believe in lies? I am a writer, not a scholar. Proclaiming my version of the truth to the masses is my job. My only responsibility is to be honest about it."

She looked away. "And I can hear in your voice that you think my scholarly work is pointless." She looked down at the floor. "Sometime I think the same thing." She swallowed more of her whiskey then turned back toward me, her eyes hard, and her jaw set with resolve. "But there's no point going into that. Our immediate problem is that Derek seems to have the same drive you do, and he is likely to suffer for it."

"I agree. He's going to suffer because Ferris and Goodson have a different agenda in mind for him. They're going to be deeply disappointed and angry after tonight."

She looked back at me. Her expression had softened. "I don't want to see him hurt."

"Neither do I."

She finished her drink and stood. "I think we should say goodnight. Tomorrow we'll both see what America thinks after hearing Derek's words this evening."

I couldn't argue with that.

***

The next morning the newspapers were alive with reactions to Derek's interview on the Norman Wycroft show. To my shock, the American public was split in its reaction. A quick poll taken by CNN after the show, indicated that half of the viewers thought Derek was a hero… not for having served in Vietnam, but for saying what he said during the interview

The columnists for the Washington Times and the Wall Street Journal, never bastions of liberalism and now solidly in the camp of the administration, were less sanguine about Derek's performance. Tom Edwards led the charge with an editorial blasting Derek himself as a "sixties era anti-war veteran of the John Kerry type whose credentials as a hero were suspect anyway, since, by his own admission, he had been wounded by friendly, and not enemy fire." Good ol' Tom went on to point out that yours truly, whom he identified as "a biased anti-American reporter who was fired by this paper," had taken Derek under my wing and was leading him down the garden path toward subversive ideas. He hinted that I and a few others had set up a "cell" in which we were trying to manipulate Derek to our own ends, which, he hinted, were to undermine the government's War on Terror and "give succor and comfort to the enemy."

Edwards' column was written as much for the benefit of the Feebs as for the general public and I knew we could expect a knock on the door by government investigators as soon as they figured out where we were.

Karin, apparently unused to the late night she and I had just enjoyed, greeted the rest of us like a cranky moth emerging from its chrysalis. The moment she heard Josh read Tom Edwards' words of criticism regarding Derek's academic support group, she metamorphosed from her persona as a Lepidoptera into that of a stinging wasp, outraged at the columnist's accusations, which painted all of us who served as Derek's advisors as radicals and terrorist fellow travelers.

"We've done nothing but provide Derek with an unbiased set of facts about the world," she seethed, pacing the parlor where we'd all gathered for morning coffee, as if she were Captain Queeg, striding his deck and ranting about missing strawberries. "Just because Derek dared to disagree with the official party line about the so-called war on terror, this ass tries to paint him and all the rest of us as disloyal Americans."

"What does it make you feel like doing?" I asked, so obviously baiting her that I felt guilty as soon as I asked the question.

"I want to denounce the damn conservatives, like Edwards and Wycroft, who equate telling the truth with disloyalty," she spat out. As soon as the words left her mouth, her face was transformed, as if she suddenly realized what she had said; that she was voicing the words of radicals—such as her mother and father—and me. "I value the truth," she said, weakly, her eyes cast, self-consciously, toward the floor.

"As do the rest of us," I answered, though I was unsure whether I was informing her of a truth or making a self-aggrandizing point. Fortunately, we were interrupted by Derek entering the parlor.

Derek seemed energized. He had scanned the papers, or so it seemed, for his first words were in reference to the reports of the public's reactions to his interview with Norman Wycroft. "The American consciousness is not so unyielding as I had imagined. I had thought I would be another voice crying in the wilderness, like my cousin." As soon as he mentioned his cousin, his face became sad again, as it had been the evening before.

The mention of Robert N'gomo sobered us all. Each of us, in our own way, wanted to take Derek's mind off of his cousin's fate.

"Let's not bask in our success and forget to do our exercises," Josh said, an undertone of anxiety in his voice.

"And eat breakfast. You're still gaining strength," Tina said, "and nutrition is important." She leapt up and strode toward the kitchen, her slight figure bent forward with purpose.

"I will eat presently," Derek said, holding up a hand to halt Tina's determined progress. He looked fondly at the two therapists. "You needn't worry. I am saddened by my cousin's death, but neither surprised nor disheartened. In some ways his murder serves to focus my purpose. With my cousin gone, the great continent of Africa—my ancestral home—has lost a spokesman. Perhaps I can direct the world's attention toward the plight of my brothers in Africa."

"The Ferris administration has ignored Africa, so far as its public policy," I said. "But there is a war going on within the continent and it is being fought by secret armies—al Mout li

Kafir on the one side and the intelligence services of the West on the other. The governments of many African nations are being treated as pawns in this behind the scenes war. No one in the administration, nor even in the European Union, wants the world to focus its attention on Africa."

"The wrong war is being fought. The battle should be to defeat AIDS and Malaria, to feed the millions of starving women and children, to stop the flow of resources and capital from the people who labor for them and into the hands of the multinational companies who return nothing back to the African people and prop up totalitarian regimes who keep the people uneducated and in poverty."

"The West wants to make sure Africa does not become Muslim before it extends a helping hand." Karin said, her voice rising. "That has been the history of European involvement in the continent—in the lives of the non-Western indigenous populations everywhere." She took a breath and tried to calm herself, but she was unable to stop the words that tumbled from her in bitter anger. "The first step is to strip a land of its traditions, including its religion, which is always branded as pagan and primitive, then to undermine public education and political institutions and replace them with the mechanisms of European commercialism in the guise of enlightened, paternal, guidance. Before the Europeans, the Arabs did the same, though they were less interested in colonization and more interested in controlling the trade and raping the country of its resources. Now the Muslims have decided they too want to control the continent. It has been labeled a struggle for the African soul, but no one cares about the souls of Africans, they just want their diamonds and oil." Her eyes were wet with tears and she was breathing as heavily as if she had just run a marathon. "I'm sorry," she said. "I got carried away."

Though I sensed that something glacial had shifted within Karin, I withheld any comment, difficult as it was to keep myself from reflecting on her transmogrification into the embodiment of a political radical, afraid that my callous exultation would trigger a reaction formation, driving her into an even more heightened form of her previously dispassionate self.

"It is your knowledge that drives your emotion," Derek said. He smiled as fondly at Karin as he had Josh and Tina a few moments before. "Perhaps other Americans would care if they knew what you know."

"And perhaps other Americans would want to have whoever says such things arrested and banished to perpetual darkness for exciting such thoughts in the minds of an innocent American public," I said to Derek. "Do you want to tell them these things?"

"It might be helpful. I seem to have been given a platform because of my unusual medical condition."

I thought about Tom Edwards' column in that morning's Times. "The government has not interfered with your speech so far, but if you continue to challenge them they may."

"I will only speak the truth."

"That's not what they would like anyone to hear."

"Is this country not still free?"

"Not for some time," I said.

I looked over at Karin. She was nodding her head in agreement. I wondered if Josh or Tina had slipped some form of liberal-erecting Saltpeter into her morning coffee.

"Then something must be done," Derek said, looking over at Tina. "I guess you are right, Tina. I will need my strength. Let us all have breakfast and plan what we must do."

Chapter 20

"I thought you said Stewart was going to be in our corner," Jervis Donovan said. He and the Reverend Merrill Goodson were in Donovan's office in the West Wing of the White House, seated opposite each other in leather wingback chairs in front of the presidential advisor's desk. Donovan had a broad scowl on his face.

Goodson shrugged. He didn't completely trust Jervis Donovan. The presidential advisor claimed to have been raised a Catholic, and Catholics were always suspect in Reverend Goodson's mind. They owed their allegiance to the Church and not to Jesus. Goodson didn't need any intermediary, like the pope, to tell him what God wanted him to do—it was all written right there in the Bible for anyone to see and there wasn't anything complicated about the message. Nobody had been able to find a contradiction or a falsehood in the Holy Book— he'd never actually checked that claim himself, but knew it must be true because God wouldn't contradict himself—and God's word was loud and clear for anybody to read. The Catholics just wanted to gain political power so they turned religion into something complicated and bureaucratic with their priests and their pope and their ridiculous philosophical arguments, all written by scholars with Ph.Ds. like Donovan.

But Jervis Donovan wasn't a strong Catholic, Goodson had to admit that. Donovan was political through and through. Goodson was pretty sure that the presidential advisor paid lip service to fundamentalist Christian values only because he thought it was politically expedient. Deep down, Goodson was convinced that Donovan had very little respect for him or his religion. And now Donovan was implying that it was his fault that Derek Stewart hadn't rolled over and played dead for Norman Wycroft. He wasn't going to let Donovan throw the blame on him. "There was no reason to think that Stewart wasn't going to be supportive of the administration—not based on what he'd said to me," he told Donovan. Actually Derek Stewart had said almost nothing to the minister, but he wasn't about to admit that.

"Do you call what he said last night on Wycroft's program supportive?"

"Wycroft wasn't smart. He tried to trap Stewart and he underestimated him."

Jervis's expression was dismissive. "He underestimated Stewart because you told him he was on our side. You told *us* that, too."

"What's the big deal" the minister asked, his tone one of irritation. "So we can't use him to drum up support for our position, but nobody's going to take him seriously after his performance last night."

Donovan responded with his own irritation. "Take your head out of your Bible for a minute, and read the newspapers. Half the country agreed with Stewart."

"I read Tom Edwards. He put Stewart in his place. And he also pointed out that he's been getting advice from a group of left-wing radicals, who've poisoned his mind. You can't blame me for that, can you?"

"Edwards says what we want him to say. Some yo-yo over at CNN conducted a poll and found out that half the country favored Stewart's version of reality more than ours."

"So what? We have control of the media. We can freeze Stewart out. Wycroft won't have him back on his show again and neither will anyone else... and that guy at CNN will be out of a job before the end of the day."

Donovan's expression softened. "I'm not sure that's the best strategy, Merrill." Donovan refused to call Goodson "minister" and usually referred to him by his first name, which he knew infuriated the minister. "There are enough subversive media outlets, even though they're small, to keep what Stewart started, going. He's started people questioning what we've been telling them and that's dangerous."

"So what do we do?" Jervis Donovan was the master political strategist and Reverend Goodson had learned to listen, albeit grudgingly, to what he had to say.

"We get Stewart to say even more."

"What do you mean?"

Donovan had a calculating look on his face. "Those advisors he's hired have turned him into a flaming radical. All we have to do is give him enough rope and he'll hang himself. The American people can put up with some questioning of our War on Terror, because they're war-weary. But you know better than anybody that they're not going to listen to anyone who sounds as if he's backing Islam against Christianity."

"And you think he'll defend the Muslims?"

"Of course. You heard him last night."

"How do we get him to go further? Put him back on Wycroft's show?"

"How about on your show?"

"My show?" Reverend Goodson had a weekly inspirational show on which he featured different celebrities who provided a testimony as to how their lives had been turned around by Jesus Christ. Occasionally his guest was a converted Muslim who told the audience how he had been brainwashed by the Muslim Imams and threatened with eternal damnation if he didn't subscribe to belief in Islam. Invariably, the repentant guest recounted how he had been "saved" by the intervention of a Christian influence that showed him the depravity of his former beliefs and pointed him toward the path of salvation in Jesus.

"You know Stewart's position. You can push him to say what he really believes in front of millions of viewers. Nobody can unmask an unbeliever like you can, Merrill."

Goodson was nothing if not susceptible to praise. He liked to think of himself as a modern crusader—a knight at the forefront of the fight against the forces of evil that were always threatening the domain of Christ. He would like nothing better than to have the entire nation, perhaps most of the Western world, watch him strip Derek Stewart of his anti-Christian pretensions. "You're right, Jervis. I'm probably the only one who knows exactly how to handle Stewart."

"Of course you are." Donovan could tell he'd pushed the right buttons. Appealing to the minister's ego was a strategy that rarely failed. He just hoped that Goodson was up to the challenge.

"I'll get him on the show tomorrow night."

"Good. The sooner the better." Donovan stood up to signal Goodson that it was time to end their meeting. Now that the minister had agreed to take the next step, Donovan didn't need him sticking around anymore. There was much more the presidential advisor needed to attend to. Foremost was the contingency plan, in case Derek Stewart was a better interviewee than Goodson was prepared for. With Iran poised to take the bait and send a nuclear missile screaming toward Tel Aviv, the administration needed full support from the populace for what they were about to do in response—annihilate three Islamic capitals. If Stewart was responsible for developing an alternative voice to that of the government's he would have to be silenced—and Donovan knew just how to do it. An assassination of the recently awakened war hero by a Muslim terrorist would serve the purpose of silencing Stewart and proving, once and for all, that America's enemies were too ruthless to be treated with anything but the most deadly force the free world could muster.

Chapter 21

The Black U.S. Customs official at Logan Airport stared hard at Mohammed Sahadi's face. "You were not born in France."

The French passport Mohammed was carrying, under the name of Maurice Aziz, listed his place of birth as Beirut. "I was born in Lebanon, but I am a French citizen." Although the name of Mohammed Sahadi was on every watch list in the Western world, his picture appeared nowhere. The name and birthdate of Maurice Aziz had been taken from the records of infants killed in the violence in Lebanon during the Israeli occupation.

"The purpose of your visit?" The customs officer's face was arranged in a broad scowl as he continued to stare at Mohammed with suspicion.

"I am here to visit friends. Then I plan to travel to see as much of your country as I can before my visa expires."

The customs officer looked like he was weighing Mohammed's words. His eyes narrowed. "What is your religion?"

"I am Christian."

"You converted to Christianity?" The skepticism was apparent in the man's voice.

"My family has always been Christian—both in Lebanon and in France."

The customs man continued to look skeptical. The man in front of him was clearly an Arab and weren't all Arabs Muslims?

"One fourth of all Lebanese are Christians." Mohammed explained. He knew that most Americans were unaware of the fact. Anyone who looked like he was an Arab was assumed to be a Muslim. My God, he thought, shouldn't a customs officer at least know such things? Were Americans as ignorant as most Europeans claimed them to be?

The skeptical look didn't disappear from the customs officer's face. "Really?"

Mohammed smiled. "We even have thousands of Jews in Lebanon. It is a melting pot." He couldn't resist the last statement, since he knew Americans often described their nation similarly. "But I have not been in Lebanon since I was an infant. I am French."

The officer sighed, as if he still didn't believe Mohammed, but he stamped his passport and allowed him to zip his suitcase closed. Mohammed had not been so stupid as to bring any weapons with him on the airplane. There would be ample opportunity to purchase what he needed to make a bomb right here in the United States.

The customs officer dismissed him with a wave and he moved ahead into the terminal.

Mohammed took a taxi to South Station and purchased an Amtrak ticket for Washington, D.C. He boarded the train and marveled at the lack of security inside the country. He appeared to be able to go anywhere without being searched, especially if he didn't take an airplane. He would keep that in mind when he was fleeing after his mission was complete. More like a clever criminal than a terrorist, he always planned his escape, even before he knew the details of his plan. Mohammed was no suicide bomber. He wanted revenge for the death of his parents, but he had no illusions about reaching heaven and meeting up with 72 virgins as a result of the deaths he was causing. He would more likely end up in hell, if either heaven or hell existed. He didn't really care.

As he watched the fall landscape of bleak orchards and barren fields speed by outside the window of the train, he was surprised at how much open space was in America, once the cities were left behind. It was not desolate, like the Middle East, where the landscape included lonely stretches of mountain and desert almost absent of people, but it was not so crowded as Europe, which often reminded him of one continuous suburb. He had heard that before the World Trade Center and New York Subway system attacks, many Lebanese prospered in this country. He remembered his childhood days when relatives from America came to Lebanon to vacation with the families they had left behind. They brought presents and tales of success and, sometimes even fortunes from their adopted land. Most of them had only good things to say about their new home.

But everything had changed in the last ten years. Travel from America to the Middle East was restricted for ordinary citizens of Arab or Persian descent. Arab-American Muslims were no longer able to practice their religion openly, since it had been labeled a source of international terror. Mosques had been boarded shut or torn down—or worse yet, burned to the ground. Many Arab and Persian Americans had converted to Christianity in an effort to avoid constant harassment from their government and fellow citizens. If Mohammed had identified himself as a Muslim, he might not have been allowed into the country. Certainly, he would have been put under surveillance.

As he looked through the window at the fields and orchards flashing by, at the small towns in the distance, he was amazed at the lack of visible poverty. In his training to prepare for this trip he had read that poverty existed only in certain geographic areas of the United States and only among certain ethnic groups. When he reached Washington he would be able to see inner city poverty and the plight of Black people in America, but he already suspected that American poverty was no match for what he saw in any Middle Eastern city. He had noticed a similar difference when he had lived in Europe. Although he had melted into the vast, disadvantaged North African and Middle-Eastern immigrant population that inhabited the poorest section of most European cities, he always had to remind himself that his fellow immigrants were poor by European standards, not by the standards of the Middle East. He had never traveled to Africa, but he had heard that sub-Saharan Africa made even the slums of the Middle East look opulent.

The thought of Africa brought his thoughts to Robert N'gomo and the image of the severed head, sitting in its pool of blood on the platter, staring up at him with its lifeless eyes. Mohammed was still reeling from his encounter with N'gomo— not so much because of the shock of seeing his disembodied head, but because of the force of the African's presence when Mohammed had watched him being tortured. N'gomo had resisted Mustafa al Adim's efforts to break him. The old African man had some kind of strength inside of him that Mohammed was not used to seeing. He had seen the resilience and defiance possessed by zealots, such as al Adim, but not the quiet confidence that N'gomo was able to summon, even when his own death was imminent.

Mohammed wondered if he would be able to face his own death with such courage. Mohammed had risked his life many times, but when putting one's life at risk to carry out a hazardous mission, the thought of death was only a ghost at the back of one's mind—a fleeting thought that one held in abeyance so that it did not interfere with the task at hand. But what if death were certain? What if there was no chance to resist? What if he had time to think about the moment his life would end? If such a moment came, Mohammed hoped he would be tortured because he knew that the source of whatever strength he possessed was his anger. He would be strong if he was being tortured, if he could hate those who were about to kill him. Robert N'gomo did not appear to hate his captors and yet he was not afraid. Mohammed did not understand such a man.

He wondered about the man he was traveling to Washington to kill. What kind of man was he? He was N'gomo's cousin and a man who struck fear in the heart of Mustafa al Adim. Mohammed was supposed to get close to Derek Stewart before he killed him—to be sure he was the man N'gomo had prophesied would follow him. The thought was deeply disquieting to Mohammed. Every time he had killed, his victim had been a stranger to him. This time things would be different.

Chapter 22

After Derek's performance on Norman Wycroft's interview show, the last person I expected to contact him was the Reverend Merrill Goodson. But it had only been two days since Wycroft's TV show and the steadfast Mr. Erskine, Derek's attorney, had contacted us with Goodson's offer to be a guest on his weekly television show.

I was opposed. Since there was no way that providing Derek a platform for offering his anti-establishment opinions profited the government and Reverend Goodson was nothing if he was not a government stooge, I could see the ominous jaws of a trap in the corpulent minister's offer. The vague parameters of the Patriot Act III allowed any evil minded or even just witless FIIEB henchman to issue arrest orders based upon any statement that didn't echo the patriotic platitudes that characterized all public speech these days. I said as much to Derek. But from the moment I voiced my objection, I knew I was fighting a losing battle.

"I cannot live my life in fear," Derek said. "This is an opportunity to have a frank discussion with a man who shapes both public opinion and the decisions of government."

He and I were alone, discussing Walter Rodney's, *How Europe Underdeveloped Africa*, the intellectual tour-de-force of the martyred Guyanese historian and political figure who was assassinated by the Guyanese government, when Mr. Erskine's call came in.

"Goodson's a dimwitted demagogue who wouldn't know a frank discussion if it jumped in his lap and called him 'momma,'" I answered. "He is only hoping to bring you down— to expose you as a subversive influence so he can slap you in irons."

"Why be silent now, if that is the government's intention? I have no agenda that favors waiting until some later date to speak my mind. Wouldn't it be worse to have them figure out a way to arrest me before I have a chance to say anything more?"

Derek had a point. "What do you intend to say?" I asked.

"That depends upon what he asks me."

"His program is a religious one—although I use the term loosely. He'll want to talk to you about religion." I was actually puzzled by Goodson's invitation. I assumed that he wanted to bait Derek into saying something illegal, but wasn't sure he didn't still harbor a hope that he could enlist him in the administration's crusade against the Muslims.

"Religion? Well, I'm sure the reverend and I shall find a good deal to talk about," Derek said, a barely perceptible smile on his face.

"May I ask you a question?" I said.

"I thought that was what you did for a living?" Derek said, smiling. "But I guess you mean a question about something sensitive or personal."

"I am your biographer, and I don't know anything about your religious beliefs. In this day and age, that is an important part of someone's biography."

He gazed at the wall, as if my comment had provoked a heavy thought. I hoped I had not pushed too far into his private life.

"My grandmother was what I would call a spiritualist," he began, for one of the few times, not looking me in the eyes. It was as if he was consulting some inner text. "She was in search of something, and I think she thought she had found it—at least at certain times of her life. But she was adamant that I find my own inner truth. I listened to some amazing men and women, each of them voicing something different, something unique and, in many cases, something brave." He refocused his gaze on me. "All I did was learn to listen…and to choose. Listening is wise and choosing is brave. Choosing without listening is foolish and listening but failing to choose is faint-hearted." He looked at me as if his explanation was complete.

"I'm still not sure if you're telling me about your religion," I said, completely perplexed by his answer.

"I have only voices of other human beings and the freedom to make choices. I have nothing else to tell you about."

"How do you make a choice when there are so many voices?"

"I try to discern the truth."

"What is truth?" I asked.

"Truth is what I look for at all times. Finding it is mostly a matter of avoiding self-deception."

"What you are describing is not what most people would call a religion."

He smiled. "No, I am afraid it is not. But it is enough to guide my life."

"What about God—a supreme being—or at least something greater than yourself?"

"There are many things greater than myself—the laws that govern the universe, for instance, or the common good, or even great music or a poem, some remarkable ideas."

"But nothing spiritual? Nothing you would pray to?"

"To what or to whom would I pray? To what end?"

"Reverend Goodson will be disappointed."

Derek smiled. "Let's see what he believes in, shall we?"

***

Karin and I had prepared Derek as well as we could by providing him with copies of Reverend Goodson's speeches and sermons, which Derek consumed with his usual alacrity, which seemed less mind-boggling to us this time, since most of the material was written at a pre-literate level. As he read the minister's various homily's, Derek did not try to disguise his incredulity, nor could he suppress an occasional chortle. We also supplied access to a voluminous amount of historical material on the conflicts between Christians and Muslims, Christians and Jews, Jews and Muslims, Shiite Muslims and Sunni Muslims, Muslims and Hindus, Hindus and Sikhs and even between Protestants and Catholics. If we'd had more time, I'm sure we could have unearthed simmering tensions between Seventh Day Adventists and Jehovah's Witnesses or Wiccans and Voodooists. Derek's reaction to this material was devoid of amusement. In fact, his study of the subject appeared to provoke a profound sadness, which he visibly made an effort to shake off in the days before his appearance on Reverend Goodson's show.

Despite my constitutionally jaded attitude toward most of life, the ability of people throughout the world and throughout history to justify their most base motivations by invoking spiritual inspiration provoked a level of disgust in me that astounded even myself. The most benevolent religious doctrines were routinely cited as the justification for barbaric practices directed toward non-believers. Buddhism admonished its followers to "hurt not others in ways that you yourself would find hurtful," and Islam asserted that " no one of you is a believer until he desires for his brother that which he desires for himself," while Christians and Jews solemnly proclaimed that "you shall love your neighbor as yourself."

" 'Persecute those who don't agree with you,' appears to be how the Golden Rule is translated in practice," I declared after skimming the final tome in our mini-library of religion. "The human race's ability to generate so much hate from so much profundity is truly impressive. Ain't spirituality wonderful!"

By the evening of the show, which was broadcast live to everyone on the East Coast and on tape to those in the West, Derek was as ready as he was ever going to be. He appeared neither excited nor anxious, but his melancholy mood had lifted. Josh and Tina kept close to him as we entered the Washington television studio in which the show was recorded, none of us having completely allayed our fear that the request from Reverend Goodson might be a ruse to take Derek into custody for his earlier remarks to Norman Wycroft. Although they mounted a formidable interference for Derek, he had ordered both physical therapists to put up no resistance if anyone tried to arrest him. I had my doubts about their intention to follow his order.

Following a young blonde tenor, one of the show's regulars, singing *God Bless America*, in the program's customary opening, succeeded by the young man's stirring rendition of the Bach adaptation of the Martin Luther text, *Savior of the Nation's*

133

Come, the show's theme song, Derek was the minister's first guest. Reverend Goodson greeted him like a long-lost relative—perhaps hoping to suggest the return of the prodigal son.

"The whole nation is grateful that one of our heroes has been returned to us," Goodson began, smiling benevolently in Derek's direction. "I believe that God had a purpose in waking you from your long sleep at this very moment in our country's history. Wouldn't you agree?" The "preying" minister held his hands in their usual clasped position in front of his chest, as if he was hoping to summon God at that very moment.

"I only know that I woke up," Derek answered, smiling politely. His low voice was warm and friendly.

Goodson's smile remained but it was more strained. "I think most of my viewers would agree with me that your waking was God's will. This country is in a prophetic battle with conscienceless thugs who will do anything to prove that their religion is greater than ours. I'm sure you want to help your country in its greatest fight of all time."

"What do you mean when you say '*our*' religion?" Derek asked. There was no accusation in his voice. He sounded genuinely curious.

The minister appeared confused. "Christianity of course. This country was founded on Christian values. They are embedded in our Constitution."

"I was not aware that our constitution favored one religion over another," Derek answered, as if the minister's comment had left him puzzled.

"Things have changed while you were in your coma."

Derek gazed at him without saying anything.

"You must believe in Christian values," Goodson stated, though it sounded as if he was asking a question. The minister had given up on enlisting his guest's support and was clearly baiting him.

"Do you mean loving our enemies, turning the other cheek, offering the shirts off our backs, and valuing charity above faith?" Derek asked, the look of curiosity still on his face.

Goodson's face showed his irritation. "Of course I include those values, but I was referring to defending our country against the nations that deny that Christ is God and who want to make us believe in their heathen prophets."

"America no longer believes in religious freedom?"

Goodson wrestled his anger to a dull roar before answering. "We are a free country except to those who try to destroy democracy. It is our enemies who are not free. While the Muslims, whom you want to compare to us, impose their strict censorship on every aspect of life in their countries, it is an undisputed fact that every Christian nation in the world is, and always has been, a democracy." The minister leaned toward his guest and jutted out his multiple chins, as if daring Derek to challenge him.

Derek continued to gaze at him with unruffled composure. "Perhaps you are forgetting Germany and Italy during the second World War, Chile under Pinochet, Portugal under Salazar, Spain under Franco, Yugoslavia under Milosevic, Liberia under Charles Taylor, and of course the years of tyranny by the White Christian government of South Africa?" His comment was phrased as a question. He leaned toward the minister with an earnest expression of interest.

Goodson's red face showed his anger in full bloom. "You have cited a few isolated aberrations. I could counter with the names of Godless Communist dictators if I wished, but our enemies now are the Muslims, who are out to convert the world to their heathen religion and their primitive laws. There can be no democracy in such societies."

"The challenge to democracy lies in the imposition of a state religion, not the mere detail of which religion is the one imposed." There was no malice in Derek's answer, though he was clearly challenging the minister.

The smile had left the face of Reverend Goodson. "We cannot allow religions in this country that preach the overthrow of our democracy."

"When we become prisoners of our own defenses, we no longer need an enemy," Derek said. His tone expressed his dismay at the minister's statement.

"Are you denying that our enemies are real?" Goodson asked.

"I think we have used the existence of enemies as a justification for taking away the freedom of our citizens and for pursuing our conquest of the rest of the world."

"That is treason," Goodson said, his voice cold.

"Can the truth be treasonous?" There was a note of pity in his voice, as if Goodson's shallow thinking made him feel sympathy more than anger.

"Your opinions are treasonous and you can be jailed for voicing them." There was a threat in the minister's tone.

"You mean my opinions provoke such fear that our government would imprison me rather than allow me to speak freely?"

"Our way of life must be protected."

Derek gazed at Reverend Goodson for several seconds before responding. "Those are the words of a police state, Reverend. I hope your listeners understand that." For the first time, the sympathy was absent from his voice. Instead, his words sounded as if he was giving the minister a warning.

'We shall see what they understand," the Reverend said, looking toward the camera to signal the end of the show. He looked as if his confidence had been shaken in the face of Derek's unyielding resolve. "My listeners are loyal Americans and their faith will guide their understanding." There was a note of pleading in his voice that appeared to surprise even him.

"I hope the desire for truth will guide their understanding," Derek said. Those were his last words as the program's director stepped in and signaled for a commercial break.

"You have not showed wisdom tonight," Reverend Goodson said flatly as he stared at Derek across the table. "You have misjudged the attitude of your fellow citizens."

Derek's face showed his sadness. He stood and without saying anything, turned and left.

I was cheering wildly from the wings.

Chapter 23

Jeremy Swift stood in the shadow of the low building that housed the café across from the beach in Jaffa. He was dressed in a dark sportcoat and slacks, his shirt open at the neck in the Israeli fashion. Despite the darkness around him, he wore shaded glasses. He watched the cars as they slowly cruised by, loaded with boisterous young Israelis out on the town for the evening, looking, for all of their dark eyes and deep-voiced Hebrew intonations, like young people from anywhere in Europe or America. The reverberations from rock music drifted up the beach from the bars farther down the road that ringed the bay. That scene was in stark contrast to the subdued atmosphere of the café in the building next to Jeremy, where old couples drank coffee next to housewives conferring with each other while taking a few hours to escape from the confines of husband and children, and where solitary students bent their heads over thick textbooks, while they scribbled notes or typed into laptops.

A white van slowed, and from the front passenger seat a reedy, middle-aged, man, balding and wearing glasses and a rumpled suit stepped onto the sidewalk. He glanced down the street in either direction, then furtively hurried around the side of the building. When he nearly ran into Swift standing in the dark, he startled.

"Sorry to surprise you, sir," Swift said in an even voice. "I appreciate your coming."

Ari Yeshuen stepped back and took a long look at the man in front of him. Other than their similar ages, they could not have looked more different—Swift with his debonair appearance and Ari looking like a staid bureaucrat. Both of them knew that Ari's harmless exterior masked a more dangerous and cold-blooded warrior than Jeremy had ever been. The two went back many years, to the time when Ari had been an officer in the Mossad and the American had been a CIA operative attached to the U.S. Embassy in Jerusalem. Together they had worked on more than one dangerous mission. But the aide to the Israeli Prime Minister's duties had changed and Jeremy Swift was no longer stationed in Jerusalem. A meeting of this kind was more than unusual—it was unprecedented. "You said it was urgent," Ari said to his old colleague. "The prime minister is eager to hear what you have to say."

The two men walked down the dark passageway between the buildings until they reached the alley. Swift's SUV was parked against the back of the café. Swift unlocked the door, and they both got in. Jeremy started the engine. "Let's drive around, if you don't mind."

Ari nodded.

"I am violating the trust of my government by being here," Jeremy said, edging the SUV through the traffic and driving away from the raucous strip of road along the beach.

Ari blinked, then removed his glasses and cleaned them on his tie. "I don't understand."

"My country is ready to sacrifice your people. I don't want that to happen."

Ari put his glasses on and stared at Swift. "Tell me."

"I overheard a conversation between someone high up in my government and a key figure in the Lebanese government. The Lebanese asked if there would be retaliation by America if Iran attacked Israel with nuclear weapons."

Ari continued to stare at him. "What was the answer?"

"The Lebanese was reassured that there would be no retaliation. The American representative said that he agreed that Israel needed to be taught a lesson."

The Israeli's face, even in the shadows of the automobile, looked stunned. "How close to your president was the American?"

"Close enough to speak for the president. What he says becomes American policy."

Ari looked out the window. The sea was only a distant ribbon. Traffic was light this far from the water. "Did the Lebanese talk about an imminent attack?" His voice was weak, and his words emerged as if he had had difficulty getting them unstuck from his throat.

"He was vague. He talked of rumors. But he talked of a concerted plan by Kharrazi, Aphta, and Hezbollah. They are feeling the threat of al Mout li Kafir gaining strength among their people. All the Arab leaders want to show that they are as militant as Mustafa al Adim."

Ari searched the face of his old colleague in the dark interior of the car. "Why are you telling us this?"

"Israel is an ally of my country. We should not treat an ally this way."

"But you have committed treason."

"You can do something to spoil Kharazzi's plan. You can attack him first."

"That could be disastrous if you are wrong."

"I'm not wrong."

They had arrived back at the café. Jeremy stopped the car. "I don't know how long you have before Iran decides to launch an attack."

Ari opened the door of the SUV. "I will bring it to the attention of the Prime Minister tonight."

Swift nodded.

The Israeli closed the car door and walked back down the alley. When he reached the street the white panel truck appeared out of the traffic and came to a brief stop. Ari Yeshuen got into the passenger seat and the truck moved back into the flow of traffic.

Chapter 24

Tina was up frying bacon and making pancakes for the rest of us when I came down the stairs, dressed, but still sleepy-eyed and looked around for coffee. An almost full pot was sitting in the coffee machine. Tina herself drank only herbal tea.

"I don't know how you stay in shape with the kind of breakfasts you fix," I said to Tina. Although she was slim, she had shapely, trim hips and small, delicate breasts. Her shoulders, revealed by a pink tank top, were hard and muscled.

She smiled shyly. "This for the rest of you. I have eaten my morning soup already."

I knew she was referring to the bowl of noodles she had each morning and which, along with rice, seemed to form the heart of each of her meals. On occasion Josh could get her to eat a big American dinner along with the rest of us, especially when he cooked his special ribs and I knew she also loved both pizza and hamburgers, but most of her meals stuck pretty close to traditional Vietnamese staples except on the nights she cooked dinner for all of us and then her offerings, although still thoroughly Asian, were more elaborate.

"Anybody else up?"

"Derek has done his morning exercises with Josh and now he's in the living room having coffee. Josh went out to get a paper. Karin hasn't been down yet."

"I guess Karin and I are the lazy ones."

"Maybe you stayed up late last night?" Even behind her shyness, I could detect a twinkle in Tina's eyes.

"Only for a bit," I said, smiling. The truth was, we had sat in the living room long enough to have a nightcap and talk about the seriousness of Reverend Goodson's implied threat against Derek for speaking his mind. Both of us thought the threat was real, but we differed on whether Derek should continue to speak out as he had on the minister's television show. Although I was wholeheartedly of the opinion that what Derek chose to say was up to Derek, I was 100% behind him speaking out against the government's positions, if that was what he felt. For her part,

Karin blamed me for putting Derek in danger. She accused me of using him to voice my own anti-establishment feelings and putting him at risk for what she considered senseless reasons. I had thought she had been gaining some anti-establishment feeling of her own, but last night's conversation made me think she was right back where she started—including harboring a low opinion of yours truly.

I heard the front door open and footsteps in the foyer then Josh came lumbering into the kitchen, copies of several papers under his arm. "Bacon smells good," he said to Tina. "Morning Luke."

"Did you look at any of the papers?" I asked him.

"Not yet. I'll have my coffee before I read the bad news. You can have them if you want."

"I'm with you," I answered him. "I can't imagine anyone is going to react very well to what Derek said to Goodson last night. I think I'll wait till I enjoy my coffee too. Maybe even until after breakfast."

"I thought Derek said exactly what you wanted him to say," Karin said, descending from the stairs into the kitchen. "Are you afraid to face the problem you've created by encouraging Derek to spout your opinions?"

I hadn't even heard her coming down. She was dressed in tight-fitting black wool slacks and a yellow cashmere sweater that emphasized her figure. I noticed she had put her hair up in a new look for her and had already put on makeup. I couldn't stop myself from hoping her attractive appearance was for me, although her words made me doubt it..

"Nobody tells Derek what he should say," I answered. "Besides, from what you said to both him and me prior to the show, you agreed with everything he said." I shook my head sadly. "I fear you're retreating back into your safe, non-opinionated, academic shell. I liked you better with more fire in your belly."

She stared at me with a cold look on her face. "I couldn't care less which way you like me. I was carried away by the despicable treatment Derek received from Norman Wycroft and the silly religious nonsense that Reverent Goodson spouts to the public. But the answer to that sort of drivel is not to launch into our own equally biased opinions on the other side of each issue, especially when it could get Derek arrested."

"And you blame me for that?"

"You are the rabble-rouser. You always have been."

Before I could frame a suitably insulting rejoinder, the doorbell rang and in one rapid motion Josh deposited his armload of papers on the kitchen table and headed toward the front door. Tina was right behind him. I hadn't even seen her put down the spatula she'd been holding. For physical therapists they made a great team of bodyguards.

I followed Josh and Tina into the living room. Derek was sitting in a large Queen Anne chair, his coffee on the table next to him, looking at the door. Josh was looking out the glass window at the top of the door. The doorbell rang again.

"We must have a guest," Derek said. "Open the door, Josh. Whoever it is must be cold out there."

Josh moved to one side while Tina stood on the other side of the door so that she would be out of the line of vision when the door was opened. Instinctively, I moved in front of Derek.

Josh nodded at me. He still hadn't opened the door.

I felt Karin next to me and was amazed that she was standing at my side. She put her arm through mine and looked up at me, her face filled with a grim look of determination.

Josh opened the door with caution. A woman's voice asked if this was Derek Stewart's house.

"Who is interested in knowing?" Josh asked.

"Susan Harlow," the woman answered.

Josh turned around and looked at Derek and Karin and me.

"Let Ms. Harlow in," I said, signaling a look of reassurance to the others. I had recognized both the name and the woman's voice. Susan Harlow was a well-known figure in Washington, a professional campaign planner, fundraiser and political strategist who had the reputation of selling her services to the highest bidder. She was talented and smart, without an apparent ideological bone in her body. I had no idea why she would be at our door.

Josh opened the door all the way, although Tina remained hidden, as a middle-aged woman with a bushy mop of flaming red hair and black-rimmed thick glasses walked through the doorway into the house. She wore a trim gray wool suit covered by a long black coat, open in the front, and high, black leather boots. Although her clothes were trim, her pudgy figure gave her a slightly dumpy appearance.

"I'm surprised you're not inundated with reporters," Ms. Harlow said, looking around the room and starting to remove her coat. She eyed the cup of coffee next to Derek. "Do you mind if I have a cup of coffee? I almost froze my ass off standing on your porch for so long."

Tina stepped from her spot beside the door and came around in front of Susan Harlow. "I will bring you a cup of coffee."

Susan nearly jumped out of her boots, having been unaware of Tina's presence. Then she looked at each of the rest of us. "Hello Luke," she said to me, having been interviewed by me once in the past. "So this is the cabal that has poisoned Derek Stewart's mind." She laughed a harsh laugh.

"These are my friends," Derek said. He had stood and put out his hand. "I am Derek Stewart. Josh and Tina are my physical therapists, Luke is my biographer and Doctor Milne is my tutor."

"Tutor?" She looked quizzically at Karin.

"Karin is a professor of history. She has been catching me up on what I missed by sleeping through the last 40 years."

"A liberal-tinged history, but a thorough one from what I've seen of your performances on T.V."

Karin stiffened, while I whispered "nah nah nah nah nah" in her ear. She unwound her arm from mine and shook her head in disgust.

Tina came into the room with a cup of coffee and handed it to Susan, who took it and, without being asked, sat down on the couch. I went into the kitchen and picked up my own cup of coffee and poured one for Karin and brought both cups into the living room. Josh had gone back to the kitchen with Tina.

"Why did you think there would be reporters here?" I heard Derek ask

"You haven't read the papers this morning?" Susan asked him.

He shook his head, then looked at Karin and me, who had each taken seats—Karin on the couch next to Susan and me on a chair next to Derek. We both shook our heads.

"Tell us what the papers said," Derek asked, smiling at Susan.

She sipped her coffee and looked at Derek. "You were quite a success last night on Reverend Goodson's television show."

Derek continued to smile. "That's gratifying to hear." He looked at Karin and me. "I think my friends were afraid to read the papers for fear that I would have been pilloried by the press."

I gave Karin an "I told you so," look.

Susan laughed. "Oh some of the columnists, such as Tom Edwards in the Times, tried to paint you as a dangerous subversive. I think he accused you of being a puppet of Mr. Evangelista here, whom Edwards seems to hold in special disrepute. But Edwards was in the minority. A couple of polls showed that the majority of the viewers thought you made Goodson look like a fool—not such a hard thing to do, I admit—and people liked what you had to say."

"I spoke the truth. I had no intention of belittling Reverend Goodson."

"Goodson has a way of demeaning himself," Susan answered.

"You came all the way here this morning just to tell us what the papers had to say about Derek's TV performance?" I asked. Susan Harlow was as calculating a woman as I had ever met and she had to have an angle in coming to visit Derek.

Susan smiled and took another sip of coffee before speaking. "I came here because of what the papers had to say about the public's reaction to Mr. Stewart." She fastened her eyes on Derek. "Some of the papers were more than complimentary. They have called for you to run for public office."

Karin and I looked at each other. We were both stunned.

Derek had a placid smile on his face. He did not seem the least bit surprised by Susan Harlow's statement.

Josh walked into the room. "Breakfast is ready. Any longer and it will get cold." He glowered at Susan Harlow.

"Would you like to join us for breakfast Ms. Harlow?" Derek asked.

"I'd love to." She said, smiling back.

"Before we eat, I have a question for Ms. Harlow," I interrupted as everyone stood to go up to the dining room.

"Yes?" She arched her eyebrows, but she looked as if she suspected where I was going with my question.

"What does this have to do with you? Why are you here this morning?"

"I'd have thought it would be obvious," she said. "I'd like to organize Mr. Stewart's campaign."

"Campaign for what?" Karin asked. I could sense her bristling at Susan's presumptuous manner.

"For the presidency, of course," Susan answered, directing her gaze at Derek to gauge his reaction.

"It's an interesting topic," Derek said. "Shall we eat?"

Chapter 25

"Goodson you're an ass," Jervis Donovan said, the contempt dripping from his voice.

"Don't blame Goodie," President Ferris said, feeling a rush of sympathy for the fat minister who provided his personal religious guidance. The president was sitting at his desk in the Oval Office, and both Donovan and Reverend Goodson were seated in front of him. "The idea of inviting Stewart onto Goodie's show was yours, Jervy, and we simply miscalculated both Stewart's cleverness and his appeal to the public." He picked up a glass of water and took a sip. "But we've learned our lesson. No more invites for our Mr. Stewart. He's a momentary phenomenon, and he'll be forgotten in a few weeks."

"The Post ran a poll that showed that he would be neck and neck with you if he ran for president right now," Donovan said, the scowl still planted on his face. He didn't feel like letting Goodson off so easily.

""Well he's not running against me right now. There isn't an election for another year, and nobody will remember who he is by then." As an afterthought, the president added," And make sure whoever came up with the idea of that poll at the Post gets fired."

Donovan nodded. "That's already been done. But the cat's out of the bag. Stewart raised questions about the war and about our security measures. Now people are starting to question our whole agenda," He was no longer scowling, but his face was deadly serious.

"I answered every one of his ridiculous comments," Goodson said, glancing over at the president for approval. "People won't take him seriously when they think about what he said.

"You didn't answer anything," Donovan said viciously, "You made us sound like a bunch of Nazis and allowed him to raise questions about our fight with the Islamic world."

"We're a Christian nation, I reminded the audience of that. All we really need is some more old fashioned flag-waving and call to prayer." Goodson said, his eyes remaining more on the president than on Donovan. "Let's not forget whose side God is on in this war."

"Oh for Christ's sake," Donovan said, a disgusted look on his face.

Ferris shot a look of reproof at his advisor. "Goodie is right. This is a holy war, and we're on the right side." He stroked his chin, the classic jutting facial feature that leant him an impressive aura of authority. "But we need something soon. The real problem with Stewart's appearance on your show, Goodie is that we can't afford to undermine public support or start raising questions about our War on Terror right now. We're too close to the start of an all-out nuclear battle with the Goddamn Arabs."

"You mean they took the bait?" Goodson asked, the eagerness evident in his voice. The prospect of a nuclear Middle East war raised visions in his mind of the *last days*, the return of the Temple in Jerusalem, the devastation of Israel by their failure to acknowledge Christ, and then the start of Christ's thousand year reign. He could hardly contain his zeal at the prospect of playing a part in bringing such *end times* about.

The president was calmer in his assessment. "It looks that way. Jervy talked to them and he says Kharazzi could launch a nuclear attack anytime. "He looked over at Donovan, who nodded in agreement. "They've been told we won't retaliate if they take out Tel Aviv."

"And they believed us?" Goodson asked, a note of awe in his voice.

"I gave them the message himself—direct to Mahmoud Fakhry, who said he'd relay it to Kharazzi and Aphta," Donovan said. He was irritated by Goodson's childish enthusiasm, knowing that it was based on what Donovan considered a cockamamie fundamentalist religious theory. "Fakhry gave no indication of not believing me completely."

"Wonderful! Pope Gregory has prepared the Euros," Reverend Goodson said. "He says they'll be solidly in our corner if we counter an attack on Israel with an attack on the Middle Eastern capitals."

"And the American people were solidly in our corner before this Derek Stewart came along. Now they could turn on us if they don't believe in the legitimacy of our war effort," Donovan said, his expression glum. "We need to gain some ground with the public before any nuclear war gets started."

"We're not controlling the time table. The genie's been let out of the bottle and it's all up to Kharazzi and his military advisors now. Who knows when they'll decide to launch?"

Donovan looked glum. "Maybe I can do something to get them to hold off. I can talk to Kharazzi again. Then we need to do something here at home." Donovan said. "And I mean do something right now."

"I can go on television and make some speeches, rally the people behind our Christian mission. Deep down, Americans know all Muslims are pagan fascists—they just need to be reminded of it," Goodson said, he still was bubbling with enthusiasm.

"Too little and it'll take too much time," Donovan snapped. "We need something more dramatic," he stared at the president for a moment before continuing. "We need another terror attack on U.S. soil."

"I'm not going to kill a bunch of Americans to get public opinion behind us," the president said, although his tone was less than emphatic, as if he might, indeed, be considering just such a option.

Donovan looked offended. "Of course not, sir. And I wouldn't recommend such a thing unless we were in more dire circumstances. I'm talking about an assassination—killing just one man."

"You mean we engineer a terrorist assassination?" the president asked. His eyes glittered in anticipation. "Who would be the target?"

Donovan smiled in satisfaction, as though he had been waiting to spring the punch line to their conversation. "Derek Stewart—our new American hero."

Chapter 26

Mohammed Sahadi knew how to avoid drawing attention to himself. He had lived most of his adult life in Europe and had carried out numerous assassinations without ever having his face identified by Interpol or any of the European security agencies. Even after his latest mission, in which he had detonated a bomb in the midst of a meeting of the European Union Finance Ministers, killing three ministers and several of their aides, he could walk the streets of any European capital without fear of being apprehended.

Mohammed's lack of familiarity with Washington D.C. was a handicap. He knew the capitals of Europe well but he had only seen Washington in movies. Up close, the government buildings, the hotels, and the Georgetown neighborhoods were as impressive as they were on film. But away from the glamour of money and government, the inner city was as dirty, dangerous, and chaotic as any he had seen in Europe.

Mohammed knew that, as a Frenchman and as a Christian, his visit would not prompt any undue surveillance. His appearance, which was distinctly Middle Eastern, even though he wore Western clothing, might prompt suspicion from the people with whom he interacted, and he would have to avoid drawing the attention of the local police, who, he had been warned, might arrest him on almost any pretense, just because of his ethnicity.

The easiest section of the city within which he would blend would have been Georgetown, where Middle Eastern students, businessmen and diplomats were an everyday sight. His target lived in Georgetown, so that was where he wanted to be anyway. The problem for Mohammed was that he was on a limited budget, and he didn't want to attract any official attention by hanging around Stewart before the two actually met. Mohammed's problem was figuring out how he was going to contact Derek Stewart and how he would earn his trust,

Sitting in a café in Columbia Heights, on a street lined with trees, barren of leaves in the winter, Mohammed sipped his tea and read the newspaper, trying to quiet the anxiety that he felt about his mission… about just being here in the United States—in its very capital. This neighborhood was of mixed ethnicity, with newly arrived Africans and Middle-Easterners, mostly fleeing their countries for political reasons, and African-Americans, some of whom had lived in the neighborhood for generations. As a new face, even one with Middle-Eastern features, Mohammed attracted no attention as he eagerly read the mainstream papers—not making the mistake of reading an ethnic language paper in public—looking for what he could find out about the man he was planning to kill. Derek Stewart was a headline topic in both the Times and the Post, although the two newspapers depicted radically different views of the man.

Stewart had become a rallying point for the disenfranchised liberals in the country who were suspicious of the War on Terror and opposed the Draconian security measures which had been instituted as part of that war and which had led to the outlawing of the Islamic religion and the jailing of thousands of Muslims under suspicion of aiding the overseas terrorists. Mohammed felt his anger rising as he thought about what had happened to his fellow Lebanese in the United States under the Ferris administration.

The Post was cautiously optimistic about the emergence of a new figure in opposition to the administration of president Fremont F. Ferris. Without commenting on the accuracy of Derek Stewart's comments while on Goodson's show, the editors of the Post suggested that the newly awakened war hero might present an alternative to Ferris and his supporters, and that questioning of the administration's foreign policy might prove a popular stance in a war-weary United States.

Mohammed felt himself beginning to tremble. He had not seen Stewart's performance on television the previous night, but from the newspaper account it sounded as if he had voiced views similar to those that his famous late cousin had been known for espousing—especially in his anti-war stance. Why was Mohammed being asked to kill a man who didn't want to continue the U.S.'s War on Terror?

Mohammed took several deep breaths and allowed his muscles to relax, then turned to the Times. Perhaps the other paper portrayed Derek Stewart in a more dangerous light. In fact, it did—but more dangerous to America. To Mohammed's consternation he found that the paper's most vocal editorial writer, Tom Edwards, declared Derek Stewart a menace to the American way of life because of his "pacifist and frankly Middle-East-leaning stance" and urged his prosecution as a dangerous subversive.

Mohammed could feel himself losing his resolve and the feeling frightened him. Although he had never known any of his targets personally, he was familiar with each of their public stances and the danger they posed to Muslims. But with Stewart he could see no danger. Mohammed knew that it had been a mistake to bring him this close to his target—to expect him to get to know the man and gain his confidence. As he felt his will beginning to lessen, he made a conscious choice to thrust his sympathetic thoughts about Stewart from his mind. His role was not to question his orders. Along that path lay chaos and weakness. He must be strong and do what he had been told to do.

As Mohammed focused his mind on his mission, he thought about how to get near his target. He had read that, although Stewart was now employing a well-known, in fact notorious, political strategist to plan his campaign, his other advisors were a small group of more or less amateurs who had been with him from the day he had awakened from his coma or even before that. None was a seasoned political campaigner nor had any of them any experience in foreign affairs. Mohammed had lived in the Middle-East, throughout Europe, read and spoke several languages, and had no strong political beliefs other than his hatred of Israel and any country that supported it. He was the ideal candidate to become a part of Stewart's little team of amateurs. He could, in fact, provide a level of expertise about world affairs at a personal level, that was exactly the level of knowledge upon which Derek Stewart appeared to thrive and upon which he was basing his appeal to the public.

He finished his tea and paid and left the restaurant.. He had read that Susan Harlow had simply appeared on Stewart's doorstep one morning and announced her desire to manage his political campaign. The strategy had worked for her, perhaps it might also work for him. It would be a gamble because, unlike Susan Harlow, he was dark skinned, he spoke with an accent and he was not a United States citizen. Neither did he have any credentials to back up his claims of expertise in world affairs. He could be arrested. But he had no other strategy.

When he reached Georgetown and the address he had been given for Stewart, Mohammed rang the doorbell on the townhouse. The door quickly opened to reveal a massive, muscular Black man with a ferocious scowl on his face.

"We don't want any," Josh Mannerly announced.

The physical therapist's manner would have struck fear in the heart of any other person, but Mohammed had not felt fear since the day his family was killed in Lebanon. The muscular bodyguard merely presented a tactical problem.

"I have information," Mohammed managed to get out before Josh shut the door.

Mannerly stopped before he had the door closed. A look of suspicion crossed his face. "What kind of information?"

"I am a Muslim."

No one announced his allegiance to Islam any more. Such a statement could land a person in jail within a matter of minutes. Josh tried to figure what this man, who stared him straight in the eyes without any indication of fear, wanted. Was this a terrorist who had come to blow himself up, and Derek Stewart and the rest of his small entourage with him? Did suicide bombers announce themselves first?

"What do you want?"

"I want to help Mr. Stewart. I want to work with him to put America on the right path." Mohammed's expression contained no threat. He acted as if he was making an ordinary request.

Josh wasn't sure what to do. The young man's confidence irritated him at the same time that he was becoming even surer that the man presented no immediate threat. He was about to ask the young man in front of him to leave his name and a phone number when he felt a presence behind him.

"Let the young man come in, Josh, " Derek said. He stood just behind the physical therapist's shoulder. Josh hadn't even been aware that he was downstairs.

"We don't know who he is," Josh said. In his opinion Derek was much too trusting of everyone. His hiring of Susan Harlow, just because she showed up at his front door, was a perfect example. Was he going to do the same thing again with this young man?

"We can't find out who he is unless we invite him in to tell us," Derek said. He stepped past the physical therapist. "I'm Derek Stewart. I'd like to hear what you think you could offer me," he said to the young man at the door.

Mohammed was struck dumb. He hadn't expected to be face to face with his target so quickly. Every other important person he had ever met had layers of intermediaries in between himself and the public. Mohammed struggled to say something. Finally, he just nodded and, responding to Derek's gesture of welcome, stepped through the front door.

Chapter 27

There was nothing left to do. What happened from this point forward would be in the hands of the Israeli Air Force and Prime Minister, Benjamin Dalert could only wait—and pray that the results were what he had desired when he had given the order to bomb the nuclear facilities in Iran. Dalert had provided the Americans no warning of his country's precipitous attack. The Prime Minister had been outraged when he had found out that President Ferris had not only guaranteed the Iranians that they would not be punished for attacking Israel with nuclear weapons, but that the president of the United States had encouraged them to do so.

Dalert could have gotten on the telephone and talked directly to President Ferris, but he had rejected that course, almost immediately. The very fact of Ferris's collusion with the Lebanese, Iranians, and Syrians, was enough to convince Benjamin Dalert that the Americans could not be trusted. Suddenly their promises of support and their lofty words of encouragement for Israel's brave defense against constant Arab attacks on innocent Israeli civilians were revealed as empty platitudes or worse, evil deception. Dalert had a suspicion regarding what Ferris hoped to gain by conspiring with Israel's enemies. If an Arab-Iranian assault on Israel took place, the Americans could use such an attack as a justification to confront the Islamic nations directly. There was no chance that the Americans were actually allying themselves with any of the Middle Eastern countries—Ferris and his advisor Reverend Goodson, not to mention the American allies in Europe and their champion, Pope Gregory, were determined to destroy Islam as a world religious power. How could Kharazzi and Aphta have forgotten that? What Benjamin Dalert wondered was whether the American antipathy toward non-Christian nations extended to the Jewish state.

Did the Americans want to take over Israel?

The prime minister's telephone rang. The jets were in the air. In less than fifteen minutes they would be over the Iranian nuclear facility, 100 miles from Tehran. The Israeli planes were not armed with nuclear weapons. If Dalert had wanted to attack Iran with nuclear weapons he would have launched a missile, and not only the Iranian nuclear facility but Tehran itself would be gone by now. That was not his intention. He only wanted to remove a threat, not destroy a country.

***

The first images came in from the VEGA spy satellite orbiting over Israel. Five American-made, Israeli Air Force B-2 Stealth bombers, designed to be invisible to radar, but, unbeknownst to the Israelis, containing a single strip of engineered metal to which the VEGA radar had been programmed to respond, were detected as they took off from Yavne, the secret airfield located near the Palmachim Air Force Base on the coast of Israel south of Tel Aviv. The satellite radar continued to track the five planes as they tore across the sky over Jordan, then Iraq, and finally into Iranian air space. Each B-2 bomber had fired off its payload of 2,000 lb. Global Positioning Guided GBU-36 bombs, leaving nothing but a massive array of craters where the Iranian nuclear assembly plant and launching facility had previously existed, and headed back to Yavne, before U.S. CentCom had even determined the object of their mission.

Ten minutes later, President Ferris was roused from bed and given the news. Within half an hour he and his top advisors were in the situation room deciding what they should do.

"What the hell could have possessed Dalert to do a thing like this?" the president ranted, his face twisted into a furious scowl as he paced back and forth behind the long oval table at which were seated Jervis Donovan, the Reverend Merrill Goodson, Raymond Decker, his National Security Advisor, Consuela Madrid, the Secretary of State, Albert Rutherford, Secretary of Defense, Nathaniel Broadmoor, the Director of the CIA and Air Force General Mathew Corey, Chairman of the Joint Chiefs of Staff.

"It's not like the Israelis to do something behind our back," Secretary Madrid commented in her soft voice. The short, dark, plump Secretary of State was past middle age, but her round features still spoke of her earlier beauty. Around her mouth and eyes were lines from years of smiling, a reflection of her open and engaging personality, the personality that had brought her into public service. Now her eyes were worried. Her petite mouth was set in a look of grim frustration.

"They're not a Christian country," Reverend Goodson said, as if that explained everything.

"They are our allies," Consuelo Madrid answered, trying to hide her impatience with the overweight minister, whom she regarded as a virulent influence on the president.

The president glanced at his Secretary of State with a barely hidden look of disdain. The Mexican-American former Harvard professor was an excellent negotiator with other countries, who uniformly respected her opinions, and enjoyed her warm frankness, but within Ferris' cabinet she was rarely taken seriously. The president had only brought her into his administration as a token to lure the Hispanic vote during the last election. Since then he'd managed to deport or jail enough illegal Hispanic immigrants that there was no way of securing their vote during the next election, no matter what he did. Goodson had almost convinced him that even the legal Mexican immigrants were disloyal because they were more Catholic than American, and they still had allegiance to both the pope and to their native country. Maybe it was time to round the whole lot of them up and send them back where they'd come from—Consuelo Madrid included. But he was getting distracted from the matter at hand.

"What do the rest of you think?" the president asked.

Raymond Decker, the National Security Advisor gave a knowing look toward Jervis Donovan. Decker was more than a match for Jervis Donovan in austerity. He had the physique of a marathon runner, which in fact he was, and a perpetually intense, wired look about him, as if he might be on some kind of stimulant medication, except that he was known to not even drink coffee. He was a dedicated Christian—dedicated to ridding

America of non-Christian influences and in his role as National Security Advisor, he extended his religious cleansing campaign to every corner of the world touched by American foreign policy. Only Decker, President Ferris, Donovan, Broadmoor and Reverend Goodson knew that the administration had given the green light to Iran to use its nuclear weapons against Israel. All five of them were thinking the same thing: Israel had discovered what the Iranians were about to do. But Decker didn't know how that could have happened, and he couldn't say anything in front of the other people in the room. "The real question is what the Iranians are going to do in response," the National Security Advisor said.

"Have we heard anything from Khafry in Lebanon?" the president asked, an edge of anxiety in his voice. The question had a double meaning. Khafry was a known friend of the United States, so it would be natural that he might be in contact with someone in the administration. But Ferris also knew that Khafry had been given the message that the United States would support an Iranian attack on Israel and now the Lebanese Speaker of the Parliament, as well as the leaders of Iran and Syria, must be wondering if the United States had double-crossed them.

"I've talked to him," Decker answered. "I've reassured him that we had no prior knowledge of the Israeli attack on Iran. I think he believes me, but he doesn't think he can dissuade the Iranians and the Syrians from launching a full-scale invasion of Israel."

"Shit!" the president exploded.

"We can't let the Muslims take Jerusalem," Reverend Goodson said. He was speaking in his oratorical voice.

"Perhaps we could convene emergency talks with Khafry and some of the other Middle-Eastern leaders who aren't directly involved, such as Aphta in Syria," Secretary Madrid offered.

The president gave her a dismissive glance. "Nate," he addressed the CIA Director, ignoring his Secretary of State's suggestion, "Do we have any intelligence to suggest that the Islamic countries are getting ready for an assault on Israel?"

"It's only been a hour since the Israeli attack, sir. We've got satellite data on a lot of military activity, but whether it's defensive or offensive, it's too early to tell at this point."

"Mustafa al Adim has issued a statement, Mr. president," Jervis Donovan said. All eyes turned to the presidential advisor. "He is demanding a response from the Islamic countries in the Middle East. He says that they must drive Israel into the sea." Donovan looked around at the others' faces. "He also has called for a renewal of his Jihad against any country that supports Israel. He means us. He has urged suicide bombers to strike against us here in America."

"This is our chance, Mr. president," Reverend Goodson said. He was so animated that the rolls of fat around his neck shook in waves, like bread dough sliding up and down a conveyor belt. "We've been looking for an excuse to finally have it out with the Islamofascists, and now they're about to give it to us. We have to defend Israel. It's our obligation as a Christian nation to not let the Holy lands fall into the hands of heathens. This could be our chance to destroy the Islamic governments once and for all. It's our opportunity to mount a modern Christian Crusade."

"Jervis?" the president looked at his chief advisor.

"I have to agree with Reverend Goodson on this one, sir. We can't afford to stand on the sidelines if the Arabs and the Israelis go at each other. We would look as if all of our rhetoric was just empty talk and if the Israelis lost, we'd lose our only ally in the Middle East and the Muslims would have the best recruiting tool they could ever have hoped for. Al Mout li Kafir will take the message of Western weakness to Africa, and we'll find ourselves and Europe isolated from the rest of the world."

"I doubt that the Israelis want an all-out war, Mr. president," Secretary Madrid said, although no one had so much as even looked in her direction. "They are likely to reject our offer of assistance. It would be better for them if things returned to normal."

"We're not going to ask them if they want our help," the president answered. "We're going to give it whether they want it or not. And this is going to mushroom into a bigger fight and the hell with what the Israelis want. We run our foreign policy, they don't."

The president looked at General Corey. "I want full mobilization of whatever size force we're going to need to win this thing, General." He scanned the other faces at the table. "And I want our nuclear missiles put on ready. We're not going to put any limits on what we're willing to do to win this one. We're not going to fight another Vietnam, leaving one of our hands tied behind our back."

The general looked the president squarely in the eyes. "I understand, sir."

Chapter 28

"You've got to take advantage of the situation," Susan said, her voice urgent, although she was trying to control her natural tendency to become irritatingly strident. "People need to hear a new voice."

We were all seated in the living room of Derek's townhouse—Derek, Susan, Karin, Maurice—the young Lebanese-born Frenchman who had shown up at Derek's door several days before—Josh, Tina and myself. We were watching CNN's coverage of the explosive Middle East situation. Syria and Lebanon were massing troops on Israel's border. Iran was rattling its sabers—or in this case, its Russian-made jet bombers—threatening to retaliate for Israel's surprise attack on the Iranian nuclear facilities.

"The Israelis have said they don't want any help from the United States," Derek answered. While his face showed his concern, he had retained his calm amid the atmosphere of crisis that characterized how the rest of us were reacting to the Middle East situation.

"Ferris and his crew don't want to be accused of sitting on the sideline," I said. "They're dying to get into the fight and this would be the perfect excuse for them to take out a couple of Islamic governments like Syria and Iran—all in the name of protecting Israel. That boob Goodson has gone on record saying that Jerusalem should be a one hundred percent Judeo-Christian city and he probably wouldn't mind dropping the Judeo part. He's not going to let Jerusalem fall into the hands of the Arabs."

"Then you've got to take an opposite position," Susan insisted, looking at Derek. "Be the champion of letting the Israelis and the Syrians and Iranians hash it out among themselves."

"Because that will help my candidacy?" Derek asked, a smile playing around the corners of his mouth.

"Of course," Susan snapped, losing, for the moment, her control over her own ambitious anger. "You'll be the voice of the independents—the man who's not afraid to defy the government."

"Or the man who will say whatever it takes to win the support of the public?" His voice was gentle, though his words revealed the underlying point of her argument with relentless precision.

Susan was crestfallen—but only momentarily Her Machiavellian nature was remarkably resilient. "I didn't mean you should say something you don't believe in. But I thought you were generally against the country going to war." She looked up at him shyly. "Aren't you?"

Watching Susan Harlow play the bashful ingénue caused me to suppress a guffaw.

"You're right, Susan," Derek smiled at her. "But standing on the sideline, as Luke puts it, isn't going to stop the fighting."

"It's not America's war," Maurice joined in, his voice tense with emotion. "Israel made the first move, now the Israelis have to take the consequences."

Several eyes in the room glared at the young Frenchman. We knew he was a Muslim, but Maurice's prejudices against the Israelis were so obvious they made the rest of us uncomfortable.

"That's one point of view, Maurice," Derek answered. His own expression contained no hint of anger at the young man's opinion. "But if there's a way to settle disputes without people killing each other, that is preferred, wouldn't you agree?"

Maurice shifted his gaze to avoid eye contact. He looked confused. "Do you really think the Arabs and the Israelis can settle their differences by talking? There's too much hate on both sides." With a start he seemed to notice that he was sounding too impassioned. "Isn't there?" he asked meekly.

"What do you think about that mutual hate?" Derek asked, his voice still gentle as he looked, with what seemed innocent inquisitiveness, at the young Muslim.

Maurice stared Derek in the face, his own jaw set resolutely. "It has been earned. There have been many atrocities committed by the Israelis against Arabs—both the Palestinians, whose homes they took away from them and others such as the Lebanese, whom they attacked repeatedly."

"That's a one-sided view," Karin surprised me by answering. She was not one to engage in political debate… or I'd thought she wasn't. "Israelis settlers bought a lot of their land from the Palestinians, though I admit they simply took more of it by force when they sought a homeland after the Second World War and then took even more after the six-day war. But that was the price of attacking them. They needed a cushion between them and their hostile neighbors. And Lebanon has harbored terrorists who have killed many Israeli citizens. The Israelis have had to defend themselves."

"They defend themselves by killing indiscriminately," Maurice shot back, his eyes bulging with anger.

Karin looked embarrassed, as if her own words had never been intended to cause such a personal reaction.

"It is a normal human reaction to want to avenge the wrongs against our people, or defend their honor, or exalt them to glory," Derek said, almost as if he was talking to no one. "But when we commit ourselves to the glory of a nation, or to that of a movement, or to avenging wrongs, we see individuals as expendable—as living only to serve a higher good. That is a mistake. Each person is valuable in his own right, and only in his own right. He lives only for himself or for those whom he immediately cares for."

"But people die for higher causes," Maurice said, his tone halfway between anger and pleading. "Sometimes it is necessary to defend the honor of one's people."

"Yes," Derek answered, "it can be necessary to die for a higher cause." He paused, "…although I would question the value of defending one's or one's people's honor." He turned toward Maurice. "I have a feeling that you have suffered terrible losses in your life, Maurice." His expression was compassionate as he gazed at the young man. "Would you rather avenge those losses or to not have suffered them in the first place?"

Maurice looked at him suspiciously. The young Frenchman had never discussed his background, except to say he'd been born in Lebanon. Tears were forming in his eyes. "There is no way to bring back what I have lost. Revenge is all some of us have left." He continued to stare at Derek, his whole body trembling, as if he was holding back great sadness—or rage.

"That's not true," Derek answered, returning the young man's stare. His voice was gentle. "You have a great deal left besides revenge. There are millions of young people with families who love them and whom they love, but whom they will lose because of war. You can do something to protect those young people from those losses, or you can try to satisfy your revenge and guarantee that those young people will suffer just as you did."

Maurice looked away. He brought up a fist and brushed away a tear. He shook his head, but no words issued from his mouth.

"Holy shit," Josh Mannerly said, interrupting the silence that had descended on the room. We all turned our heads. He was staring at the television screen.

The CNN announcer was talking while the screen showed pictures of the worst carnage and destruction any of us had seen since 9/11. The scene was the U.S. Embassy in Ghana. The building had been completely leveled. So had an entire four-block area surrounding the American compound. Bodies lay everywhere. While pictures of emergency vehicles, bleeding people, mangled bodies, and smoking husks of buildings paraded across the television screen, a tinny voice spoke in Arabic. As we listened to the halting translation of what was being said, it slowly became clear that we were listening to an al Mout li Kafir tape declaring responsibility for the bombing. The words across the bottom of the screen listed an estimated death toll of over 900 people.

"It is the voice of Mustafa al Adim," Maurice said. "He is saying that he is spreading the Muslim holy war to Africa."

Chapter 29

"This attack in Ghana is exactly what we've been looking for," Jervis Donovan said. Although his voice was low and controlled, his eyes gleamed with intensity. "Al Mout li Kafir has widened the war and shown the world, once again, that their methods are nothing short of barbaric." He was addressing the president in the Oval office. The only others in the room were Reverend Merrill Goodson and the National Security Advisor, Raymond Decker.

"This is our opportunity to act," Decker said, his eyes on the president. Decker, part of the presidential "inner circle," was nearly as religious as Reverend Goodson and had been a chief architect of the administration's overall Middle East strategy, which called for military overthrow of militant Islamic governments and "democratization" of their countries, defined as replacement of their rule by elected secular governments, friendly to the United States. His plan extended to Africa where elected or not, any Muslim rule was considered hostile and a potential target of military intervention. Although there had been occasional drone and even manned air strikes by elements of the U.S. AfCom, the African Command, which had been formed back in the early years after 9/11, overt use of military land forces on the continent had always been considered too risky in terms of its reception by the world's opinion as well as public opinion at home. Decker saw the bombing of the U.S. Embassy in Ghana as an invitation to initiate the second phase of the War on Terror— the one that would spread across the African continent.

"What do you all recommend?" President Ferris asked the three others in the room. Most of his decisions were made with the advice of his inner circle.

"This is our chance to target those countries where militant Islam has taken hold," Decker answered, his eyes bright with enthusiasm. "Somalia would be a good place to start. I say let's target the government buildings in Mogadishu and the terrorist camps outside the city. It'll give a message to al Mout li

Kafir and any government that tries to shelter them, that we mean business."

"We're still talking about air strikes aren't we?"

Decker nodded. "We could take out their leaders with drones, like we've done in Yemen, but I recommend massive strikes this time, not just precision attacks against high-level targets. We want to send a message to the rest of Africa."

The president looked at Donovan and Goodson to see how they reacted to Decker's suggestion.

Donovan eyes were still bright. He nodded vigorously. "No one gives a damn about Somalia anyway and most people think it's being run by al Mout li Kafir. I say let's do it."

"If we don't do something we'll be considered soft," Reverend Goodson added. "But I don't want to stop with Somalia. Can't we go after some of the more influential Islamic countries like Ethiopia or Senegal?"

"Holy shit, Goodie, those countries are our allies," Ferris said, scowling at his religious advisor.

"But are they Christians?" Goodson exclaimed, his confusion showing on his face.

"Ethiopia has more Christians than Muslims," Donovan answered. "Anyway there are a lot of friendly countries in Africa that aren't Christians. Besides, if we attacked those countries we'd be condemned by every other country in the world, including our European allies and the whole of the African nations. Anyway, Ethiopia and Senegal are just as threatened by militant Islam as we are. They're firmly opposed to allowing al Mout li Kafir to operate within their borders."

"But the reverend is right that we don't want to be content with just an isolated attack on one country that no one cares about," Decker added. "We want to establish a foothold in Africa that will send a message to those governments that have let the Islamists have too much influence—like Sudan for instance or Nigeria. For some reason al Mout li Kafir seems to have retreated from Sudan recently, but both Sudan and Nigeria have become almost theocracies because they've let their courts be run by judges who follow Sharia law."

"Then let's do it right in Somalia," Jervis Donovan said. "Make our response big enough and bloody enough that it makes those other African countries think twice about allowing the Islamists into their midst. We want to scare the hell out of 'em, like we did with Gaddafi when we invaded Iraq. If we don't get some other countries, like Nigeria, throwing in with us and kicking the terrorists out, then we'll go after them, too."

President Ferris nodded. "Ok that's what we do. We bomb Somalia back to the stone age and make it absolutely clear that anyone who is friendly with Moustafa al Adim and his organization is going to get the same treatment from us."

"What about spreading Christianity?" Reverend Goodson asked.

"In time, Goodie, in time," President Ferris answered. "Remember the story about the mule-trainer who was hired to get the farmer's mule to do what he was told? The trainer said it was all in how you talked to the mule. He then picked up a two-by-four and hit the mule square between the eyes, knocking the mule to its knees. After that he whispered in the mule's ear and the mule did just as he was told. The farmer asked why he hit the mule if the secret was in the message he whispered in the mule's ear. The trainer said, 'first you have to get the mule's attention.' That's what we're doing here, Goodie, we're getting the Africans' attention."

"And let's not forget the most important point," Donovan said, his eyes narrowed in concentration. "Al Mout li Kafir's attack in on our embassy in Ghana gives us a good reason to get involved in the Middle East. This is our chance to take down the governments of Syria, Lebanon and Iran, without bothering about whether the Israelis invited us or not. It's not just their fight now. The attack in Ghana was against us. We can use that attack as a reminder of the danger of Islamic extremism, and nobody's going to question us attacking those Middle Eastern countries that are known to harbor terrorists."

"You mean the Little Bang option?" President Ferris asked, a hopeful look in his eyes. He had been displeased ever since he'd lost the reason to exercise what he thought was the best plan yet for getting rid of the Muslim threat.

"Why not?" Donovan answered. "That was our goal in encouraging Iran to use its nuclear weapons. This gives us another chance to use our own nukes." He surveyed the others for signs of dissent.

"We can't just destroy Tehran, Damascus and Beirut out of the blue," Decker objected.

"We'll get the congress to declare war," Ferris answered. "We've just lost a Goddamned embassy for Christ's sake," he looked sheepishly at Reverend Goodson. "Excuse my language Reverend, but I have strong feelings about this."

"Armbruster can get the votes," Donovan said. "We don't need to ask the congress to let us use nuclear weapons; just get them to give us carte blanche to fight the damned Muslims where they live."

"After their conscienceless attack on our embassy I don't see how congress can refuse," Goodson said.

"They won't refuse," Donovan answered. And, he thought to himself, if they need greater justification, we'll throw in the assassination of Derek Stewart, an event that he was confident was about to happen, although only he knew that for sure.

Chapter 30

Troy Raynham referred to himself as the "oldest hippie." In 1968 he had hitch-hiked from Seattle to Chicago to join the protests outside the Democratic Convention. After his candidate, Eugene McCarthy, had lost his bid for the presidential nomination, Troy had continued to protest the war in Vietnam. He'd taken to the streets, carried placards, sat-in at his university's ROTC building and had burned his draft card. He'd been part of a national movement. He'd been carried to heights he had never dreamed of by a wave of revolutionary fervor that had brought purpose and excitement to his life, just at a time when he would have floundered helplessly looking for his identity. Then the wave broke. He had found himself alone.

A crook had won the election, the disgraceful war had ended disgracefully, the world had returned to normal and most of Troy's fellow radicals had gotten hair cuts, traded in their sandals for wing-tips and gone to work for corporate America.

Troy had retreated from political involvement too, but not by joining Wall Street. He and a small coterie of dyed-in-the-wool anti-establishment types, finding each other in the coffee houses and wandering like lost sheep across college campuses that had been battlegrounds against authority and now were back to being training grounds for jobs with high salaries and pensions, had retreated to their communes, turned from protests to pot and then on to even more life-altering drugs. When his own draft number had finally come up, he'd fled to Canada, where he'd remained for 15 years before slipping back into the United States.

Now, after years of cynical retreat from any involvement in the nation's future, replaced by a lifestyle characterized by heavy drug use and career instability, he was taking to the streets again, protesting his country's imminent escalation of the War on Terror as it extruded itself into Africa. Troy's placard read, "HANDS OFF AFRICA," and, holding it in his wrinkled, liver-spotted hand, he pumped it up and down as he walked back and forth in front of the fence surrounding the White House. He knew that all the shouting and marching he and his fellow protesters were doing was a preamble to the real event of that Sunday afternoon—the appearance of Vietnam war hero, Derek Stewart.

Troy had been enticed back into political protest because Derek Stewart was, to him, a reminder of that "one brief shining moment" in which he and his fellow activists had felt as if they could control the destiny of the country. It was a feeling he had not had since the late 1960's, and he knew it was a feeling many of those younger people around him had never had in their lifetimes. Just like them, he was relieved to finally have someone he could believe in, someone to lead him in a fight for control of his country and his own life. Each of those young people, along with Troy, was relieved enough to risk imprisonment by the FIIEB in one of their notorious "secret" prisons, where terror suspects and "subversives" languished without benefit of a formal charge or trial. Just like each of them, Troy wasn't frightened; he was thrilled by the element of danger in their movement.

The crowd started to flow away from the White House and toward the National Mall where Stewart was scheduled to address the crowd. Blue uniformed Washington Police glared at the protesters as they walked by, chanting, "No more war!" and "Send money, not bombs to Africa." The protesters either ignored the police officers or handed them flowers. Troy felt right at home. The whole demonstration could have happened in the 1960s. He didn't understand why he and his fellow protesters hadn't been arrested yet.

The crowd had swollen to well over 20,000 by the time it spilled onto the National Mall, everyone jostling for position in front of the small stage and podium that had been erected on the lawn. Most of the protestors wrapped themselves in heavy coats because of the cold weather and huddled together to keep warm. The sky overhead was slate-gray and if there was going to be any precipitation it was as likely to be snow as rain. Troy pushed his way to the front, muttering, "Make way for the aged," as he moved forward, his placard in his hand. When he reached the front of the crowd and looked up, Derek Stewart was already standing behind the podium, adjusting the microphones. Nearly a hundred photographers snapped pictures of the Vietnam veteran.

At the edges of the crowd, somber men in drab gray suits talked into walkie-talkies, relaying Stewart's every action and waiting for orders to move in and arrest the man who was about to address the crowd.

Derek Stewart moved to the podium. He looked out over the crowd, seeing thousands of eager faces, their expressions betraying their desperate need to find a savior, a leader to bring them back to the halcyon days of "power to the people," and to overcome the repressive forces that characterized the society in which they found themselves.

"I think I remember you from 1970," Derek said, looking at the faces in front of him, and focusing particularly on the wrinkled visage of Troy Raynham with his salt and pepper ponytail, whom he did not actually remember, but who had clearly been in the crowds protesting the war in which Derek had been wounded, 40 years earlier. His remark provoked a solid round of laughter and then applause from the crowd.

Agent Edward Wilson, standing on the crowd's periphery and listening to the chatter of his fellow FIIEB agents and superiors in his ear, was chagrined. How did a traitor like Derek Stewart get away with entertaining this crowd of hopeless apologists for the terrorists, these anti-American weaklings who had no stomach for standing up to the heathens who wanted to destroy the United States and everything it stood for? Why wasn't he being ordered to move in and arrest him? Stewart was getting too much airtime from the television stations that were covering his speech. Wilson put his hand on the gun, holstered under his left arm and waited for his orders.

"I know you're all here because you're looking for an alternative to the kind of leadership our government has provided you," Derek continued. "Many of you probably see me as that alternative. But before you follow me, I'd like to tell you a story." He scanned the audience in front of him, as if he was trying to memorize every face. The mostly young faces waited in breathless anticipation.

"There once was a young man who lived in a village on the side of a mountain where every winter there were great storms containing hail and snow and lightning. No one ventured outside during those deadly winter storms, but this young man, being young and foolish, took no heed of the wisdom of others and walked out into the midst of a powerful storm and was engulfed by an avalanche that buried him under 20 feet of snow, immediately freezing him. Everyone in the village thought he was dead. But that spring there came one extremely hot day when all the snow was melted in a matter of hours, and the young man thawed out and came back to life. He was hailed as a great hero, a man who must be blessed by the Gods, and he immediately assumed the position of village wise man, despite his young age."

The faces in the crowd looked confused. No one was sure where Derek was going with his story. Edward Wilson couldn't believe that the traitor was being allowed to prattle on. Troy Raynham tried to recall who Derek reminded him of—someone he'd read or visited with during the foggy years of his retreat into drugs.

Derek looked up at the gray sky above him, as if he were seeking inspiration or guidance. He continued with his story. "Now this young man, despite his brush with death, had become no wiser. The next winter, believing the villagers' tales about his invincibility and his favored position with the Gods, again he walked outside in the middle of one of the worst storms in the village's history. Everyone in the village came to his window and watched with amazement at the young man's courage, though none of them was willing to take a similar risk himself. As the young man walked down the main street of the village, with snow and hail falling all around him and thunder rolling across the sky, he was hit by a bolt of lightning and killed. After that no one ventured out into the winter storms again."

Derek looked at the sea of people in front of him, staring at the upturned faces Most of the crowd looked confused. Still others shook their heads in irritation, thinking that this man, from whom they had hoped to hear words of wisdom, had nothing better to tell them but a long and tedious non-sequitor. Troy Raynham waited for an explanation.

"The things that happen to a man—when they are not of his own doing—do not make him smarter, wiser, nor more blessed than any other man." Derek said to the crowd. "I awoke from a 40-year coma, and some of you believe that makes me special and my words more important than those of others. I am a recipient of an accident of nature, no more and no less."

He looked out over the crowd. "Each of you is a thinking person who has an obligation to examine the world in which you live and ask yourself one simple question: Are my actions making this world a better place? If you leave that answer up to the judgment of anyone else, be he your president, your religious leader, or even me, then you will never achieve the kind of world in which you want to live. Each of you must look beyond what you are being told and make decisions for yourselves and act upon them."

The crowd stood in silence, each person trying to discern the message he had just heard. Were they being chastised or challenged? Was Derek Stewart attempting to lead them or abdicating any claim to leadership? They stood waiting for him to tell them. Troy Raynham felt himself becoming whole again. He felt himself, after years of wandering, once again finding the right path for his life.

Derek walked away from the podium.

Edward Wilson was given the order for which he had been waiting. Along with six more agents, three stationed, like him, at the edge of the crowd, and three inconspicuous until now in parkas, and headbands in front of the podium, he descended upon Stewart as he stepped off the stage.

Josh Mannerly and Tina Nguyen stepped in front of Derek. As one FIIEB agent reached for his gun, Josh delivered a mighty blow to the man's ear, knocking him to the ground. Edward Wilson grabbed for his own gun. In less than a second, Josh had Wilson spun around backwards and his neck in the vice-like grip of the Black therapist's arm. Tina grabbed the hand of the next young FIIEB agent who reached for his gun and immediately disarmed him, twisting the man's arm behind his back and not letting it go.

"Do not fight them," Derek commanded. Three more FIIEB agents had their guns drawn, ready to fire on the two physical therapists. "I will go with you people. Let my friends go—they are only trying to protect me."

With great reluctance, Josh and Tina let their adversaries go and stepped back. They both were immediately grabbed by the other FIIEB agents, who had out handcuffs and tried to shove their two captives to the ground.

"Let them go!" Derek commanded again. "I will go with you, but if you arrest my friends and create a scene, you will have 20,000 people to contend with. Put your guns away and we will walk as colleagues from this place to wherever you wish to take me."

Wilson and the other agents looked at each other. In Edward's ear his supervisor was telling him to get Stewart out of the crowd with the least attention possible. Wilson nodded to the others. They let go of Josh and Tina, holstered their guns and surrounded Derek, then began walking away from the crowd.

Chapter 31

Frederick Armbruster raised his heavy, ex-football player's body from his chair and walked solemnly to the podium in the front of the Senate chambers. Over the years since his football days his belly had swollen to voluminous size, but he managed to carry it well. He had always had small, almost delicate feet, which as a halfback, had propelled him elegantly down the football field, dodging tacklers right and left. Despite his bulk, he still walked with the athlete's lightness on his feet. He carried no prepared speech, but he knew exactly what he was about to say, and he was aware of the monumental importance of being able to convince his colleagues to vote for the president's war plan. Although the president had the authority to launch an attack on Syria, Iran and Lebanon, the three countries which were now waging a furious war with Israel, he had been persuaded by Armbruster to ask Congress for a full declaration of war. The Jewish state had not asked for American help, but the recent attacks in Ghana against the American Embassy had made it absolutely clear to President Ferris, and to the Senator, that America could not stand on the sideline in the war against the Islamic states. Now was the time to act before world wide Islamic extremism took over all of the Middle East and Africa.

"My esteemed colleagues," Armbruster boomed in his slow, deep Alabama drawl. He had the voice of a Southern judge, which is what he had been before being elected to the Senate, and he spoke with commanding authority. "Our allies, our long-time allies, the Israelis, are locked in a struggle for the very survival of their country with the militant extremists who control Iran, Syria and Lebanon. We have resisted joining the fight. But now, those same Islamic terrorists who are trying to destroy Israel have had the audacity to attack our own embassy in Accra, Ghana. Hundreds of innocent civilians, including American government employees, were killed in the vicious African attacks."

Armbruster looked around the Senate chambers, catching the eyes of several colleagues who were nodding in agreement. He noted with satisfaction their angry expressions. His words were hitting home. "The attack in Ghana was our modern Pearl Harbor. It was a second 9/11, but on foreign soil." His voice raised in tenor and in decibels. "The American people have been attacked. Brutal Islamic cowards have declared war on the American way of life—a declaration of war on freedom and peace and Christian values by those who subscribe to a heathen philosophy of death and destruction." He paused for effect, then looked forward, as if he was gazing into the future. He spoke more slowly and quietly, his teeth clenched in resolve. "We have no choice, my friends, but to fight back. We are a peace-loving people, but the time comes when we have to take a stand, when enough is enough. We have already responded in Africa with attacks on the al Mout li Kafir training camps and on the headquarters of the Somalian government that supported them. But that is not enough. We must strike the extremists where they live and that is in the Middle East. We are obliged—no we are required—to do everything in our power to rid the Middle East of Islamic extremists before they destroy us. I ask you to vote for this resolution to endorse the president's plan to declare war on Syria, Lebanon and Iran."

Armbruster's plea was greeted by a thunderous ovation and calls of "here, here" as half of his fellow senators pounded their desks in assent. But to Armbruster's consternation the other half of the senate was silent, and as he walked back to his seat, the senator from Alabama wondered what had gone wrong. Were people really defecting from the president's camp? Even members of his own party? He couldn't believe it.

Almost immediately, Armbruster was replaced at the podium by Oregon Senator Jack Williamson, the young, independent-minded former internet tycoon who had been elected to his first term in the senate in the last election. He was not a member of the president's party, and he was known to be a vocal opponent of many of Ferris's positions. But up to now, he had not had the experience to take a position of leadership among his more senior colleagues.

Armbruster breathed a sigh of relief. If Jack Williamson was the opposition, the president had little to fear. He almost laughed as he stared at the young senator with a look of hostility that contained a promise of the retribution that was sure to come to someone who challenged the senior senator from Alabama.

"I had an interesting experience last week," the fresh-faced young Senator began. Like Armbruster, he spoke without notes and looked out over the senate chamber, scanning the faces in front of him. Most of his colleagues were curious. Many had never heard him address the chamber before. When Williamson's gaze fell upon Senator Armbruster, there was no hint of antipathy. He looked past the Alabama senator as he spoke.

"Out of curiosity, mostly, I joined the crowd that was assembled on the National Mall to listen to Derek Stewart, who you all probably remember, is the Vietnam war veteran who was in a coma for forty years and just recently woke up. I stood next to a man who was Stewart's age and who, forty years ago, protested against the very war in which Stewart had been wounded. Like most of the people there, the man next to me had expected to hear a speech against going to war—against all wars, in fact. But Stewart didn't give that speech. Instead he reminded each person in that crowd of 20,000 that they had a responsibility to examine every issue facing this country with absolute honesty and to look for the truth and act upon it. Before he was arrested by the Feebs, Derek Stewart told us the importance of searching for the truth, of not making decisions based upon half-truths, or upon falsehoods, or unexamined beliefs, or because the majority seem to think it's the right thing to do."

Williamson paused to swing his gaze around the senate chambers. "What is the truth about the war in the Middle East? Well, we know that Israel attacked Iran. Israel says that their attack was a preemptive one which was necessary because Iran intended to attack them with nuclear weapons. Every piece of intelligence we have says the Israelis were right. Following the Israeli air strike Syria, Iran and Lebanon counterattacked against the Israelis. Though the truth is somewhat murky, a discerning eye would say that the Israelis' position is one of self-defense and the position of the Muslim countries, who were preempted before they could launch their own first strike, is one of aggression. I have no problem offering Israel help in such a situation. They are our ally, and they are defending themselves. But Israel has not asked, nor given any indication of wanting our help."

"Last week, al Mout li Kafir attacked the American embassy in Accra, Ghana, declaring that they want to challenge America and the West and to take their war to Africa. Our president responded by bombing the terrorist training camps and sending a message to the Somalian government that has harbored them. I have no quarrel with that response either, although the U.S. response was perhaps on a greater scale than was necessary to send a message to Somalia or any other African government. But America was attacked and a nation that is attacked has a right to respond. But now the president and my colleague, the honorable Senator Armbruster, have gone even further. They claim that the attack by al Mout li Kafir in Africa is the same as an attack from any Islamist country in the Middle East. In their view, a Muslim is a Muslim and such an attack demands that we declare war on every Islamic country, whether they are clearly connected to al Mout li Kafir or not. But what is the truth here? Iran is a Shiite country that has declared al Mout li Kafir illegal within its borders. Although al Mout li Kafir operates in Lebanon and Mustafa al Adim has his headquarters in the Bekaa Valley, Lebanon's war against Israel is championed by Hezbollah, who control much of the politics of the country and who are political enemies of al Mout li Kafir. Syria has a primarily Sunni population, although its leaders are Shiite. But Syria is adamantly secular and against Islamic fundamentalism. Al Mout li Kafir confederates are routinely imprisoned in Syria. Do these countries sound as if they are allies of Moustafa al Adim? "

"The president's resolution—the one Senator Armbruster asks you to endorse—is asking you to respond to an attack by one group with an invasion of the territory of another. If we want to take on al Mout li Kafir, then we should do so, but not by attacking other Muslim countries who are as hostile to that terrorist group as we are. If we want to support Israel, then let's respond to an Israeli request for help if one comes—which it hasn't at this point—but please don't confuse the attack in Africa with the conflict in the Middle East. If you do, our declaration of war will be a sign to the world of American ignorance and prejudice against all Muslims. It is absolutely necessary that our behavior in this current situation is based upon truth, not upon muddled fictions. I urge you to vote no on this resolution and not give the president permission to start the wrong war."

Williamson's voice had risen to an oratorical pitch with his last words. When he ended his speech and looked out across the chamber, the response was overwhelming. Several members of his own party and a few from the opposition stood and clapped. Senators were pounding the table.

The president of the Senate asked for a vote. The resolution to support the president's request to declare war against Lebanon, Iran and Syria, was defeated by a margin of 54 to 46.

Armbruster was both shocked and furious. If the senate vote reflected the sentiments of the American people, there had been a tsunami-magnitude change in public opinion. There was only one person who could be held responsible for such a change and that was Derek Stewart.

Chapter 32

Troy Raynham pumped his placard in the air and leaned toward the microphone. He wasn't used to addressing crowds, and he had felt a wave of anxiety when he had stepped to the podium and looked out on the crowd. Over 100,000 people crowded together on the grass alongside the reflecting pool on the National Mall, many of them waving placards just like his, which said, "Free Derek Stewart." Troy cleared his throat. "Thank you all for coming and showing solidarity with our cause." He paused for a moment, then shouted into the mike, "Free Derek Stewart!" The crowd took up the cry and began chanting in unison.

After 20 seconds, Troy held up a hand and the chanting gradually died out. "We can make a difference!" he shouted. The crowd erupted in cheers.

"Our speaker today is the United States Senator from Oregon who has led the fight to keep America out of a Middle East war." Troy turned and looked at the young senator, dressed in a suit and tie, his eyes bright, and his manner showing no effect from the 42 degree weather outside. "He is also leading our fight to free Derek Stewart from his unjust and unlawful imprisonment by a federal government that has shown total disregard for the rights guaranteed us by our constitution. Let me introduce Senator Jack Williamson!"

Most of the crowd applauded, placards were raised, and there were scattered shouts of praise. Many of the young people who had gathered on the Mall were in their twenties and were suspicious of anyone in government and they were waiting to make their own judgment about Williamson.

"Derek Stewart was seized by the FIIEB right here on this spot," Senator Williamson said, his voice loud and steady as he looked around him on the stage erected in front of the Lincoln Memorial. "And what was his crime?" He looked out over the heads of the young people on the lawn in front of him. "Nothing, he said softly, answering his own question. "In this day and age it is a crime to speak out against the government and

Derek did not even do that. He told a parable about at man who was thought to be a god. And he urged each of you to think for yourselves." He paused to let his words sink in. "And for that," he continued, "he was arrested and imprisoned without a trial."

Spontaneously the crowd began chanting, "Free Derek Stewart!"

The young senator stood patiently until the chanting subsided. "I have asked—no I have demanded—that Derek Stewart be either freed or brought to trial. I have sponsored a resolution in the United States Senate demanding the same. I have also asked that Mr. Stewart be brought before our Senate Committee on Homeland Security and asked to testify as to what his motives are, so the whole country can decide if he is a threat." He paused again for emphasis. "I don't think Derek Stewart represents a threat to our country. I think Derek Stewart represents hope—the hope that every American will do more than listen to what this administration tells them, will look beyond the headlines and the media images to try to understand what is really happening in the world. An informed citizenry is no threat to a democracy, in fact it is necessary or there can be no such thing as democracy—only rule by manipulation of public opinion, as we have had for the entire tenure of the present administration. I want every American to have a chance to hear what Derek Stewart has to say." He looked out over the 100,000 young faces. "You have listened and you are here. When Derek Stewart is free, others will listen also. We must free Derek Stewart."

The youthful senator stepped back from the microphone and Tory Raynham took his place, leading another chant of "Free Derek Stewart." This time the chant went on for a full two minutes. When it was over, Troy addressed the crowd with one simple message, " Let's take to the streets!" The crowd let out a cheer and then, as one, began to move forward, past the podium and out onto Constitution Avenue, then up 17th street toward the White House. Uniformed police, mounted on horses and motorcycles, cruised alongside the crowd. FIIEB men in suits relayed information through cell phones back to their command post. Both the police and the Feebs were under orders to observe only and not to arrest anyone unless it was absolutely necessary. The less attention the demonstration attracted, the better.

Troy Raynham marched at the head of the crowd, his arms linked on either side with the two young women who were responsible for bringing out a crowd of this size. Troy had not felt this good for a long time. It was as if the forty years that had intervened between now and 1970 had been wiped out. He was back in the streets again, surrounded by eager young women and his cause was just. He didn't know what Derek Stewart represented or if the Vietnam war veteran had any potential, let alone interest, in leading the battle against the repressive conservative forces that had ruled the country for the last decade, but he knew that Stewart made him feel strong again, as if his destiny was back in his own hands. To regain that feeling he would march for anyone.

Chapter 33

Tina surprised us all by suggesting we decorate the house as if we were having a party. We all had experienced her playful side before, usually in terms of her droll comments delivered with a deadpan facial expression. But her humor had always been on a small scale and intimate, usually only among the group during dinner or in private conversations with one or another of us. Now she wanted us all to join in a more expressive demonstration of our mutual elation that a Federal judge had intervened and ordered the government to either bring charges against Derek or let him go. The Feebs had chosen to do the latter, and Derek was coming home.

In Derek's absence, our number had risen by one. Troy Raynham, the aging hippie demonstrator who had almost singlehandedly, brought public attention to Derek's plight, had shown up one day on our doorstep, much in the same manner as had Susan and Maurice, and volunteered to help Derek's cause, "whatever that might be," when Derek was freed. We all felt a deep debt of gratitude to Troy for his efforts on Derek's behalf, and Susan, in particular, was eager to capitalize on the popular base Troy had assembled and use those newly radicalized young people as a nucleus of what she thought would become a grass roots movement to launch Derek's candidacy for national office.

"Do you really think he'd run for office?" Troy had asked. "He doesn't seem like the type to me." Troy had already told us that he'd developed a new political allegiance—after forty years of political nihilism—to Senator Jack Williamson, the young Oregon senator who had joined in the fight to free Derek and who Troy thought was the new leader of the opposition to President Ferris.

"Derek hasn't agreed to anything... yet," Susan said, cagily, "but I believe I can convince him. Much as I abhorred the fact that he was in prison, his imprisonment has kept him in the public eye for the last several weeks, and his appearance before the Homeland Security Committee in the Senate will only add to his exposure. Derek will be able to do whatever he wants with the publicity he's going to have."

"But does he want to run for office?" Troy asked, the skepticism evident in his voice.

"He will," Susan said, matter-of-factly.

Troy looked around the room for confirmation from the rest of us. We all shook our heads. In each of our opinions, Susan's ambition was Susan's, not Derek's.

"Derek is too committed to the truth to be a politician," Karin said, making no effort to conceal her disgust at Susan's blatant attempt to use Derek for her own ends. Since Susan's arrival, Karin had treated the political operative's overtures to Derek as if she were the devil offering him a Faustian contract. Strangely, or perhaps not so strangely if I allowed myself the indulgence of some flights of Freudian theorizing, Karin had shown an immediate affinity for Troy, who, in my opinion, had assumed the role of a stand-in for her long-absent father.

"That's a naïve opinion I would expect to hear from one of your students instead of from you, Professor," Susan snapped back. She was easily provoked and had, undoubtedly, the shortest fuse of any of us, with the exception perhaps of Maurice. She became agitated every time anyone questioned her political ambitions for Derek.

"Here they come," Tina cried. She had been watching from behind the living room curtains for Derek's car to pull up in front of the house, with Josh driving and Derek beside him. Unfortunately, a drove of reporters and cameramen were also waiting on the sidewalk in front of Derek's Georgetown townhouse. All of us inside the house trooped down the front steps and out to the curb to form a corridor of interference for Derek when he emerged from the car.

Reporters shouted questions and cameramen snapped shots, but Derek stepped calmly from the car, a broad smile creasing his face as he saw Karin, Tina, Susan, Maurice and myself waiting on the sidewalk. He walked slowly through the crowd of media people and climbed the steps to the front door of the townhouse.

"It's good to be home," Derek said, looking around the room at Tina's decorations. A bottle of champagne stood in a bucket of ice on the coffee table. He noticed Troy standing behind the rest of us. "A new addition to our family, I see. Welcome." He didn't seem surprised at Troy's presence. Maybe he'd seen the demonstrations on television.

"How do you feel?" Susan asked. Despite her obvious desire to use Derek for her own purposes, she was as genuinely concerned about his welfare as were the rest of us. We all had our glasses filled with champagne, except Tina, who didn't drink alcohol, and Troy, who had finally reached a state of abstinence after years of drug and alcohol abuse.

"Refreshed," Derek answered. "They had me in isolation and I slept nearly the whole two weeks."

"No intense grilling, waterboarding, no time spent on the rack?" I asked, surprised that he had been left alone.

"What could they question me about? I don't know anyone but all of you and it's common knowledge where I've been for the last 40 years."

"Were you able to get any news?" Karin asked.

"No."

"So you don't know that the president's request for congressional approval to declare war on Iran, Lebanon and Syria is barely treading water right now? You didn't hear about the demonstrations to get you out of prison?" I asked.

He shook his head.

"Troy here is responsible for the demonstrations," Susan said. "He got 100,000 people onto the National Mall to protest your arrest."

"Then I have you to thank," Derek said, looking at Troy. "I think I remember you from the demonstration in which I was arrested. Am I right?"

"I was there," Troy answered. "I didn't know you saw me."

"You were the only other person there who was my age," Derek said, smiling.

"Senator Jack Williamson spoke on your behalf at our rally," Troy said. "He's been leading the challenge to the president's request for a declaration of war. Senator Williamson is the one who invited you to speak before the senate committee tomorrow." Troy realized that Derek might not even be aware of his scheduled appearance in front of the senate. "Did you know about that?"

Derek nodded. "Josh told me on the way here." He looked over at Karin and me. "What's happening in Africa?"

"No more attacks by al Mout li Kafir and we've bombed the hell out of their training camps in Somalia," Karin answered. "In fact we bombed the hell out of every human habitation in Somalia. We're rattling our sabers in the direction of Nigeria too, but right now the administration is trying to build support for going after Iran, Lebanon and Syria." She had the intense expression of a lieutenant reporting to her superior officer.

"Any more word from Moustafa al Adim?"

Karin nodded,. "He's pledged to take down the government in Ghana. It's pretty clear he's running Somalia already. For some reason, he's letting Sudan alone."

"My mother was from Ghana," Derek said, a faraway look in his eyes.

"And your cousin, Robert N'gomo was a Ghanaian also," Maurice volunteered. We had told him about Derek's connection to N'gomo while Derek was in jail. Maurice seemed as deeply affected by the African leader's murder as Derek had been, though none of us was able to fathom why.

"I consider it a second home, although I have never been there," Derek said, his voice solemn. "My people in Ghana have worked very hard to build a country that provides freedoms to its citizens. Muslims and Christians have lived side by side, along with many indigenous religions left over from the Asante traditions. I fear for them if Mustafa al Adim is trying to disrupt their land."

Maurice, who was sitting on the couch next to Derek, was shaking his head as if he was puzzled.

"You look confused," Derek said, looking sympathetically at the young man.

"You sound as concerned for Africa as you are for America." Maurice said.

Derek's nodded. "America can defend itself and al Mout li Kafir has no real foothold in this country. Every African nation, even a relatively stable one such as Ghana, is fragile because none has a history free of the undermining influence of European colonialism. Tribal and religious differences within each country are just beneath the surface, and the forging of democratic institutions is in its infancy. When these factors are combined with pervasive poverty and ill health, I worry much more about Africa than America."

Maurice still looked puzzled. "But you are an American."

"That does not make an African tragedy any less painful than an American tragedy. We are all brothers in this world." He put a hand on the young man's shoulder. Although Derek often touched each of us when we talked, he had always avoided touching Maurice, probably sensing that the young man was highly defensive about his personal space.

Maurice appeared to relax under Derek's touch. His expression was thoughtful, but he asked no more questions.

Karin's eyes shown with admiration.

The look on Troy Raynham's face indicated that he was as surprised as Maurice to hear Derek's words. "Man, those are sweet words for someone like me to hear." The old hippie turned toward Susan. "But American voters like their candidates to wave the flag and sing the tune of America first. Most of those young people in the crowds aren't going to take to the streets to support a candidate who is concerned about the rest of the world more than the good old U.S. of A."

"I'm not a candidate for anything," Derek said, looking back and forth between Troy and Susan. "But if what you say about the American youth is true, that is a shame."

"But you haven't ruled out being a candidate either," Susan said, a hesitant smile on her face.

Derek kept his gaze on Susan for a moment then looked at the rest of us. "I guess I'd better prepare for the senate tomorrow." He gave us all a benign smile. "I'm really glad to be back with all of you."

We reciprocated with congratulations and well-wishes.

Chapter 34

Frederick Armbruster was the Chairman of the Senate Committee on Homeland Security and Governmental Affairs. He banged his gavel and stared imperiously down either side of the dais behind which the other members of the committee were arrayed. At the far right end of the semi-oval platform sat the committee's most junior member, newly elected Oregon Senator Jack Williamson.

"These hearings are called to order," Armbruster announced, his face frozen in a paradigm of seriousness designed to convey the gravity of the hearings. "We are here to examine the views of Mr. Derek Stewart, formerly a private in the United States Army, on the subject of the authority of the government to regulate speech and behavior that threaten the nation's security. Do you have an opening statement, Mr. Stewart?"

Derek was sitting behind a small table on which were two microphones, one of which had been temporarily silenced. The second microphone was reserved for a witness' attorney, but Derek had declined the offer to bring along his attorney, although I, and several other members of our "family" were disappointed, principally because we were denied a chance to see the elusive Mr. Erskine, with whom we'd only communicated by email or telephone. "I await your questions," Derek answered.

Armbruster nodded and began speaking. "As Chairman of this committee, I shall exercise my prerogative and begin the questioning with myself. In the first place, are you aware that thousands of Americans, chanting your name and carrying signs with your name emblazoned upon them, have been demonstrating in the streets of our capital and in several other American cities? These demonstrators have demanded that our country not send troops to the Middle East and, in fact, have demanded the withdrawal of those troops we already have in that region—a position advocated by our enemy, al Mout li Kafir." The senator's glare made it clear that his statement was an accusation.

"I have been told about the demonstrations, Mr. Armbruster, although I neither participated in them nor observed them while they were happening, as I was being held in solitary confinement by the FIIEB."

Derek's statement took the wind out of Armbruster's sails, but he quickly recovered. "Can you tell us why you were being held by the FIIEB?"

Derek shook his head. "I was never informed of the reason."

Armbruster's fleshy face revealed his frustration but he plodded forward. "Right, but when you were arrested, were you aware that you were violating our Patriot Act III laws?"

"No."

"You were urging your fellow citizens to disobey their president and their government were you not?"

Derek thought for a moment. "I was urging them to follow their own minds."

Armbruster rustled his papers and looked down at the one in his hand. "Did you not tell the crowd, 'you must look beyond what you are being told by your president and make decisions for yourselves and act upon them.'?"

He nodded. "That is a paraphrase but is reasonably accurate with regard to my meaning."

"Well, weren't you advocating disobeying the government directives?"

"I was advising those who were listening to me to listen to their own consciences and their own good sense." Derek's tone was reasonable, as if he and the Senator were having a regular conversation, perhaps in one of their living rooms.

"Well I guess the FIIEB agrees with me that your words were treasonous because they arrested you that day."

"As I said, I was never told why I was arrested." Derek smiled politely at the Senator. "I also thought that treason was a matter for the courts to judge, not the FIIEB."

Armbruster looked as if he was about to lose his temper. "We live in a Christian democracy, Mr. Stewart, and our way of life is under attack by Islamic extremists who want to impose their primitive laws and beliefs upon us." Armbruster had calmed himself and was looking into the television camera. His face had taken on the resolute look he maintained during his campaign stumps. "They fight us by sending suicide bombers and terrorists onto our soil and trying to create havoc. Your words have given new hope to those extremists, who see our country losing its will to fight for our way of life. In your name, young people are refusing to support our military effort—the very effort that has kept us free of domination by Muslim groups such as al Mout li Kafir." His gaze returned to the witness. "Do you think you are being loyal to the United States of America, Mr. Stewart?"

Derek stared calmly into the eyes of Armbruster. "I have never thought that I was acting disloyally, Senator."

Armbruster let out a long sigh of frustration. He looked as if he wanted to say more, but his time for questions had expired. The next Senator to address Derek would be the ranking member from the opposition party. Senator Warren Normandy. To everyone's surprise, Senator Normandy yielded his time to Senator Jack Williamson. There were murmurs from the gallery, and Chairman Armbruster had to pound his gavel to bring quiet to the room.

"I'm honored to meet you, Mr. Stewart," the young senator form Oregon began. "We have actually met before because I was in the crowd at the National Mall the day you were arrested."

Derek smiled. "I'm pleased that you took the time to be there, Senator."

"I believe there is some confusion regarding the meaning of your words on that day. I think I know what you were saying, but others have interpreted your words differently and, I have to admit, what you said could be subject to multiple interpretations. What I would like you to do today is tell us what you were saying to the crowd that day and what message you would like to tell those who have been demonstrating to free you since that day."

Senator Armbruster exploded. "I do not intend for this hearing to become a platform for Mr. Stewart to express his anti-American views!"

191

"I thought this hearing was to determine if Mr. Stewart's views *are* anti-American. I hope you haven't pre-judged the issue before hearing what his views are, Mr. Chairman," Senator Williamson said, his face deadpan and not a trace of irony in his voice.

Armbruster glared at the young senator. "Go ahead," he said, gruffly.

"Thank you Senator, " Derek said, politely. "My ancestors were Asante from the west coast of Africa. The Asante have a tradition of speaking in proverbs and parables. I have inherited that tradition, so I will tell you a story—one that has been passed down for many years among the Asante." He scanned the faces on the dais in front of him. Most of them looked uncomfortable, some were irritated and more than a few appeared bored.

"Many years ago in Central Africa a child was born, a baby boy in a family of boys. On the very day that he was born, the family discovered that their land lay over a rich vein of gold. The family became wealthy beyond all imagining, and the parents credited their youngest son, the one who had been born the day they discovered the gold, with their good fortune. As he grew up, his mother and father bestowed control of the family's riches on their youngest son, and his older brothers became jealous. The boy wasn't bothered by their jealousy because his parents told him he was special. He believed that he was favored by the gods and that his wealth was due to him. Every time he needed money, it was at his fingertips. His father, who was a clever man, made wise business investments, though he believed their success was due to his youngest son's favored position with the gods. When the boy's parents died, the youngest son inherited 80 percent of the family's riches while his four brothers each received only five percent. He believed that it was his fate to be rich and better off than his brothers, and he refused to consult them in managing his father's businesses. Within a year he had lost his entire fortune. He came begging to his brothers to take pity on him and take him in. But the brothers had hardened their hearts against him, and they refused him help. Eventually he died, penniless."

Derek had been looking at Senator Williamson as he told his story, but now he ran his gaze down the line of faces of the senators in front of him. "The story that the young man's parents told him and that he believed about himself was not true. His family's fortune had nothing to do with his birth, and he held no favored position with any gods. In truth, he was just a lucky young man who fell into riches but neither learned nor possessed any wisdom regarding how to retain them. And of course the truth, not the fiction the young man believed about himself, was what determined his fate."

Derek looked hopefully at the faces of the senators in front of him to see if they understood his words.

Senator Armbruster snorted in disapproval.

"Your answers still require some interpretation," Senator William said, his quizzical expression revealing his puzzlement. "Can you provide a concise statement of the point of your story?"

"A way of life based upon fictions is doomed to failure."

"Does this mean we are living on fictions here in America?"

"Wait just a damned minute," Chairman Armbruster sputtered.

Derek held up a hand and stared at the chairman, as if he was commanding the Senator's silence.

Armbruster clamped his mouth shut, as if in obedience, his eyes bulging in surprise.

"I can only give you my view of what is fact and what is fiction. It is up to each person to make that determination himself," Derek said.

"Well, can you give us your view?" Senator Williamson asked.

Derek's face was serious, devoid of the trace of humor that often lurked behind his expressions. His voice, when he answered, was deep and melodious, as if he knew he was speaking to a larger audience. "We live in a complex world, Senator Williamson. There are few simple truths. But it is difficult to deny the reality of millions of poor Africans and Asians dying of poverty and disease, while the bulk of the world's resources are consumed either for the pleasure of a few or for the sake of waging war. It is also difficult to avoid the conclusion that peace can only be achieved by bringing enemies together and not by each side trying to destroy the other. Anyone who denies these truths is making up fictions."

The young senator nodded. "Thank you, Mr. Stewart. I yield the microphone back to the Chairman."

Armbruster was furious. He asked for and got permission from the second ranking member of his party on the committee, Senator Robert Winthrop from Delaware, to yield his time so Armbruster could again address the witness himself. "Senator Williamson may think your meaning is opaque, Mr. Stewart, but it was crystal clear to me. You are accusing the United States of stealing the world's treasure and building the supremacy of our nation on the back of less fortunate nations. You are stating directly that God is as much on the side of the heathens who don't believe in Jesus Christ as he is on ours. And you are predicting the defeat of our country and calling our foreign policy a fiction. Isn't that what you're really saying, Mr. Stewart?" He glowered across the table at Derek.

"I have told a story and each of you can find his own meaning in my words."

"You mean you aren't willing to take responsibility for your own opinions. Well, we'll see about that. You don't have immunity for your responses to this committee, Mr. Stewart and when this hearing is over I'm going to ask the FIIEBs to reopen your case and determine whether or not you have violated laws against sedition."

There were cries of protest from the galleries, causing Chairman Armbruster to pound his gavel in fury.

Derek Stewart sat motionless a look of placid calm on his face.

Chapter 35

The signal was unmistakable. A message left on Mohammed's cell phone, identifying itself as a caller reaching a wrong number but using the emergency phrase, "I had thought I was dialing Mr. Kensington," known only to Mohammed and those close to Mustafa al Adim, himself. Mohammed waited five minutes then dialed a number he had memorized long before he had arrived in the United States.

"Your visa will expire, and you have not conducted your business," a gruff, deep voice stated as soon as the connection was established.

"My business is my own. I will countenance no interference from corporate headquarters," Mohammed answered, making no attempt to conceal his anger. Contact with an assassin in the field, such as Mohammed, was strictly forbidden except in emergency. Mustafa al Adim's impatience did not constitute such an emergency.

"Do you require any assistance?" the gruff voice asked.

"I transact my business alone," Mohammed hissed. "I do not appreciate this contact."

"The market is right now very favorable. We only want you to know that."

"I understand. Please do not contact me again. I will conclude the transaction shortly and come home."

"I will relay that message to corporate headquarters," the voice answered, then hung up.

Mohammed was fuming. The cell phone conversation he had just concluded increased his level of risk by more than 100 percent. Who knows who might have access to calls coming from the man on the other end of the line? It was well known that the NSA monitored all telephone calls coming into the country from the Middle East or from suspicious sources anywhere else in the world. Every contact between agents in the field was a potential source of surveillance by the enemy. And how could anyone assist him? He was the most skilled assassin in the entire al Mout li Kafir network, and he *never* required assistance in his work.

Despite his anger, he knew that he had delayed completing his mission well beyond the normal limit for such a task. In fact, he had been in position to eliminate Derek Stewart for nearly six weeks and had done nothing except locate where he could buy supplies to build his bomb. But he had bought nothing. Even without using a bomb, he had had multiple opportunities to kill Derek. To be sure, there had been two weeks when even he had no access to Derek because of his imprisonment, but he slept in the same house as the man, and he had walked beside him at public events where security was completely absent for those among Derek's inner circle. And Maurice was within that inner circle. What was holding him back?

Mohammed knew the answer and every day he fought against it. Derek Stewart was the one person Mohammed now believed might lead humanity out of what he was beginning to see as a pointless cycle of violence, leading no one anywhere.

Mohammed had been struck, not just by the words Derek had spoken, for sometimes the long, wearying stories were too oblique for Mohammed to follow, but by something else about Derek—something Mohammed had glimpsed in Robert N'gomo. Derek was sincere in his commitment to change the world and yet accepting of his fate. N'gomo had shared the same outlook. Even when the African had faced torture and death, he showed neither surprise nor fear and continued to express hope for peace. Derek had the same quality. Mohammed was, himself, familiar with acceptance of fate. It was why he risked death without fear, himself. But Mohammed's commitment had grown from his losses and his sense of betrayal, like a cancer metastasizing within his body, so that it could only be satisfied by venting of his anger and seeking revenge. Derek Stewart and Robert N'gomo shared something that Mohammed desperately wanted to understand. He had no illusions about achieving what they had, but he needed to understand it for he knew, deep inside himself, as much as he had ever known anything, that their path was superior to his.

He was no longer sure that he would kill Derek. The way of al Mout li Kafir was the way of revenge on the West—the allies of the hated Israelis—and Mohammed had dedicated his life to its mission. But he no longer was convinced that the way of al Mout li Kafir was his way.

Chapter 36

"The Feebs aren't going to do anything," Frederick Armbruster said, the frustration palpable in his voice. "They got so much flak last time they arrested Stewart that Director of Homeland Security Dolan refuses to arrest him again."

"I'm not talking about arresting him," Jervis Donovan said, his voice low and even. They were sitting in The Oval Office. Also in the room were President Ferris, Reverend Merrill Goodson, and CIA Director, Nathaniel Broadmoor, the cigar-smoking ten-year veteran of his post, a former business leader known for his ruthless approach to corporate success, and a political appointee from Ferris's first term. Under Broadmoor, the CIA had expanded its activities to include surveillance and intercession of domestic terrorist activities, despite clear-cut laws prohibiting such actions on American soil. The CIA and the administration always denied that the CIA was operating within the borders of the country, and no one had yet challenged them on it. None of those who had directly witnessed such CIA operations were any more around to voice such complaints.

"What then?" Armbruster asked, a look of puzzlement on his broad, fleshy features.

"Mr. Stewart has left himself conspicuously vulnerable to our enemies," Donovan answered in the same even voice. He looked across the room at the CIA Director. "Tell us about it, Nate."

The CIA Director, a short, rotund, ball of a man with a shiny bald head and a dark complexion and heavy beard, that always, even when he was freshly shaven, made him look sinister, rubbed the stubble on his chin and took in a deep breath before speaking. He looked around the room as if checking to be sure he wasn't being overheard. Broadmoor was known to be paranoid, a characteristic considered advantageous in his current position. "We've identified one of Stewart's inner circle as an al Mout li Kafir agent—in fact we suspect he might be that organization's most notorious assassin."

"You mean Stewart is connected to al Mout li Kafir?" the president asked, disbelief evident in his voice.

Broadmoor shook his head. "We don't think Stewart has any idea the man is a terrorist. We think the agent is there to kill Stewart."

The president couldn't resist smiling. "You mean al Mout li Kafir is going to do our job for us? This is too good to be true."

"I see the hand of divine providence," Reverend Goodson added.

"It does sound too good to be true," Donovan said. He was happy, but he didn't allow himself the freedom to gloat the way the president and his spiritual advisor had.

"But why hasn't this man killed him, then?" Armbruster asked, sounding confused. "How long has he been close to Stewart? And who is this man?"

The CIA Director ran his hand across his shiny pate, as if he was smoothing imaginary hair. He squinted his eyes before he spoke, as if to signal that what he was about to say was partially speculation. "It's a puzzle to us, frankly. If this is who we think it is, he's known for getting in and getting out quickly when he makes a hit. He's never gotten to know his targets as intimately as he knows Stewart."

"So who is he?" Armbruster asked impatiently. Why did the CIA always have to make things sound so secret and mysterious, he asked himself. He was already suspicious of Jervis Donovan, but involvement with the CIA made him even more uncomfortable. As far as Armbruster was concerned, Nathaniel Broadmoor practically radiated vibes that he was not to be trusted.

"We only know him as 'the technician,'" Broadmoor continued, his voice taking on a hushed, confidential tone. Since the CIA Director was always suspicious that his conversations might be being recorded, he often spoke in such a low voice that those around him had a hard time hearing him. "We can't be sure because we have no photographs of the man and only a single fingerprint that we're not even sure is his. What we do know is he is a Middle-Easterner, probably Lebanese, who has lived in Europe for the last 13 years. He is a shadowy figure but he has killed at least 9 important political figures in Europe and maybe two-hundred innocent civilians."

"And he works for al Mout li Kafir?" Armbruster asked, the skepticism evident in his voice.

"He carries out Mustafa al Adim's personal orders."

"If you don't even know his name, what makes you think he's the guy that's next to Stewart?" President Ferris asked. Even he was getting impatient with Broadmoor's secretive manner.

Broadmoor looked at each of them before speaking. His voice dropped another decibel, and everyone had to lean toward him to hear. "Two pieces of evidence: first, the NSA PRISM program intercepted a cell phone call to this man about a week ago from a source we know speaks for Mustafa al Adim here in the U.S. That level of intercept is a rarity in itself and indicated that the person receiving the call must be of immense importance. They were able to trace the recipient of the call to a man in Stewart's immediate entourage—in fact he lives in Stewart's house. Second, remember I said we had one fingerprint that might be the technician—it was removed from the site of a deadly bombing in France. The NSA turned their information over to us, and we managed to lift a fingerprint from the man who received the cell phone call and it was a match. None of that's absolutely positive, of course, but it's enough to convince most of my top intelligence experts."

The president cleared his throat. "So what do we do, wait until whoever this is assassinates Stewart?" Ferris's voice boomed in contrast to that of the CIA Director. The president's irritation was obvious.

Broadmoor shook his head, oblivious to his boss's frustration. "The name on his passport is Maurice Aziz, but we're sure that's an alias. We don't know why Aziz is hesitating; it's not his m.o. But we don't have to wait for him to act. With him being next to Stewart, if Stewart dies, then the blame is going to fall right into Aziz's lap—and if Aziz is to blame, so is al Mout li Kafir."

Armbruster nodded his head, looking pleased. "So if Stewart is killed, then the Islamists are to blame."

Donovan nodded in response, a sly smile on his face. "It would be an outrageous attack on an American hero."

"Exactly the kind of murderous act the Muslims are known for," Reverend Goodson said, his eyes bright with glee.

"And one that deserves retribution," the president added, a smile on his lips. His anger had vanished. He gazed at the diminutive CIA Director as if he were his favorite son. "I don't want to hear any more, gentlemen. If it turns out that al Mout li Kafir carries out another attack within our borders, even a single assassination, then I will be forced to go after them in their homeland. I think the American people will agree with me this time, don't all of you?"

"No question about it," Jervis Donovan answered.

"It's the only way to defend our peaceful and God-fearing way of life," Reverend Goodson chimed in.

The president nodded. "I'm glad we all see eye-to-eye. Mr., Broadmoor, it's up to your people now."

"Don't worry, Mr. president." The CIA Director, said, a sly smile creasing his dusky face. "Protecting America is what we do best."

Chapter 37

Mohammed had known for some time that Derek was being watched. Now his instincts, honed to the sharpness of those of a desert animal as a result of more than a decade of living invisibly while in complete view of his enemies, told him that whomever the watchers were, they had been watching him, too. It must have been that phone call, he thought, seething with anger. Why couldn't Mustafa al Adim have been more patient?

Mohammed knew what he had to do. He had threaded his way through the tightest surveillance nets in Europe without giving away his deadly intentions. It was all a matter of being able to watch the watchers. He became the observer instead of the observed.

The more he observed, the more he was confused. Whoever it was that was watching him and Derek was doing more than keeping them under surveillance. The watchers were setting up some type of operation. Mohammed had been through the steps enough times himself to detect the telltale signs of an assassination in the making. After an initial spate of watching Derek's and his' every move, the observers had scaled back. Now they only watched each afternoon when, as a matter of routine, Derek led his entourage on a walk around parts of the city to "get some exercise," and to "not let us get too far away from the people." It wasn't the same section of the city every day. In fact, Derek was interested in every sort of neighborhood—Black, Puerto Rican, Mexican, African Immigrant, White—both poor and rich. And every day, there were the watchers—two white men driving by in their Ford Taurus, sitting one car back on the train, buying coffee at a neighborhood Starbucks, regardless of the neighborhood. Only Mohammed noticed them. But they were there every day. And they no longer watched Derek and his "family" at any other time.

When Mohammed had detonated the bomb that had killed the French Minister of Defense, he had had watched the man until his daily routine had become completely known to him. He had selected the spot where the minister was most vulnerable and watched only the part of the man's routine that passed that spot. After two weeks, the minister walked into his favorite café on a damp, but not rainy day, deposited his furled umbrella in the umbrella box near the door and set off a massive explosion that killed him instantly as well as thirty-five other patrons of the restaurant. Mohammed had watched from across the street, a remote switch in his hand that exploded the bomb hidden in his own umbrella left in the box an hour before. In his pocket was a pistol in case the detonator failed to work.

What did these two men have in mind? They were setting a trap, but which of them—Derek Stewart or Mohammed—was their target? There was only one way to find out and that was for Mohammed to go somewhere else on one of Derek's afternoon excursions and see which one of them the two men followed.

The next day, Derek suggested that they all take the Metro train to visit the Sage Society, an ecumenical religious and contemplative organization in which he was interested, which had its headquarters just outside the beltway. Mohammed declined, claiming to have errands to do in the city. Free of the rest of the "family," he treated himself to a long-awaited opportunity to walk along the Georgetown Canal to the Georgetown Park Mall where he wandered, mesmerized among the posh boutiques, gazing at the clothing, jewelry, books, the restaurants and coffee shops. Before he had come to Derek's townhouse in Georgetown, Mohammed had spent time only in Columbia Heights, where he had briefly taken a room. The contrast between the mostly poor neighborhood, which was home to newly arrived immigrants and African-Americans, and the Georgetown shopping mall was stark.

Despite his enchantment with the opulence of the mall, Mohammed's interest in his affluent surroundings occupied only a tiny corner of his mind. The bulk of his attention was devoted to determining if he was being followed. So far he had seen no one and if his practiced eye could not detect his watchers, they were not there. If the two men did not surface by the end of his trip to the mall, then he could conclude only one thing—a thought that filled him with the deepest fear and anger he had ever felt—the watchers were watching Derek Stewart and not him. It was Derek who was being set up, Derek who was to be killed.

***

"There's a lot of grass root support for your candidacy for president," Susan said, approaching her favorite topic more timidly than usual.

"There are others both more qualified and more likely to win an election than me," Derek answered. We were all eating dinner, having arrived home mid-afternoon from our trip to the Sage Society. Maurice, who had not accompanied us, had arrived home shortly afterward and everyone was now seated at the dinner table.

"I think you underestimate your current popularity among the American public," Susan persisted. She was not one to give up easily.

Karin heaved a loud sigh and took in her breath as though she was about to make a comment.

Derek held up a hand to signal Karin to wait. He looked across the table at Susan. "If you are correct, I am mystified," he said.

Susan's expression showed her surprise that Derek, all of a sudden, seemed willing to talk about the subject she had been badgering him about for weeks. "There are millions of people in this country who have been watching Ferris and his group take away their freedoms, and they haven't had any idea what to do about it. No leader has emerged to question the administration's policies. Everyone is afraid of being branded a traitor or a coward or anti-Christian by Ferris and Goodson and their lap-dogs in the press. You've changed all that." Susan was pitching her campaign speech, but the admiration for Derek that shone in her eyes was real.

"I'm not aware that I have challenged the administration on anything," Derek said, looking quizzical yet unperturbed. "I only asked people to look at the world with open eyes and make decisions based on their own judgment."

"That's enough," Susan said.

"It's something Ferris and his gang can't allow to happen," Troy piped in. Troy was gradually warming to Susan's ambition to have Derek run for the presidency, even though the aging hippie still leaned toward support of Senator Jack Williamson. Both he and Susan admired Derek immensely, but I also knew that each of them was attempting to achieve a personal validation by championing his cause. Susan hadn't backed a winner in a long time, and Troy had virtually lost his sense of self during all those years when he had been a dropout to not just political activism, but to life itself.

Who was I to begrudge them this? If it weren't for Derek, I would be an unemployed biographer.

"But you will be in danger!" Maurice said, the urgency in his voice causing everyone at the table to stare at him. His manner, after his absence in the afternoon, which he said was so that he could do some shopping, was more troubled than usual. Maurice had a secretive side, which bothered Josh and Tina but not Derek. The rest of us were used to him looking as if he was carrying the problems of the world, but was sworn to secrecy as to their identity.

"What are you talking about?" Josh asked, his antennae raised as soon as the word danger had been uttered.

"Do you mean physical danger?" Derek asked, gently. There was no fear in his voice. He sounded as if he was trying to give Maurice the confidence to say more.

Maurice looked around the table. There was a hint of panic behind the usual, hard expression in his eyes. "The government doesn't want you speaking out. They know that putting you in jail didn't work. You must realize that they may believe you need to be silenced."

"Are you saying the government may try to kill him?" I asked.

Maurice looked embarrassed that he had become the center of attention. "I am no expert on your government, Luke.

But you know what they are capable of." His eyes became even harder. "And there are probably others who would be equally alarmed about a new American leader."

"What others, Maurice?" I asked. The young Frenchman was more of an enigma to the rest of us than was anyone else at the table. Josh and Tina still distrusted him. Derek seemed to be intensely interested in Maurice's view of Muslim opinions on any number of matters and I think that's why he kept Maurice around. I wasn't sure what I thought. Maurice was secretive and angry, but I curbed my suspicions about him with my guilt about allowing myself to adopt the stereotype of Muslims promulgated by the administration.

"President Ferris has been the perfect straw man for Mustafa al Adim's picture of the West as avaricious, belligerent, and anti-Islamic," Maurice said, speaking his words slowly and with conviction; his young face sober and almost reverent as he gazed at Derek. The rest of us listened, spellbound. "With Ferris in power, al Adim can recruit every disaffected young man in the Middle East to engage in Jihad against the evil American empire," he continued. "If Ferris is replaced by a moderate who chooses peace instead of aggression and who isn't interested in spreading Christianity throughout the world, then who are the Middle Easterners supposed to hate? And from where will al Mout li Kafir recruit its new crop of Jihadists?"

"So you think that al Mout li Kafir wants to kill me?" Derek asked, a faint trace of amusement in his voice.

Maurice lowered his gaze as if embarrassed. "I'm only guessing, but yes."

"You mean here—on American soil?" Troy asked, incredulous.

"Everyone in Europe knows that al Mout li Kafir can operate wherever they please." Maurice sounded defensive. Or maybe he felt he had said too much. I was starting to wonder how he knew so much about al Mout li Kafir's motives.

Derek stared at Maurice, but his eyes were soft and gentle and when he spoke there was a tone of almost intimate understanding in his voice. "Then it will be up to you, my Muslim friend, to see that no harm befalls me."

"Tina and I will make sure of that," Josh growled, shooting a hostile glance in Maurice's direction.

"Of course you will," Derek said. He looked around the table. "Our discussion is theoretical anyway. I have no intention of running for national office."

Susan and Troy looked profoundly disappointed.

"Maybe you will change your mind," Susan said, but her voice didn't hold much hope.

"You could still influence the election enough to displace President Ferris," Maurice said, surprising me again with his political savvy. "Your voice carries a great deal of weight."

"Then I had better choose my words carefully," Derek said, pushing back from the table. "Now I am tired and I am going to bed."

Chapter 38

The day was bright and clear and there was even a warm breeze that might have been the first signal of spring approaching. Mohammed awoke with a deep sense of foreboding. Something in his watchers' manner had changed in the last few days. They had shown greater urgency in their manner and had been making more mistakes. It was nearly a miracle that Josh or Tina or even Derek himself hadn't noticed them. Yesterday, when they were preparing to drive to the Library of Congress, to which Karin had access, one of the men had been standing next to Derek's car, hurrying away when the group stepped out of the front door of the townhouse. Both Josh and Mohammed watched him with suspicion until he disappeared around the corner. Although the man was one that Mohammed had seen watching them on numerous occasions, Josh gave no indication that he had ever seen the man before. Mohammed said nothing.

Over breakfast, Derek announced his plans for the day. In the morning he would work with Josh and Tina on his exercises, then study with Karin, who was now educating him about the breakup of the Soviet Union and the continuing conflicts between the former Soviet countries and Moscow. After lunch he wanted everyone but Josh and Tina to accompany him on a visit to the Capitol where he would meet with Senator Jack Williamson, who was considering throwing his hat in the ring for his party's nomination for president. Williamson hoped to secure Derek's support in his bid for the nomination, and Derek had surprised all of his "family" by agreeing to consider the proposal.

"Are you sure you want me to come along?" Mohammed asked. In his wildest dreams he had never imagined himself inside the halls of congress. If Mustafa al Adim had known, he would have expected Mohammed to be wired with a vest loaded with explosives. But suicide bombing had never been Mohammed's aim, and more importantly, he was interested in what Derek and the Senator would say to each other. In Mohammed's life he was used to all decisions being made from the top down and disagreement being equal to disloyalty. That two of the most powerful men in the United States would openly discuss their positions with the aim of deciding if they should join forces—and that Derek would include his friends because he wanted to hear their opinions on the matter—was unprecedented in Mohammed's experience.

"Of course I do," Derek answered. "You are our expert on the Islamic mind, Maurice. If Williamson means what he has said in public and even privately to Troy, then he and I both need to learn from you how we can open a dialogue with the Islamic leaders."

Mohammed's mind reeled with the absurdity of his situation. He was a member of al Mout li Kafir, in fact its most formidable assassin, and now he was being asked to be an advisor to a potential nominee for the American presidency. Even more absurd was that he was being invited to present the Muslim point of view to a potential presidential nominee as a genuine alternative to the mindless use of terror as a strategy for achieving the fundamentalist Islamist's aims. What had happened to him? Had he succumbed to the enticements of the luxurious American way of life? He didn't think so. He had spent too many years in Europe to become swayed by Western opulence. No, the real influence responsible for working a change in him was Derek Stewart. In spite of himself, Mohammed found himself listening to Derek's words and beginning to see the world differently because of them.

When they had finished their lunch of steaming hot pea soup, sliced cheese and bread, Derek announced that it was time to go. The appointment with Senator Williamson was at 2:00 p.m. in the Senator's office. Josh had brought the car around to the front of the townhouse before lunch and parked it on the street. Now the burly Black physical therapist was mounting an argument with Derek as to why he should be allowed to accompany the group on their trip to the Capitol. Josh didn't like Derek venturing out without either Tina or him alongside.

"The Senate offices are very well guarded," Derek explained. He understood Josh's anxiety and appreciated it, but if all of them were to go they would need to take a second car, and Derek preferred taking just one into the Senate parking lot, where he had been given a pass to park the car.

"I'm not worried about when you're in the Senate offices," Josh answered. "I'm worried about when you're out in public. Maurice told you that there are all sorts of groups out there who would like to harm you."

Derek wouldn't budge and Josh finally resigned himself letting the other five go without him. Maurice would drive.

Mohammed slipped in behind the wheel as the others climbed in the front and back of the Mercedes. Turning the key, the engine didn't start immediately. When it finally caught, the barely detectable, but familiar, series of clicks Mohammed heard sent a chill down the back of his neck. "Everybody out of the car!" he yelled, jumping from his seat and throwing open the back door and dragging Derek by the coat into the street. The others stared dumbfounded and didn't move.

"It's a bomb," Mohammed yelled. "Get away from the car."

He didn't need to say more, the others scrambled from the car, but stood only a few feet away staring at the vehicle in disbelief. Mohammed knew he had no choice. He had no idea why the bomb had not yet exploded, but the car was running and he could do only one thing. He jumped back in and put the car in gear and floored the gas pedal. The powerful German car leaped forward, hurtling thirty yards down the street before it was consumed in a massive explosion that knocked every one of the former passengers to the ground. Mohammed, still sitting determinedly at the wheel and making no attempt to escape, was blown into a thousand tiny fragments of bone and flesh.

Chapter 39

"Maurice Aziz, as you knew him, was not his real name," the burly FIIEB agent, Nicholas Schmidt said. Everyone in our little "family" was seated in a conference room in the Metro Washington Field Office of the FIIEB on 4th Street. We had told Agent Schmidt and several other officials our various accounts of what happened, and now he was telling us what the Feebs thought was the real story. His manner was gruff and matter of fact, clearly implying that he saw all of us as naïve children.

"From what we can put together, using information from other branches of the Department of Homeland Security, Maurice's real name was Mohammed Sahadi. He was an al Mout li Kafir operative, in fact their most notorious assassin. There's no doubt that the bomb that killed Sahadi was a suicide bomb meant to kill Mr. Stewart and anyone else who was with him."

"Maurice saved our lives," Derek said, softly. Sorrow was written on his face.

"It seems that way to you," Schmidt said, both his expression and his tone patronizing. "But our sources are absolutely clear that his mission was to assassinate you."

Derek didn't appear surprised. "I don't doubt that. But he chose to not carry out his mission and to save our lives instead." His voice had gotten stronger. He turned to the rest of us. "What interests me is why he did that. If the most notorious al Mout li Kafir assassin decided to save the lives of his intended victims, then it means that there is room for dialogue with our enemies, does it not?" He looked around the table to see if we agreed.

None of us whom Maurice had pulled from the car before it exploded had the slightest doubt that he had not only saved our lives, but that he had deliberately sacrificed his own life to be sure that we weren't killed by the car-bomb. In my mind, another issue was equally important. "If Maurice is responsible for saving us, then who was it that tried to kill us?" I asked.

"Jesus, you people!" Schmidt exploded, looking first at me and then at the others. "Don't any of you listen? Your

'Maurice,' as you call him, worked for al Mout li Kafir. That's who wanted to kill Derek—and any of the rest of you who happened to be with him."

"How do you know that?' Karin asked a look of defiance on her face..

"Because we traced a call to Mohammed from an al Mout li Kafir operations site."

"How long ago was that?" I asked. "For how long have you known that we had an al Mout li Kafir assassin in our midst?"

Schmidt gulped, looking first embarrassed, then angry. It was obvious he'd said too much. "I don't know. I was just told that we had evidence of a phone call."

"Thanks for having given us a heads up," I said. "You've really convinced us that our safety was your first priority. Anyway, a phone call just proves that Maurice had ties with al Mout li Kafir." I looked around the table at the others. "Would anyone say that Maurice knew that the bomb was in the car before he turned on the ignition?"

No one answered yes.

"So it's not only possible, but it's almost assured that someone else planted that bomb," I said, giving the FIIEB agent a look that implied that he was thick headed. He was either that or he was covering something up.

"That's bullshit," Schmidt said, barely able to control his anger. "You people are more screwed up than I thought."

"It leaves open the question of who wanted Derek dead," I said, looking around the table and ignoring the FIIEB agent, who sat fuming at one end.

"Maurice already told us who," Troy said. He looked defiantly at the FIIEB agent, as if Schmidt was the enemy and Troy was finally getting to fight some of the old battles he hadn't gotten a chance to fight during his younger days.

We all looked at Troy waiting to hear whom he was talking about.

"The Ferris administration…. Remember?"

Schmidt let out a loud snort. "An al Mout li Kafir assassin tells you it's really the U.S. government that's after you, and you all believed him? Brother!"

"The U.S. government, in the person of you Feebs, arrested Derek on no charges and kept him locked up in solitary confinement for two weeks," I said. "Why would we think you'd be above trying to kill him?"

Schmidt looked like he would like to kill *me*. "Because the American government doesn't go around killing people, that's why."

"You mean it doesn't kill Americans," Troy said. "Because for sure the American government kills people in other countries. We've got an army dropping bombs in Somalia, we've got drones killing suspected terrorists in Yemen, and we want to drop bombs on the capitals of three Middle Eastern countries." He looked around at the rest of us for support. "And here in the U.S. we have no idea whether the thousands of so-called terrorists who have been arrested have been killed or not."

Schmidt threw up his hands in frustration. "You people are beyond help. All I can tell you is that your pal 'Maurice' was Mohammed Sahadi and he worked for al Mout li Kafir killing people. Mr. Stewart was probably the next victim on his list, but he blew himself up by accident instead."

"Is that going to be your official report?" Derek asked.

"What else would my report say?"

Derek ignored the question. "A lot of people are going to be ready to go after al Mout li Kafir if you report that they tried to assassinate me."

"Sorry pal," Schmidt said. "We have to call 'em like we see 'em."

"This all plays right into the administration's hands," Karin said. Her voice had become shrill with anger. "Now they've got their terrorist attack to justify jumping feet first into the Middle East conflict. They don't have to wait for Israel to invite them, they can claim we've been attacked on our own soil."

"How Goddamned convenient," Troy muttered.

"Then we have to tell people the truth," Derek said, matter-of-factly.

"What truth?' I asked. "That Maurice was really Mohammed somebody and that a al Mout li Kafir assassin who was stalking you, no doubt in order to kill you, finally saw the light and stepped in at the last minute to save you?"

"That appears to be what happened," Derek answered. "Only I don't think Maurice changed his mind at the last minute. If he joined us with the idea of killing me—and I wouldn't be surprised if he did—he changed his mind about that a long time ago. The Maurice we knew for the last few weeks had no intention of killing any of us, I'm sure of that."

Chapter 40

Karin's prediction that President Ferris would use the attack on Derek as a pretext for joining the Middle East war between Israel and its neighbors was borne out within a day. The president held a news conference and expressed his "outrage" that "cowardly Muslim terrorists" had "brought the war to our own shores by attacking a genuine American war hero."

Derek's townhouse was surrounded by FIIEB agents, who refused to allow Derek to speak to the press on the grounds that he needed to be protected from further attacks. The rest of us were allowed to come and go, but when Troy gave a press conference in which he accused the government of being behind the assassination attempt on Derek, his protestations fell on deaf ears. Even the young supporters who had swarmed to Derek's camp after his earlier arrest thought that Troy was some sort of ex-hippie wacko.

Senator Armbruster moved quickly. A declaration of war overwhelmingly passed in the two houses of congress. An amendment to the declaration, forbidding the United States from using nuclear weapons, introduced by Senator Williamson, was defeated. The country was holding its breath to see if the president would order a nuclear strike on the Muslim countries that were at war with Israel. Half the people favored such a tactic. The other half vehemently opposed it.

"You have to do something," Karin announced to Derek at breakfast. "Ferris is using the assassination attempt against you as an excuse to start a nuclear war." She glared at Derek as if he was responsible for the president's actions.

"And it was an assassination attempt he probably ordered," Troy added, glumly.

"Won't you reconsider running for office?" Susan asked, her tone almost pleading. "Can't you see you're needed now, more than ever?"

Karin looked over at me and rolled her eyes. We both knew that Susan was just trying to take advantage of the situation.

She probably leapt in the air with glee when she heard that congress had declared war.

Derek shook his head, slowly. "I have no desire to run for public office," he said, with no expression in his voice.

"Then how about supporting another candidate?" Troy asked, hopefully.

Susan shot a look of fury at Troy, but the rest of us were curious.

"Who are you talking about?" I asked.

"Senator Williamson," Troy said, looking at the others' faces to judge their reaction.

"Williamson's too new in the Senate to be considered for national office," Susan said, trying to sound dismissive, though her tone came across as defensive.

"He's the most vocal leader of the opposition to Ferris, and he's vehemently opposed to this war," Troy countered. "Well?" he asked, looking at Derek.

"I have been impressed by Senator Williamson," Derek said quietly. "He is young but he is not afraid to challenge the administration and stand up for his beliefs." He looked at each of us. "Most importantly, he does not accept simple answers to complex questions."

"Jack Williamson hasn't got half the following you do," Susan said, but we could all hear the defeat in her voice. "He has no chance of challenging Ferris."

"He may or he may not," Derek answered. "But he may be able to rally enough popular opposition to Ferris to keep the president from using nuclear weapons in the Middle East."

I was surprised by Derek's comment. It was the first time I had heard him address the current political situation from a strategic point of view.

Susan looked glum. She moved what remained of her scrambled eggs around her plate aimlessly, as if she had become a rudderless ship adrift at sea. Without a political candidate to promote, she was without purpose.

"Williamson is speaking at a party fundraiser in a few weeks in Portland—in his home state," Troy said, eagerly. He had also sensed a change in Derek's attitude—a signal that, while Derek had no desire to run for office himself, he might be willing to use his influence to shape political events. "Would you be willing to go there and speak on his behalf?"

Derek looked thoughtful. "I have been a part of this modern world less than a month. I am not sure that it is wise for me to become involved in politics. Politicians must take positions on issues based on their need to be elected. I would rather avoid that situation."

"Williamson's not that kind of politician," Troy said, a note of defensiveness in his own voice. "Besides, you don't need to support him on everything. It's his position against this war that is the important thing."

"I will think about it."

"I have an alternative suggestion," Karin said.

I looked over at her. She had an intense expression on her face I hadn't seen before. I listened, intrigued.

Both Susan and Troy looked irritated.

Derek smiled at her, waiting for her to continue.

"Next week in California, the National Union of Evangelical Christian Churches is having their convention in Orange County. The topic of the conference is the war against Islam. Reverend Goodson is their keynote speaker. I'm sure you could get on the agenda."

Troy's look of irritation had transformed itself into one of glee. "Perfect!" he said. "Beard the lion in his own den."

I was still too amazed by Karin's suggestion to say anything. What had happened to the scholarly historian who had chastised me for trying to provoke the establishment?

"Why would they allow me to speak?" Derek asked.

"You are still regarded as an American hero," Karin answered. "I don't think your religious sentiments are clear to anyone."

"That is understandable," Derek answered, barely suppressing a grin.

I couldn't help but smile, myself. Derek had a way of making his statements enigmatic. He and I both knew that, if he voiced his religious—or more accurately, non-religious— "sentiments" publicly, he would never be invited to speak to the Evangelicals. "What would you talk about?" I asked.

"If I am going to speak about religion, I'd better do some more studying. Given my grandmother's ideas, I was hardly raised within the mainstream. It's time I found out what the mainstream is all about."

"You mean conservative Christianity?" I asked.

"That appears to be the mainstream in America in this day and age."

"It's the lowest common denominator to which the consciousness of this country has sunk," I offered. "The average American's version of religion is about as sophisticated as a video game with bad guys who act like monsters and good guys who act like saints until it comes time to kick ass—then the good guys and the bad guys all act the same, only the good guys earn points in heaven for doing their killing."

"If it is the people who believe such things that I plan to talk to, I will need to understand them." Derek smiled. "If I don't understand them, how can I change their minds?"

Susan surprised us all by leaping to her feet. "Well I think you are all crazy!" she said, angrily. "Embroiling yourself in a religious debate is the quickest way to alienate at least half of the electorate. You'll never be elected to anything if you go to that convention and speak out against Reverend Goodson's point of view. Even Jack Williamson won't want you campaigning for him after that."

"I wouldn't be so sure of that," Troy answered her. "I happen to know that Williamson is planning to speak there, himself.'

She glared at Troy and then at the rest of us. "You're all impossible. You're such amateurs that you're squandering political capital that's been handed to you on a silver platter. And for what? To take your anti-establishment jabs at the administration instead of mounting a sustained campaign to win the voters away from them. At the end of all this, Ferris will remain in power and you will completely ostracized from the political debate." She turned and strode dramatically out of the room.

Derek looked around at all of us. He appeared unperturbed. "Shall we organize our day? We have a lot of work to do."

Chapter 41

The privately chartered Lear jet touched down on the worn tarmac that was the central runway for Orange County's John Wayne Airport. Taxiing to the end of the runway, the jet made a sharp turn and continued its taxi off the main runway onto a side area reserved for private planes. When it finally halted in front of Midway Airlines offices, a balding, overweight and sweating man in his forties, came bustling out of the office and waited as the steps were lowered from the plane.

The weather was a dry 72 degrees, and we were all overdressed as we emerged from the private jet into the warm Southern California air.

"Is this paradise or have I just stepped into a hallucination?" I asked the others.

"Don't get sucked in by the weather," Karin said, standing beside me, and doing her level best to quell the expression of awe and relief that threatened to spread across her being. "Remember this is the home of the John Birch Society and of unqualified support for Richard Nixon, Ronald Reagan, and George Bush. That's hardly a description of paradise."

"Point taken," I answered. We were in Orange County, after all, because Derek was going to speak at the National Convention of the National Union of Evangelical Christian Churches. It was no accident that an organization such as the National Union of Evangelical Christian Churches was having its convention in Orange County. This was one of the most conservative, Christian locales in the entire United States.

"I have a place on the ocean," Derek said. He was slowly descending the stairs from the plane and was looking up at the pristinely clear, deep blue sky above us, unmarked except for the bright golden sun that, even at mid afternoon, beat down on us as we stood on the runway beside the airplane. "I asked Mr. Erskine to put us up in the most private accommodations he could find, and as it turned out, such a request required that he rent a property for us. He said it was on the ocean."

Our entire entourage piled into the sleek, black, limo provided by the charter airline, and in a matter of minutes we had left the airport and were headed West, toward the ocean, about two miles away. We passed through palm-tree lined and ultra-pricey Newport Beach, then crossed a couple of arched bridges over mansion-lined canals and finally drove onto a tiny island, connected by another bridge. A large sign emphatically labeled the island *private*. It contained only three houses, each immensely large and each fronting on Newport Bay.

The house itself was a Spanish-style stucco, three-story, nine bedroom extravaganza, which looked like a turn-of-the-century ranchero. Instead of horses there were two BMWs, one of them a yellow convertible, a long silver Mercedes, and a hulking, shiny red Hummer lined up in the garage. The house itself, in addition to having a wide brick sun porch facing the bay, encircled a copper-colored, tiled interior patio, complete with a fountain in its center, much like a small plaza in the center of a Mexican village.

I was the first one to park my bags in my room and find a comfortable patio chair on the sun porch and sit, in a pair of shorts and a Hawaiian shirt, which I had bought for the trip, and stare out at the bay. All I lacked was a Mai Tai with a small umbrella sticking out of it. I began rummaging through the cupboards to see with what kind of liquor the house came stocked. I was rewarded by finding one cupboard filled to the brink with Canadian whiskey, scotch, gin, vodka, rum and a variety of mixers. I made myself a gin and tonic, found and sliced a lime from the refrigerator, and returned to my seat on the deck.

Karin, Susan and Troy were waiting for me, which necessitated a return to the kitchen to fix two more gin and tonics for the women and pour a coke for Troy.

"Some digs, huh?" I asked the others as I sat back and sipped my drink. A 70 foot, two story yacht, roughly double the size of my apartment in Washington, chugged through the placid waters in front of us, throwing off small waves that slapped against the foundations of the deck. A darkly tanned, slim blonde, who could have been anywhere from 18 to 60 years old waved a hand toward us as if we were old friends.   I waved back.

"Friend of yours?" Karin asked.

"We're acknowledging our mutual membership in the sphere of the privileged," I answered.

"And the politically connected," Karin answered back, the sarcasm in her voice unconcealed. "The rich from this area have a lot of political clout with the Ferris administration. They bankroll his and a lot of his fellow conservatives' campaigns."

"And they can do the same for Derek if he says the right thing at the convention," Susan commented.

"Derek is here to support Senator Williamson, not to throw his own hat into the ring," Troy said, looking hard at Susan.

"Jack Williamson hasn't got the chance of a snowball in hell against Ferris," Susan answered impatiently. "Williamson is trying to rouse a liberal base that's been underground for so long they're afraid to poke their heads out. The country may be tiring of Ferris, but they're still frightened as hell of the terrorist threat and they'd like someone who will kick the living daylights out of the Muslims."

"Then it's obvious that Derek should tell convention he's in favor of bombing the Muslim countries." I said. "He'll lock up their vote for sure."

Susan turned away from Troy and looked at me. "Don't be a damn fool, Luke. Derek doesn't have to go that far. He just has to not alienate anyone and he can keep his message right down the middle of the road and as vague as he wants it to be."

"Bullshit," Karin said. She was leaning forward in her chair, her face animated, as if she were a college student eager for a debate. "Derek is the only voice of reason in this country, except perhaps Jack Williamson. It's his obligation to use the media spotlight that's on him to tell the public the truth. All this war on terror garbage and the loss of internal freedoms that's gone with it are destroying this country, not to mention creating a world situation that will lead to massive middle-Eastern bloodshed. Somebody has to tell America and that's what Derek has been doing."

"No one will listen if he gives that message to the evangelicals," Susan answered.

I was getting tired of their arguing, which had taken the same track every one of their conversations had taken for the last three weeks. "The Feebs and the CIA are going to be listening, and Derek's already been arrested once for saying what he thought. Does anyone know what he's actually planning to say at the convention tomorrow?" I looked around at the faces.

"He has to say what he believes," Karin said, her voice filled with defiance and her eyebrows knitted in earnest intensity.

"If he goes to jail again, he might not come back out," I answered her. I was feeling worn out by Karin's relentless moral stridency. She had too much of the certitude of the new convert, and even though I preferred the new Karin over the old cautious and disapproving one, I was disheartened by the fact that she'd carried the same rigid intolerance from her former role into this new one.

"Derek knows that too," Troy said. He didn't want to believe that the situation was too dangerous to allow Derek to speak out in favor of his candidate, the senator.

"And Derek probably doesn't care," I answered. "I think we need to have a plan for getting him out of the convention and into hiding if there's any hint that he's going to be arrested."

Troy and Susan looked at me as if I was out of my mind.

"Don't you think you're overdramatizing things?" Susan asked. "We're talking politics, not guerilla warfare."

Karin had jerked her body into full alertness. Her expression was fiery. "I agree we need a plan, and I've got one."

I couldn't suppress a smile. Karin was just waiting for a barricade to storm, and my warning had given her one. "What's your plan?"

"I'll tell you all tomorrow," she said, mysteriously, the intensity still in her expression. "Just pack all of our stuff into that Hummer that's in the garage, and bring it with us to the convention."

"Oh brother," Susan said in a voice laden with sarcasm.

"You don't have to be part of the plan," Karin said, shooting daggers in her glare at the other woman.

"I wouldn't miss it. Anyway, are you trying to exclude me from the group now, because I don't agree with the rest of you about Derek running for office?"

"You mean because you want to use Derek to further your own political ambitions," Karin shot back.

"And you're trying to relive some sixties experience your parents had and you missed out on because you became a safe, middle-class professor," Susan said.

Karin's eyes flared with anger and then hurt. "I'm not thinking of me," she said, but there was a catch in her voice, as if she was trying to choke back a sob.

"All right, cut it out guys," I interrupted. "Karin's plan makes sense to me. It's easier to have an escape plan than to think we can control what Derek says. And we're all in this together. Everyone can go to the convention tomorrow in the Limo and I'll bring the Hummer along later, filled with all of our luggage. I'll park it in the regular parking lot along with the convention attendees, so no one knows that it's connected to Derek. If we think we need to get away fast, I'll lead us all to the Hummer and we'll go to wherever Karin tells us to. OK?"

Susan looked skeptical but nodded reluctantly. Troy and Karin did also. Karin's eyes were bright with eagerness. I was sure she was hoping that Derek would say something tomorrow that would lead to our having to flee from the convention, the authorities hot in pursuit of us, maybe even firing away with guns as we drove into the sunset. Her dream was my nightmare.

Chapter 42

Crystal Cathedral, the glass-spired church and compound composed of school, convention center and religious retreat, was in the heart of central Orange County, only minutes from the fantasy spires of the Magic Kingdom in Disneyland. The Cathedral would have fit right into the amusement park for all of it's ostentatious fairy-tale look. It was the location of the Evangelical Ministers' National Convention. Although only 3000 delegates attended, the group's endorsement of various political positions, including prospective candidates for either party's nomination was virtually a stamp of approval that would determine the voting choices of millions of conservative Christian Americans. For the last three elections the ministers had endorsed Fremont F. Ferris.

Derek and the others had taken a rental limo ahead of me and I had stayed behind in the Newport Beach bayside mansion to load everyone's suitcases into the Hummer and follow along fifteen minutes after the others. When I arrived at the Crystal Cathedral I entered the public parking lot and parked among the other cars, then went inside.

Had I not known it was a religious convention I would have thought I was at a patriotic meeting for all of the American flags draped inside the lobby and along the hallways leading to the sanctuary where the speeches were to be delivered. It wouldn't have surprised me to see a crowd of Veterans of Foreign Wars trooping down the hallway in their funny little hats. I looked around for a statue of Jesus raising an American flag.

When I arrived at my seat, Derek was already waiting behind the curtains on the stage, which was a pulpit on Sundays when services were broadcast across the United States and throughout most of the world. Only Josh and Tina had been allowed to stay with him and I had joined Troy and Karin in the front row of the 3,000 seat cathedral. Susan's seat was empty but sitting in the same row as we were, there were five stern-looking government types, who didn't return my smile, but must have been associated with one of the speakers to merit their preferred seating. Since Reverend Merrill Goodson was on the schedule immediately ahead of Derek, I had no doubt that the G-men were part of his entourage, and that they also had the power to arrest Derek if he said anything that Goodson decided violated the Patriot Act III. I was sure that there were at least a couple more such agents behind the stage with Goodson himself.

The presence of the federal agents gave me a moment of panic as I thought about our plan to make a quick getaway, should the need arise. Since we were sitting right next to them, it would be difficult to surreptitiously leave the sanctuary and have the Hummer revved up in the parking lot without alerting the feds to our plan. I assumed that, even if an arrest was imminent, the agents weren't going to accost Derek in front of millions of TV viewers, so he would be safe until the actual convention was over. That meant that, in the general hubbub following the conclusion of the meeting, we would need to move quickly, lose ourselves in the crowd and grab Derek, Josh and Tina and sprint for the door and the waiting Hummer. Hopefully, the G-men wouldn't be expecting us to have planned a quick escape and we would catch them off guard. That is, if such an escape was even necessary.

The convention began with a series of convocations, prayers for our troops, our leaders, the attendees, and a call by the Reverend Darley Fitzhugh, the president elect of the organization to go forth and convert all the world's "heathens" to Christianity. I had to remind myself that I really was in the 21st century. Reverend Fitzhugh prayed for peace, and as a part of his lengthy prayer, reminded the audience that true peace could only be achieved through the subjugation, if not the complete extermination of all those in the Muslim world who rejected Christianity and its message of love and charity. He blessed President Ferris and asked God to continue to guide the president's decisions, even if that meant guiding him to use nuclear weapons against the Muslim infidels. The crowd murmured "amen" while I marveled at the mental acrobatics necessary for anyone to interpret the prayer as a call for peace.

A series of pink-cheeked young singers followed Reverend Fitzhugh's convocation. Most of them sang Christian hymns but a few also sang patriotic songs, continuing the convention's theme of mixing religion and politics and a general message that Jesus was on the side of the United States. Whatever happened to love thy enemies and turn the other cheek?

Senator Jack Williamson was the first political speaker and he followed Jake Gagniol, a nationally famous professional football player. Gagniol, a quarterback, described his descent into the world of money, drugs, beautiful cars and fast women until, reaching bottom, which included a year-long suspension from the NFL, he listened one evening to the message of Reverend Merrill Goodson's weekly television broadcast and realized that he had to turn his life over to Jesus. The rest of the tale was the stuff of storybooks. He gave up the drugs, the loose women and the focus on material wealth and dedicated himself to serving Jesus with a pure body and a committed mind. When his suspension was over, he returned to the NFL, won a Superbowl and an MVP award and spent his off-field hours proselytizing his fellow athletes. Had I not noticed that he had arrived at the convention in a limo the size of two of Derek's, and that he traveled with a cadre of bodyguards who appeared to be packing weapons, and that at least two beautiful young women, neither of whom I suspected were his sisters, stayed behind waiting faithfully in the limo while it was parked in the VIP zone in front of the Cathedral, his story might have impressed even a hardened cynic such as myself.

Jack Williamson was playing to a tough audience. Even the roly-poly, looks-like-your-favorite-uncle, country preachers, whose round faces and soft blue eyes glittered with brotherly love when they were introduced to you, had a peculiar facility to be transformed into bloodthirsty Crusaders when the War on Terror was mentioned.

The Senator from Oregon broke the ice with a story about his own upbringing in a devoutly Christian farming family in the Willamette Valley, and his listeners thawed a little as they learned that he had attended a small Christian college in the outskirts of Portland for his undergraduate degree. I guessed that these were the credentials that had gotten him into the convention in the first place. I waited curiously, wondering if he was going to portray himself to his audience as another one of their good 'ol boys, in order to garner their endorsement, and I shot Troy a look of skepticism to convey my fear that the aging hippie had been duped by just another politician.

My fears were short-lived as the young senator denounced, in rapid succession, war, anti-Muslim sentiment, racism, and the merging of religion, politics and military adventurism as anti-Christian. His speech was replete with quotations from the New Testament, many of them attributed to Jesus himself, but they held little sway with his audience, which became first restless, then angry, and finally began booing him. He was not deterred from closing with a resounding condemnation of nuclear war on any scale and for any reason, and a call for the election of a president who would see every leader in the world as a potential brother or sister and choose the path of conciliation as the preferred mechanism of American foreign policy, not just with our Christian allies, but with every nation on the globe, including those that were dedicated Muslims. It wasn't the kind of message of peace and brotherly love to ring a note of sympathy with the messengers of Christ seated around me. Their religious zealotry had appeared to morph into a lust for the senator's blood.

As if in answer to the incensed audience's prayers, the next speaker was the Reverend Merrill Goodson, who held up Senator Williamson as an example of naïve liberal thinking of the type that played into the hands of our sworn enemies. Not to be outdone in terms of biblical quotations, the reverend began by quoting Paul's admonition that, " Ye cannot drink the cup of the Lord, and the cup of devils: ye cannot be partakers of the Lord's table, and of the table of devils." Adding Paul's warning that "Be ye not unequally yoked together with unbelievers: for what fellowship hath righteousness with unrighteousness? and what communion hath light with darkness?" The good Reverend argued that intolerance of heathen religions, even Judaism, has a basis in the Holy Scriptures, and anyone preaching mutual understanding was undermining the Word of God. Moreover, citing the book of Joshua, where God called for the extermination of "anything that breathes," in Canaan, Reverend Goodson made the point that there was no precedent in the Bible for true followers of God to be either tolerant or lenient with unbelievers. In other words, nuclear annihilation of non-Christians was not only acceptable, it was practically God's will. I wondered if "bomb them back to the stone age," was also a phrase from the Bible, and I had just somehow missed it in my own narrow religious education.

The thunderous applause that greeted the conclusion of Reverend Goodson's speech told me that he had hit a note of accord with his more than receptive audience of Christian conservative ministers.

Into the mouth of this Christian dragon stepped Derek. I had nothing but bad vibes about the kind of reception he was about to receive from this audience. Reverend Darley Fitzhugh introduced him with the same fervor he had showered upon Merrill Goodson, describing Derek as a war hero, who "knew from a personal perspective, the experience of offering one's life for his country" and also knew what it meant to "receive a miracle at the hands of God." Fitzhugh had obviously never listened to any of Derek's previous statements regarding the circumstances of his war wound, his views on the War on Terror or his thoughts about God's role in his recovery from his coma. Some of the audience *had* been paying attention to those statements, and Derek received only a scattered and tepid round of applause.

Derek was gracious, as usual, thanking his host and the audience for inviting him to speak to them. He greeted Reverend Goodson and Senator Williamson as equally familiar acquaintances. He began with a quotation from Mahatma Gandhi: " 'The pursuit of truth does not permit violence being inflicted on one's opponent.'"

"Notice that I have quoted a man who is not a Christian, whose words are not in the Bible, and who lived and died within the lifetimes of some of you or at least your fathers," he said. "Notice also that I have talked about truth, not faith."

He looked out across the sea of critical faces, many of them scowling, but all of them listening. "My favorite quotation is actually from Albert Einstein, a man who died the year after I was born, but with whom my grandmother was well acquainted. Einstein said, 'Everything should be made as simple as possible, but not simpler.' I am afraid that most of you as well as many of your fellow Americans have built your beliefs on ideas that are too simple to be supported by reality."

His comments provoked a chorus of angry snarls from the ministers in the audience. Derek seemed not to notice. He was no longer smiling. He looked out on the audience with a penetrating stare.

"While I admit that we don't live in a world where everyone is eager to look out for the welfare of his fellow man, I hasten to add that neither do we live in a world where one half of the people believe in love, kindness, charity and virtue while the other half believes in hate, destruction, evil and fear. That is far too simple a picture of the world to be true. Most people in our world want to earn an honest living, raise a healthy family, find meaning in relationships with others and, perhaps by expressing their spiritual yearnings through a particular faith. I include Christians, Jews, Muslims, Hindus, Buddhists, Sikhs and many other followers of the world's many religions in this overall group who have the same aims and strivings as each other. Minus the spiritual yearnings, many atheists are similar."

"Within each of these groups, however, are those who want power and control, who are angry at anyone different from themselves and threatened by ideas and behaviors that do not fit into their own narrow view of what is acceptable. These persons have always been with us. They are the Jewish Sanhedrin at the time of Christ, they are the Catholic Church during the Inquisition, the American Puritans who killed women they had branded as witches, the PVDE, in Portugal under Salazar, the Red Guards in China during its Cultural Revolution, and of course in modern times, the Taliban in Afghanistan, the Morality

Police in Iran and Saudi Arabia, the Sharia courts in a number of Muslim countries, and ..." he hesitated and seemed to stare down his audience one by one before continuing, "... right here in this county, the government authorities who enforce the tyrannical Patriot Act III, and the religious zealots and militarists who call for destruction of all the nations of the world who do not subscribe to Christian theology."

The crowd erupted with an angry roar. I had a momentary fear that the Cathedral might suddenly become the site of a good 'ol Southern lynching party, but Derek held up both of his hands and somehow managed to regain their attention, filled with antipathy as it was.

His voice was deep and powerful, defying his audience to do anything but listen, whether they wanted to hear his words or not. "Actions that take advantage of our weakest fellow human beings, or wipe out entire races on the basis of narrow and vicious stereotypes, or sacrifice others for the sake of our greed for material wealth, are self-evidently evil. When entire societies embrace such actions, then we have lost the humanity that separates us from the rest of the animal world and we must look long and hard at how such a state of society came about."

The audience was quiet, though most of their faces had hardened against Derek's words. Still he persisted, his voice ringing within the glass walls of the cathedral.

"As a young man I was appalled to read the works of modern German intellectuals, who in the 1960's had forgotten the caricature of evil their own society had become only 20 years earlier. How could they not be consumed by self-examination? I look at Africa, from the time of European colonization until the present day of genocidal warfare. Even without war, the massive loss of life and livelihood as a result of famine and monumental greed and mismanagement by various governments, has created holocausts that surpass the extermination of European Jews in terms of numbers, if not savagery. Where have been our moral leaders during all this time? Aren't world leaders over all of these decades at least as culpable as those who acquiesced, albeit silently to the German Holocaust?"

231

"And now," his words continued to ring, his audience spellbound, "with anti-Semitism still rampant in much of the world, with millions still dying and being murdered in Africa, our own society has, instead of trying to remedy these evils, fomented even greater hatred and devastation with the so-called War on Terror and the labeling of the religion of half of the world's peoples as blasphemous and an excuse to bomb them and their countries into lifeless rubble."

He looked out over his audience and now his tone was as if he was pleading with them. "Where are the truly moral leaders who will question our present course of action and lead us back into a state of civilization that embraces love and respect for our fellow human beings, rather than fear and hatred? I look to our political leaders and, with the possible exception of Senator Williamson, I do not see anyone standing for morality. I listen to the leaders of our Christian religions, both Protestant and Catholic, and I do not hear words of compassion or love. What I see is a society that no longer has a right to lead the world."

Reverend Goodson shook himself free of the spell under which even he had been held and leapt to his feet, or at least struggled to them as rapidly as his immense bulk would allow him to. "That's traitorous and anti-Christian," he shouted. "There is no room in this Hall of God for the words of this man." His call at first was met by shocked silence, then others began to join him in calling for Derek to leave, or perhaps they were calling for his head. At any rate, those who were most vocal soon became the majority and a unified chant of "Get out... Get out!" soon reverberated throughout the Cathedral, loud enough that I had thoughts of the glass walls coming down around us.

It was time for me to get the Hummer.

Chapter 43

Josh and Tina, with Derek firmly in tow, burst out of the side door, just as Karin, Troy, and I screeched to a halt on the blacktop in front of the door, the Hummer's engine panting like a resting lion. Troy threw open the side door and Derek and his two bodyguards jumped aboard. We were all accounted for except Susan. Within three seconds, she appeared at the same door through which Derek had just exited, pursued by three FIIEB agents, who came flying out of the same door moments later, but they could only stand and watch with angry looks on their faces as Susan jumped in the SUV and we sped out of the parking lot and up the street to the nearest freeway entrance.

"You picked a great time to take a powder," I said to Susan. She'd almost gotten us captured because of her tardiness.

"I wanted to talk to Senator Williamson," she said sheepishly.

"Still looking for a candidate?" I asked.

"Why not? " She settled back in her seat in a sulk.

I shifted my thoughts from Susan and devoted my attention to driving. Karin was barking out directions to us as we merged into the traffic moving North on Interstate 5.

"Keep heading North," Karin commanded, sure of a plan she had not fully divulged to any of us.

"To where?" I asked.

Derek, sitting between Tina and Troy in one of the two back seats, didn't appear concerned about our destination.

"Mendocino," Karin answered.

"Is that a place?" I asked.

"It's the last refuge of what's left of the hippies from the sixties. My mother owned a house there. That was where I was brought up. The house is empty and I still own it." There was enough excitement in her voice that I was sure she was recapturing more than just a piece of real estate. She was moving back to the era of her parents—anti-establishment activists on the run from the authorities—and taking us with her. We didn't have much choice.

233

"I used to live in Mendocino," Troy said, his voice strained.

"Maybe you knew my mother?" Karin asked, an eager tremor in her voice.

"Not Tracy Milne?" Troy asked, his tone a mixture of dread and excitement.

"You knew her!"

Troy was silent for moment. Then he reached forward and put a hand on Karin's shoulder. "I think I'm your father."

Karin swung her head around and stared at Troy. "Holy Fucking Jesus," she said.

"There'll be time for reunions later," I said, trying to be as sensitive as I could be while I my heart was racing with the thought that the Feebs could descend upon us at any moment. Repeated anxious checks in the rear-view mirror had failed to show that we were being followed but I wasn't convinced that we wouldn't be as soon as the wheels of government began to move. Derek had only voiced his opinion, but he had done it on national television and he had been critical enough of the administration that Reverend Goodson's claim that he had violated the Patriot Act III had a good chance of sticking.

"You made your point," I said, catching Derek's eyes in the mirror. "But I'm afraid that's going to make you a fugitive."

"I spoke the truth, or at least the truth as I see it. I was prepared to be arrested."

"Why didn't they arrest him?" Troy asked, sounding as if it was an effort to rouse himself from his preoccupation with his new found knowledge that one of his companions for the last two months had been his daughter. "It was almost too easy to get out of there."

"It would have been on national television," Susan answered. "The administration didn't want that. They don't want Derek to be a martyr."

"So why are we running?" Troy asked. His question was directed to the group.

"Because as soon as the television cameras are gone, the Feebs won't have any hesitation about arresting Derek," Karin answered. Her voice still sounded strained. She didn't turn around when she spoke to Troy.

"Or assassinating him," I added. "Don't forget the bomb that killed Maurice."

"Give me a break," Susan sneered. "Ferris may want Derek out of the public eye, but he's not going to resort to murder."

"Where have you been the last several years?" I asked, sarcastically. "They tried to kill Derek before and they've killed a lot of others who opposed them. What do you think happens to those people who just disappear after they're arrested?"

Susan sulked instead of answering.

When I glanced in the mirror I could see that Derek was staring straight ahead, thinking. "What do you want to do?" I asked

"It is time for me to go home," he said, his eyes still fixed on something faraway and private.

"You mean back to Washington?"

He shook his head. "I will go to Africa."

Chapter 44

"That turncoat Stewart tried to one-up me again," Reverend Merrill Goodson sputtered. "I want to see him in prison. I want him shut up for good!" The corpulent minister was pacing back and forth in the Oval Office in front of the president's wide desk.

President Ferris sat stolidly behind his desk, his head sagging in worry as he listened to his religious advisor. "For God's sake, Goodie, keep your eye on the big picture, will you," he said, tiredly. "Nobody gives a rat's ass what Stewart said to that group of evangelicals. They threw him out, didn't they? The point right now is we've got bigger fish to fry than one loudmouthed ex-soldier."

Goodson's expression was glum. "He's got a lot of public opinion on his side and that's not good for us. He wants to stop fighting the terrorists and he could erode a lot of the support that we badly need for our war."

"All that's going to change, Goodie. We've got Congressional approval to do whatever the hell we want to those damn Muslim countries and we're gonna do it sooner, rather than later."

"You mean attack them? Go nuclear?"

"We're gonna have a strategy meeting in ten minutes in the Cabinet Room. I'm ready to give the order for the Little Bang option. Jervy and General Corey say the time is ripe. The whole country is bullshit about al Mout li Kafir bombed our embassy in Ghana and then attempted an assassination right here on our soil and they'll support anything we do right now ... your newly awakened war hero Derek Stewart notwithstanding."

"We wipe out Beirut, Tehran and Damascus all at once?" the Reverend asked, his eyes wide with excitement. He could hardly believe the attack was really going to happen.

"We've got to do it all at once, before anyone can raise an objection. Then if that doesn't bring the Muslims to their knees, we can threaten to widen our attack to the surrounding countries. I want those damn Arab countries to agree to smash al Mout li

Kafir, Hezbollah, and every other Muslim militant group. And I want them to agree to leave Israel completely alone."

Reverend Goodson gulped. He had forgotten about Israel. If the Jewish state remained unscathed during the war, how was the Bible prophesy going to be fulfilled? "How do we get control of Jerusalem, if we stop the Arabs now?" he asked.

"Fuck Jerusalem. We want to win the war on terror. That's the main thing. We can do that if we act now."

Goodsoon felt his skin prickle. Had the president missed the whole point? The entire struggle against the Muslim countries was part of what the Holy Bible had prophesied for the "last days." Taking back Jerusalem was part of the prophesy. The Jewish Temple had to be rebuilt, then destroyed again. Christians had to take over Israel. "We can't just leave Israel standing, Mr. president," Goodson said, aware that he sounded as if he was pleading. "We need to fulfill the Bible prophesies. Let the Muslims defeat Israel then we can bomb them and send our troops into Jerusalem to root out any left over Arabs and establish a Christian occupation."

The president looked skeptical. "That's what the Bible says is supposed to happen?"

Goodson sensed an opening. "It's clear as black and white, Mr. president. We need to make Israel a Christian country and we can't just declare war on the Israelis. God's on their side, too. We need to let them get conquered so we can save them."

The president still looked unconvinced. "Those fucking Arabs have lost every damned war they've fought against the Israelis. They'll probably lose this one, too."

"We don't need to let the war go on till it's over. We can just wait for at least one Arab victory on Israeli soil, then we can blast Damascus, Tehran and Beirut to kingdom come and send our troops into every one of the Arab countries and Israel too."

The president shook his head. "I've got to talk this over with General Corey and Donovan and some of the others. Shit, Goodie, we're right on the brink of winning this whole damn war on terror by dropping a few nukes on those Middle Eastern capitals. Why do you have to complicate things?"

"I'm only trying to make sure we're doing God's will," Goodson said. He lowered his head as if in prayer.

Ferris looked at him with irritation. "OK Goddammit. I'll talk to the others."

***

The Cabinet meeting room was crowded with Secretary of State Consuelo Madrid, Chairman of the Joint Chiefs of Staff, General Mathew Corey, National Security Advisor, Raymond Decker, Secretary of Defense, Albert Rutherford, CIA Director, Nathaniel Broadmoor and Special presidential Advisor, Jervis Donovan. Vice President Daryl Rogers was on the secure speaker phone and president Fremont F. Ferris was presiding. His religious advisor, the Reverend Merrill Goodson sat at his side and next to him was Chairman of the Senate Committee on Homeland Security and Governmental Affairs, Senator Frederick Armbruster.

"Thanks to Army here, we've got Congressional approval to do whatever needs to be done to go after those damn Muslims in their own territory," the president began, flashing a tight smile at Senator Armbruster.

"And that includes a nuclear attack," Armbruster reminded him.

The others around the table nodded. Only Secretary of State, Madrid looked troubled by the suggestion. "It's an approval for doing whatever we think is necessary," she said, her voice steady, but quiet. "It's not a mandate to drop bombs on anyone."

"It's a Goddamned mandate to win the war," Armbruster answered, clearly irritated by the Secretary of State's comment.

"Army is exactly right," Ferris said. "We want to win this damn war once and for all, or at least deal a fatal blow to those damn Muslim thugs. They blew up our embassy and we're not going to tolerate any more of their terrorist shenanigans."

"That was al Mout li Kafir," Secretary Madrid said, her voice shaking. She knew she was a lone voice in a room full of men ready to go to war.

"It's our policy and it has been for more than ten years to go after those countries that harbor and support terrorists," boomed the voice of Vice President Rogers over the speaker phone. "We've got incontrovertible evidence that Lebanon, Iran and Syria have made themselves safe havens for al Mout li Kafir. Where do you think those fucking sand monkeys get their arms and money from? It's those Muslim governments—that's where."

"The vice president is 100% correct," interjected CIA Director, Broadmoor. "Al Mout li Kafir has their headquarters in the Bekaa Valley in Lebanon and they're getting supplies and money from both Iran and Syria."

"It's the same as if the attack came directly from those three countries," Rogers added, his disembodied voice echoing in the room. "They deserve to be blown off the map."

"I believe the feeling is unanimous," Jervis Donovan said quietly, his first comment since the meeting began. "The quickest and most decisive way to defeat the terrorists is to attack the Muslim capitals with a force so lethal that every other country in the Middle East is afraid to side with the terrorists any longer. The Egyptians and Saudis will hunt Moustafa al Adim down themselves, just so they don't risk an attack from us. I think the CIA and the military would agree with me, wouldn't you gentlemen?" He looked at both Director Broadmoor and General Corey for confirmation. They both nodded.

"Reverend Goodson wants us to hold off a spell," the president said.

"This is a military matter, not a religious one," Donovan said, looking daggers across the table at the minister.

"The War on Terror is a religious war," Goodson said. "If we forget that simple fact, we're doomed to lose it." He spoke in his most weighty and intense voice, as if he was making a pronouncement given to him directly from God.

"The longer we wait, the more we expose ourselves to more terrorist attacks," Security Advisor Decker spoke up for the first time. "Moustafa al Adim knows we're going to go after him and he'll try to inflict as much damage as he can as fast as he can. Do I need to remind anyone that the attacks have come in bunches in the past? This Ghana embassy thing was just the first round."

The president turned to Reverend Goodson. "Tell them what you want to do, Goodie. Make your case."

Goodson spoke without hesitation. "I just want to wait until we have at least one Muslim victory over the Israelis so we can send in troops to secure Jerusalem. There's no point in this whole thing if we don't emerge with Christians owning Jerusalem and we need some pretext for sending in an occupation force."

Donovan exploded. It was the first time anyone at the table had seen the presidential advisor lose his temper. "Are you nuts? The point of this whole thing, as you put it, is to maintain the security of the United States, which we are unable to do so long as a bunch of Arab suicide bombers are running all over the planet."

Consuelo Madrid had a look of alarm on her face. "The Israelis are our allies. It has never been our aim to occupy Israel."

Several of those present, including Jervis Donovan, Senator Armbruster and the president himself glanced at each other, just a hint of sheepishness on their faces.

"Of course it hasn't been," the president said, clearing his throat and casting an irritated glance at Reverend Goodson. "We have no designs on Israel itself. We would only enter the country if we were needed for its defense against the Muslim states."

Jervis Donovan was still agitated. "This discussion is diverting us from our goal. We need to come to a decision about a nuclear attack against Lebanon, Iran and Syria."

Reverend Goodson started to object, but the president shot him a withering look that made it clear he wanted the minister to be quiet.

"The time to strike is now," Security Advisor, Raymond Decker said. He looked at General Corey and the Defense Secretary, Albert Rutherford for affirmation. They both nodded.

"You have my vote," the CIA Director, Nathaniel Broadmoor said.

"Mine too," added Senator Armbruster.

Donovan looked at the president for a decision.

"Daryl?" the president asked, staring at the speaker phone at the center of the table.

"You know my recommendation, Mr. President," the vice president's voice boomed over the telephone. "This is the time to show those dust monkeys we mean business."

"Consuelo? Goodie?" The president looked inquiringly at the Secretary of State and then at his religious advisor.

Her eyes showed her fear, but Consuelo Madrid fixed her face in a grim look. "I disagree," she said, then quickly looked down at the table.

"You know I'd rather wait," Reverend Goodson said, "but in principle, I agree."

"Then we go ahead," Ferris said, putting both of his hands flat on the table, as if to signal that the discussion was over. "Jervy, Army, we're gonna get some flack about this. Get ready for it and Jervy get your speechwriters working on something for me to say on television as soon as the attack is over. Nate, Consuelo, start putting out overtures for concessions from the other Arab countries as soon as this goes down. We don't want to have to drop any more nukes than we have to end this thing. Our conditions are that every Arab county disavow al Mout li Kafir and rid themselves of any safe havens. I want every Muslim terrorist in jail or dead, including Moustafa al Adim... understand?"

"Absolutely," the CIA Director said, nodding his head vigorously.

Secretary of State Madrid nodded silently, still avoiding the president's gaze.

Ferris slapped his hands on the table. "Meeting over," he said.

As they filed from the room, Ferris put a hand on the CIA Director's shoulder to hold him back. Jervis Donovan was standing behind his chair and had made no move to leave the room. "We're gonna get a lot of backlash both at home and abroad," the president said, after the last of the others had left the room. "We can put up with whatever the Europeans and the Chinese and the Russians say because they can't do a damn thing about what we do. But I don't want anyone leading a fight against us at home." The president eyes were red and tired. He heaved a long sigh. "Get rid of Derek Stewart. This time I mean really get rid of him. I don't want him saying anything in public against us."

"What about Senator Williamson?" Donovan asked. "He's gonna get a lot of national attention and you know he's gonna go ballistic when we launch this attack."

"Then get rid of him too."

"You mean you want him dead?" the CIA Director asked, his face expressionless. His job was to carry out orders, not to question them.

"I just don't want him saying anything. Arrest him, or eliminate him. I don't care and I don't need to know any more about it. Just do it."

Both men nodded.

The president turned and left the Cabinet Meeting Room.

Chapter 45

We'd crossed the Golden Gate Bridge, then left Highway 101 just north of Santa Rosa to cut over to Highway 1, and, traveling up the coast on the winding two-lane highway, had just passed Little River, a tiny community of mostly lodges, inns, and bed and breakfasts overlooking the rocky and tumultuous Little River Bay. Karin and Troy were having some sort of emotional redintegration. After sharing a good hour's worth of guilt and anger —the guilt Troy's and the anger Karin's—related to Troy having left his wife and baby to escape to Canada and avoid the draft, they appeared to have let bygones be bygones and were now firmly bonded and busily decrying the commercialization of the spectacular coastline they both remembered from their separate pasts. Much of the scenery consisted of pine-forested mountains tumbling down to a sweeping coastal plain that ended abruptly in soaring cliffs, towering above an angry sea. Occasionally the tortuous road would drop to sea level and we would round a corner to discover a pristine beach where the mountains had been eroded away by a sparkling stream that for eons had cut its way to the ocean, leaving a grass-covered valley in its wake. All of us. except Karin and Troy, were content to ignore the roadside convenience stores, liquor stores, video-rental stores and the small clusterings of mobile homes that marred the otherwise awe-inspiring landscape. We had never experienced the more desolate coast that had been the environment of Karin's childhood and the days Troy had spent living with her mother before he had left. However, as we entered Mendocino, even the two of them ceased to grumble and, instead, marveled at the unchanged character of the coastal village with it's uneven and faded wooden sidewalks, its hardware and produce stores peeling paint from their weathered sides and the populace of sixties era hippies, aging, but still suitably seedy, wandering the streets. Karin directed us to a lone, boarded up three-story Victorian house near the edge of town, overlooking an expanse of heath that would have rivaled the most forbidding English coastline and which stretched to distant, sheer, slate colored, sandy cliffs overlooking a ferocious gray sea.

"It's the same house!" Troy exclaimed as we pulled into the driveway.

"You mean you lived here with Mom?" Karin asked, her voice filled with emotion.

"Long enough to conceive you. You weren't even born when I left." He hung his head. "But I knew Goddamn well that your mother was pregnant."

"Well now we can share it," Karin said cheerily. Troy was fortunate that they'd discovered their relationship after she'd made her transformation into a rebel. Her intellectual and emotional empathy with both of her parents had already been established.

"The county that time forgot," I quipped, as we unloaded our belongings from the Hummer. Josh was already noisily knocking the boards off the windows with a 10 lb. sledgehammer he had found in the garage. The rest of the group was sweeping away cobwebs and dust.

"How did this house remain unoccupied for years without it being trashed?" Susan asked, as she flopped into a massive velour easy chair from which she'd just spent ten minutes knocking the dust.

"My mother had a friend who ran a real estate firm in town." Karin answered. "After mom died and I inherited the house, I paid the lady's agency to watch over the place, except in the summers when I usually spent a couple of months here. During the winters the agency pays the local sheriff to run anyone off who tries to squat in the place."

""You'd better give that agency a call and tell them you're here," Troy said. "I'm sure that Sheriff will come by as soon as anyone reports someone in the house." He turned and parted the curtains on the window, furtively eyeing the road leading past the house. "You can bet the Feebs have sent something out to every law enforcement agency in the country about us."

"Don't you think you're being paranoid?" Susan asked, in a dismissive tone.

Troy's expression showed his irritation. "They're gonna come after Derek; you can bet on it. The whole country saw him and heard what he said. Ferris isn't going to let Derek run around free and continue stirring up criticism of the government. He'll arrest Derek for violating the Patriot Act III as soon as he figures out where we are."

I thought Troy was right. Derek had stepped over the line in his speech to the Evangelicals, and his words had gone out over the national airwaves. Ferris and Reverend Goodson weren't going to let Derek say another word to anyone. They'd either quietly insure that he disappeared or make an example of him by arresting him and blasting a denunciation of his sins across all of the media.

I turned to Karin to echo Troy's advice about calling the real estate agency and realized she was no longer in the room. Josh was still outside making a racket clearing away the boards he had taken from the windows, and Derek had gone upstairs to unpack. I could hear someone rummaging in a back room and went to check. I heard Karin calling for Troy. He and I followed the sound of her voice to the back of the house.

"What are you doing?" I asked Karin, who was in the back of a walk-in storage closet, bent over one of several boxes that were strewn about the floor.

"Are any of these yours?," she asked, looking at Troy with a broad grin on her face. She pulled what looked like a discolored rag from one of the boxes and held it up, her eyes shining in triumph. "My mother's old clothes." What had looked like a rag, was actually a tie-dyed slip-over blouse, looking like something worn by a new-age freak at a Renaissance Faire.

"Holy shit," Troy exclaimed. "Are those really left over from the old days?"

"They were mom's." Karin's eyes were shining. "I kept them, but I was never sure why. Now I know why." She looked at both of us mischievously. "We can wear them as disguises!"

"Who wears that one?" I asked. "Troy or me? ... or Josh?"

Karin frowned. "There are men's clothes here too, you idiot—in other boxes. If we wear these we can go into town and no one will recognize us. They'll just think we're some of the locals." She stole a shy look at Troy. "And maybe some of the men's' clothes actually were yours."

Troy reached down and gave her a fatherly pat on the back. "It's going to be just like the old days when I put these things on. Let me know if you find any pot in there."

Karin looked alarmed. We both knew that Troy had given up drugs and alcohol years ago.

"Just kidding," Troy said, winking at his daughter.

"You may be kidding, but I wouldn't mind having a drink. Is there any liquor in this house? I asked..

"No," Karin answered. "But there's a great bar in the old Mendocino Hotel. Mom and her friends used to hang out there and listen to folk music."

"Ah, I remember it well," Troy said, a smile on his face. "Especially a night about… when were you born, Karin?"

"April 19, 1973"

"About nine months before that."

Karin blushed.

"You think these hippie clothes will really work as disguises?" I asked.

"Didn't you notice?" Karin answered. "That's how most of the middle aged people around here dress."

I shrugged. "I guess I don't have to miss out on the sixties after all." I remembered Troy's worry about the sheriff. "Troy said you need to call the real estate agency and let them know we're here so the sheriff doesn't come by to check on the house."

Her expression changed. " He's right. I need to call the agency right away. They'll let the sheriff know I'm here, and he doesn't have to check on the house any more. That should keep him away."

We were surprised by Derek entering the room. I think I and everyone else had thought that he was resting upstairs. We

246

forgot that he had amply demonstrated that he needed less rest than any of the rest of us.

'My compliments to you, Karin," Derek announced, standing in the middle of the room, surveying the boxes of clothing and the newly dusted furniture. "This is a very comfortable house in a picturesque setting—a perfect place to getaway. What are all these clothes? They look like they're left over from the sixties. Are these your mothers?"

Karin blushed but nodded. "I thought if we wore them we might attract less attention. This is still the type of dress people around here wear."

"So you think we need to hide," Derek said, looking straight at her.

"They're going to come after you," I answered.

"These people are paranoid," Susan said, entering the room and shooting a disgusted look at Karin and me. "If you go into hiding, your message to the American people is dead in the water."

"Paranoid my ass," Troy piped up. "As soon as the Feebs find out where we are, they'll send their jackbooted storm troopers right to this house. There's not going to be any chance to give any message to anyone. The only question is whether they'll arrest Derek or blow us all off the face of the planet as soon as they find us."

Karin and I nodded. We were watching Derek to see how he reacted.

Derek had been looking down at Karin, who was sitting on the floor, still absently going through her mother's clothing. He straightened up and looked past us and out the window. In the distance the surf was pounding against the outcroppings of rocks that jutted from the cliffs. Rhythmic fountains of white spray exploded above the turbulent gray sea. "This is not the destination I would have chosen if I was aiming to make a statement to the American public. I made that statement in Orange County, and now it's up to others such as Senator Williamson to carry that banner." He looked at us with the familiar twinkle in his eyes. " I believe the applicable phrase is 'a prophet is without honor in his own country.'"

"So you consider yourself a prophet?" I asked.

Derek thought for a moment, then shrugged. "I neither know the future nor speak for anyone greater than myself, though my words are influenced by those who came before me."

"Where will you go if no one is listening in this country?" Even though I asked, I knew his answer before he said it.

"I am going to Africa," he replied.

"What will you do in Africa?"

"I will start with trying to get my people to stop killing each other."

When he mentioned "his people," there was ring in Derek's voice that I had not heard before. It was the voice of someone who had a mission.

Susan's face showed her horror. "The power to make a difference in this world lies with America. How can you give up a chance to have that power?"

"Anyone who can stop the cruelty of one person toward another or prolong the life of innocent children or their parents will be making a difference. I believe I can do that where the need is greatest. That is in Africa."

Susan let out a long, defeated sigh.

"How do you get to Africa from here?" I asked.

Derek smiled. He walked back out of the storage room to the dining room where there was a worn armchair from which Tina had spent nearly a half-hour beating the dust. He sat down and looked up at the rest of us. "I plan to sit here and wait until the fervor over my speech subsides, then book a flight from San Francisco. In the meantime, I will weigh the wisdom of disguising myself as a hippie and walking the streets of this delightful little village."

Susan snorted in disgust and stormed out of the room. I decided it was time to pick out a pair of ragged jeans and flannel shirt. Maybe I could use one of those tie-dyed T-shirts for a do-rag. But what was I going to do for sandals?

Chapter 46

Nathaniel Broadmoor had an almost innate distaste for Jervis Donovan. Broadmoor considered himself a man of action and he found Donovan's arcane conniving abhorrent. Still, the presidential advisor had the ear of President Ferris and that made him more powerful than Broadmoor—and a man who had to be listened to.

"We know where Stewart is hiding," Donovan said. He was standing at the president's side, emphasizing his role as Ferris' right hand man, while he looked down his nose at the shorter CIA Director. Only the three of them were in the Oval Office.

"How can you know where he is? Neither my men nor the FIIEB have been able to find him since he left Orange County," Broadmoor asked. If Donovan really had found Derek Stewart, the CIA Director would be even more irritated at the pompous advisor.

"We've been able to infiltrate his closest group of advisors." Donovan answered. His face remained expressionless, so it was unclear if he found any satisfaction in having one-upped the CIA Director, but the fact that he used the word *infiltrate* gave Broadmoor the distinct impression that the presidential Advisor was implying that he'd done what the CIA was supposed to be doing. "Our person inside of his entourage called us and told us where he's hiding."

"How do you know that person can be trusted?" Donovan's matter-of-fact manner was even more irritating than if he had gloated. Broadmoor hoped that the advisor's information turned out to be a false lead and Donovan would end up with egg all over his face.

"I believe that's something your agency can ascertain." Donovan answered, looking for all the world as if the CIA Director's question was hardly worth his consideration.

"Why not use the FIIEB? I assume he's still in the United States. They can arrest him for violating the Patriot Act III in his speech in Orange County."

Donovan glanced at the president, who had been silent so far. The president gave his advisor a knowing look and turned his back to look out the window. Raindrops were streaming down the window panes, and nothing was visible through the heavy downpour outside.

"We don't want him arrested.," Donovan said. "We don't want any attention given to Stewart at all. We want him to disappear." He looked down at the swarthy CIA Director. "I believe your agency can handle that task—or have I overestimated your capability?"

Broadmoor's dark complexion deepened in color. Donovan was deliberately pushing him and he didn't like it. "We can do it. But isn't he with others?"

"They will all have to disappear."

"What about your informant?"

"Everyone."

Broadmoor glanced over at the president, who was still gazing out the window, as though he was absorbed by the pattern of raindrops on the glass. He was acting as if he was no part of the conversation, which was happening within three feet of where he was standing.

"Where is Stewart?" The CIA Director asked.

"Mendocino—the Northern California coast. They're in a house on the edge of the town. One of them, Karin Milne, the Georgetown professor, has a house there."

"How old is your information?" Broadmoor asked.

"We got a phone call this morning. They plan to stay awhile, then Stewart is going to leave the country and travel to Africa."

"And you want everyone taken out."

"Successfully this time. No attempts that have to be explained later." Donovan stared the CIA Director in the eyes, as if to make sure his meaning was clear. They both remembered the failed attempt to car bomb Stewart earlier.

"I don't need to be told how to do my work," Broadmoor answered through gritted teeth.

Donovan nodded. "Then get your people up there and do it."

The CIA Director nodded, waiting to see if the president was going to finally turn around and acknowledge the conversation that had just taken place. The president continued to stare at the rain on the window. Broadmoor nodded in the direction of the president's back and turned and left the room.

President Ferris turned around. "Once Stewart is out of the picture, there's no more excuses. I'm giving the order to nuke those Godless Muslim bastards," he said to his advisor.

"It's what we agreed on, Mr. president."

"With Stewart out of the way, there will be no credible voice of dissent left. We'll be able to do what I was elected to do—protect democracy."

Chapter 47

So far so good, I thought to myself, even though I felt like a pinhead in the outfit I was wearing. My faded jeans had holes in both the knees as well as in the butt and I had on a flowing orange and pink, long-sleeved cotton shirt, that I left unbuttoned so that my chest and belly were visible. Already, in just three days, I'd acquired a suntan and I had a good start on a beard. I still hadn't found any sandals, but I was wearing a pair of moccasins that were floppy enough to fit me and gave the appearance I wanted. No one even looked twice when I passed them on the sidewalks of Mendocino.

Derek had only ventured out a couple of times. He seemed content to walk the cliffs each day or sit on the porch looking out at the sea; I guess visioning his African roots or something like that. Karin and Troy accompanied me nearly every time I went to town, which had been a couple of times each day, partly out of boredom and partly to get supplies and see if anyone was talking about us being there. Nobody was.

Josh and Tina stayed at home to cook and watch over Derek. Susan was the only one of whom I wasn't sure in terms of what she was doing with herself. When I saw her at meals or when we all sat out of the porch or accompanied Derek on one of his walks, she looked pissed at all of us. She refused to wear one of the sixties costumes, and I knew she had gone to town a few times wearing her normal clothes. But she only looked like a tourist and I assumed her face wasn't well enough known for anyone to spy her and conclude that Derek must be nearby.

On our fourth afternoon in the town I found out I'd been wrong.

The Mendocino Hotel was well over a hundred years old and it had a suitably antique look, with a bar that was cozy and comfortable and was the gathering place for a lot of the locals and for soaking up town gossip. Karin and Troy and I pulled up chairs at our usual table in a dark corner of the bar and ordered drinks. Troy was still on the wagon, but Karin and I both ordered pints of the local beer, which had already made enough of a positive impression on me that the fact that the hotel bar had it on tap was sufficient to make me a patron in the middle of the every afternoon.

Troy had been haranguing the two of us on his favorite topic, which was how the Ferris administration was going to start a nuclear war before anyone who was against such a war or wanted to unseat the current group in power in Washington had a chance to do anything about it.

"I don't doubt that you're right about them wanting to do that, but would they really do such a thing if they knew public sentiment was against it?" Karin asked. Despite being a college professor and an expert on modern history and politics, Karin had begun deferring to Troy's opinion. I assumed her behavior was a way of acknowledging his paternity and I gave her a pass, though I ordinarily would have jumped all over her for not stating her own opinion more forcefully.

Troy enjoyed having an audience—especially his daughter. "They don't give a damn about public opinion unless it's going to get them booted out of office. They think God is on their side. This whole thing is less related to protecting us from terrorists than it is to defeating Islam as a religion and kicking the Arabs out of Jerusalem."

"What about the Jews in Jerusalem?" I asked. "Conservative Christianity has only been friendly to Jews since they decided that they needed Israel intact in order to fulfill the last days prophesies. But that will end up with only Christians in the Holy Lands, if I understand it right." I wasn't sure that I *did* understand conservative Christian beliefs and I wasn't even sure they *could* be understood.

"Luke makes a good point," Karin said, "surprising as that is." She gave me a saucy smile.

"I hate you," I said, giving an appraising look at her ghastly hippie apparel. "And your mother makes you wear funny clothes."

I expected to provoke a laugh, but when I looked at Karin's face, I saw that she was staring at the bar with a look of alarm. Two well-dressed men in dark suits had entered from the street and were walking toward the bar. Unless there was a film crew outside doing a remake of "Men in Black," the two were either Feebs or were from an even more sinister government agency. They scoured the afternoon clientele with their blankly accusing gazes but the three of us, looking like rejects from "Easy Rider" must have passed muster, so they turned to the bartender, a burly chap with tattoos on both arms who looked across the bar at them with a broad scowl on his face. Mendocino townies didn't like to be hassled by Feebs.

We were in earshot enough for me to hear one of the government men ask the bartender about new faces in town and to hear him answer back that it was tourist season and everyone in town was new. The agents didn't pursue the subject and left.

"We're in deep shit," Troy growled. "You can be sure they're looking for Derek."

"How could they know we're here?" Karin asked.

"Maybe it's routine," I said, not very convincingly. "Maybe they're just hassling the place because it's so full of anti-establishment types."

"Then they wouldn't have asked about new faces," Karin answered. She was right.

"Let's get back to the house and warn Derek." Troy said. "It's time for us all to leave."

"Leave for where?" I asked. "Where in the fuck can we go? This is the edge of the Goddamn world." I couldn't figure out how the government had ever picked Mendocino to look for Derek. Despite Karin's and Troy's nostalgia about the place, it was so out of the way that I as sure it was no more on the government's radar than was Dog patch, USA.

"We can get Derek out of here," Troy asserted confidently. "Let's just get the hell back to the house before the Feebs, or whomever they are, get there."

We paid and left the hotel. The three of us had walked to town, it being only four blocks from the house and because we'd decided that the Hummer was the most obvious sign of Derek's presence, especially since it belonged to the agency that had rented us the house in Newport Beach, so it had no doubt been reported stolen. As we came around the corner of a building we saw the two government agents ahead of us. They weren't alone. Four more clones were with the original two, gathered around a pair of black SUVs with their heads together in conference. We were only two blocks from Karin's house, and they were all looking in that direction, as if they were plotting their strategy.

"Let's take another street," I said. "We can circle back to the house from the other side.

Karin and Troy both nodded, and we walked as nonchalantly as we could in the other direction until we were out of sight of the six agents. Then we took off at a jog in a direction that would take us a few blocks away from them but eventually bring us to the other side of Karin's house. I was fervently hoping that Derek and the rest of our group were at home. We'd have to get out of there fast.

I was in better shape than I'd thought I was and so was Karin, but Troy was about to suffer a stroke or some other equally cataclysmic event by the time we reached Karin's house from the opposite side from the one the Feebs were on. I had to drag Troy up the side steps and into the kitchen. Karin was already inside and she'd gathered everyone together.

"The Feebs are here in town and they know where we are," I said. "We've probably got a matter of minutes before they descend on us."

"The rest of you don't need to be here," Derek said, his expression not the least bit frightened. He seemed absolutely calm in the face of looming disaster. "They want me and if you all go, they probably won't bother to come after you."

"They're not going to arrest you this time," Troy wheezed. He was still bent over and breathing in gasps. "They'll kill you, like they tried to do with the bomb in DC."

Derek didn't argue with him. "All the more reason for the rest of you to leave now," he said.

"What about Africa?" I asked.

My question took him off guard. He looked thoughtful. "I don't see how I can do that right now."

"You won't do it ever if they catch up to you," I answered. "I think Troy is right. They're going to kill you, not take you in."

"If they found us here, they'll have the airports covered for sure," Karin volunteered her face twisted in fear. "There's no way we can get Derek out of the country."

Troy put his hand around her shoulder. "Maybe your old man's got an idea," he managed to say between deep breaths.

"If you've got an idea, let's hear it," I said. "Before you keel over."

Troy looked over at Susan. "I don't want to talk in front of everyone."

"What are you talking about" I asked.

"The Feebs didn't just stumble on us," Troy said, his eyes still on Susan.

"Why are you looking at me?" Susan asked. Her voice was shaky.

"Those government men knew right where we were. They even seemed to know about this house," Troy said, his tone getting more and more angry. "I think you told them, Susan."

Susan's face showed her panic but her voice was defiant. "You're crazy. Why would I do that?"

"Because you know that you're not going to get Derek to run for office, and you don't want to throw away your career for a non-candidate," Troy answered, staring her down. "I think they offered you your own brand of 30 pieces of silver—probably a place in Ferris' next campaign—and you took it."

Susan was backing away from the group, her eyes searching the room in desperation. Josh advanced toward her and Tina began to move along the edge of the room to block the door.

"Susan, why don't you go," Derek said, holding up a hand to signal Josh and Tina to stand down. "You're future isn't with me or these people anyway."

Susan looked at Derek. "I'm sorry. You could have had it all. I would have helped you. I could have gotten you elected." She looked as if she was about to cry.

"Watch out," Derek said. "If those people were going to kill me, they won't want any witnesses. They'll try to kill you too, Susan."

"Troy's right. They offered me a job... in the next election," she said, helplessly.

"Be careful," Derek said. He sounded genuinely concerned for her.

Susan turned and went out of the kitchen. We heard the front door close.

"It'll take her about five minutes to reach the Feebs and tell them we're leaving," I said. "We've got to leave now. Troy you can tell us your plan when we get in the Hummer. I hope you really have one."

Josh was out the door and within seconds he had the Hummer out of the garage and parked at the side of the house with the motor running.

"Let's go," I said. "Leave everything behind."

We trooped out of the house and crammed ourselves into the Hummer. We all had just the clothes on our backs.

"Where to?" Josh asked.

"Take the highway north to Eureka," Troy said. "They bring in oil from overseas and unload it there. There's an oil tanker from Nigeria that leaves tomorrow for the Panama Canal and then back to Port Harcourt in the Gulf of Guinea."

"You've been reading the shipping reports?" I asked.

"I had this as a back-up plan. I've been keeping watch on all the ports, including San Francisco and Coos Bay up in Oregon. There's a lot more shipping traffic out of San Francisco, but Eureka's closer and I think the Feebs are less likely to think of it."

"For an old man, you amaze me," I said.

"I left here once myself, remember," Troy said.

"Port Harcourt is a good place to begin," Derek said, solemnly.

"Begin what?" I asked. I'd barely heard of the place.

"To stop the killing. In Nigeria it is one African killing another—mostly to obtain an advantage in the competition for oil revenues. The West is fueling the fight, but the local tribes have turned an economic war into ethnic battles that have killed thousands of people."

"What can *you* do?" I asked. I was experiencing a growing sense of dismay. It seemed to me that Derek was leaving the scene of the real issues here in America and heading off to tilt at African windmills. I suddenly realized I was thinking like Susan. I waited to hear what Derek had to say.

Derek was looking out the window. The mountains had receded to the East, and we were driving along a long low plateau that was increasingly populated with mini-malls and small towns as we reached the outskirts of the capital of Humboldt County. Occasionally we could glimpse the ocean off to our left. "I am the cousin of Robert N'gomo. My cousin is still known throughout Africa and he spoke of someone coming behind him. I will be that person. I will assume the mantle of my cousin's successor, and the leaders of the warring factions will meet with me. I will talk to them about peace. I will talk to them about making Africa strong."

"And you think they will listen?" Karin asked. She was pointing toward the exit for the Port of Humboldt Bay. Josh turned off the highway to follow the signs toward the docks.

Derek smiled then shrugged. "It is what I must do. I was given a second opportunity at life. I do not want to waste it on easy accomplishments." His smile became broader, as if he were sharing a joke with us.

"The United States will hunt you down," I said. "They have a heavy presence in Africa. You will be labeled a terrorist if you upset what Ferris and his cronies call the 'balance of power' in that region."

He shrugged again. "They will kill me if I stay here. The United States wants oil from that region of the world. Local wars and oil thievery are driving up oil prices in Nigeria. Why should the U.S. stop me if I try to stop the wars?"

"Maybe Senator Williamson can help you here in the U.S." Troy said. His face was serious but his voice was eager. "I'm going to make my way back to Oregon and join his campaign. If he can stay out of jail, he may be able to change things."

"That is a good place for you to be," Derek said, smiling at Troy. "Your voice is an important one, and Senator Williamson is a good man. He will listen to you."

I looked at Karin. She seemed frightened. She was still busy showing Josh how to find the port, but she was listening to Derek's words. She looked at Troy. I could see she was torn between her newfound relationship with her father and her allegiance to Derek. I was glad I didn't have such a conflict. "I'm going with you to Africa," I said.

Derek looked at me for a long moment. "Of course. How could you stop recording my biography when I am just embarking on my most significant journey?"

I was surprised. I had thought I would have to fight to remain with him.

"I am going along also," Tina said quietly. "My job is to protect you. It does not matter where I do that."

"Me too," said Josh from the front seat. "Africa is the home of my people, too."

"You are both most welcome to continue at my side," Derek said. "You only make me stronger."

There was a silence in the car. Finally it was broken by Karin directing Josh to park the Hummer. We had arrived a small pier lined with fishing boats.

"We can't go through the Port Authority," Troy explained. "We can charter a fishing boat to take us out to the tanker in the bay. We will negotiate directly with the Captain. It will be a matter of money, not official papers."

"You've done this before?" I asked, impressed by his knowledge of how to stow away on a merchant ship.

"This is how I got to Canada. I took one of these ships to Vancouver. I did some checking around town. This is how it's still done when people need to get out of the country unofficially."

"So much for port security," I said.

"I'll take the Hummer with me," Troy said. We were all sitting in the car, wanting to delay our parting. "I'll probably ditch it and find another way to get back to Oregon though. The Hummer's probably pretty hot by now."

I looked at Karin. She hadn't said what she was going to do.

"What is it? Africa or Oregon?" I asked. I didn't want to see her go, but finding her father after all these years had made her happier than I'd ever seen her.

She looked over at Derek, who laughed and gave her a knowing look as if they shared a secret and it was about me.

"What?" I asked.

"I'm going with you."

"How are you going to tutor with no library at your disposal?" I asked.

"Who needs to tutor? I'm going so I can be next to the man who is most important to me."

I was shocked. I knew she respected Derek, but I'd thought that her relationship with Troy was stronger. My surprise must have shown on my face.

"She's talking about you, Luke," Derek said, the smile still on his face.

I looked back at Karin. She was beaming at me. "Derek figures everything out." She looked over at Troy. "Is that OK?"

He was beaming at her like the proud parent that he was. "Sure," he said. "I like thinking of you and Luke together. He reminds me of me when I was younger."

I looked out at the oil tanker sitting at its mooring in the middle of the bay. At the dock a fleet of fishing trawlers beckoned. A small, weather-beaten general store that sold fishing gear and groceries stood at the top of the gangway leading down to the docks.

We piled out of the Hummer and headed toward the docks. All of us gave Troy a hug. We left him and Karin alone for a few moments. When she joined us there were tears running down her cheeks.

"OK, let's get on the boat," Karin said.

"Let me stop at the store first," I said .

"Beer?" Karin asked. I was encouraged that she didn't sound disapproving. It bode well for our future relationship.

"A pen and paper," I answered. "It's time to start writing some of this down."

Coming Soon!

Morality: Book Two—The Peacemaker

Chapter 1

A bright light flared briefly on the darkening Talusian horizon, like a fiery meteor cutting a luminescent swath through the atmosphere. For the length of a few seconds all eyes in the planet's Western hemisphere were riveted on the blazing evening sky. When the light died as suddenly as it had appeared, the Talusian population - 99% Aphorian natives and a lone contingent of Falstinian settlers from Talus' twin planet, Noruna - went back to making its preparations for the upcoming Talusian night, the mysterious illumination in the heavens having been dismissed and forgotten.

Like a cat stretching after a deep nap, Jason, having just been awakened after his long interstellar voyage in suspended animation, stretched his muscles, rubbed the heavy sleep from his eyes and worried for a moment that he might be sick, but then he remembered that he had been told to expect some vertigo and nausea upon waking from cryogenic sleep. He forced himself to ignore the agitated feeling in his intestines and to wait, motionless, until the dizziness in his head subsided, like a top slowly spinning to a halt. Then he deftly began to work the controls of his landing craft. His shallow deceleration had slowed the vessel sufficiently to allow the protective skin of the craft to cool and no longer to send angry flames of heat into the thickening atmosphere around it. The coordinates for his landing had been preprogrammed by the council scientists, and as the craft's proximity to the planet increased, the guidance of the ship would come under the complete control of the automatic pilot. Jason had nothing to do but to wait. The landing represented the goal for which his intense training had been aimed, from the time of his childhood until his departure on this flight.

When the landing craft had settled, crouching on its six leg-like supports as if it were a giant insect, with each of the intricately synchronized systems that had guided its delicate landing shut down and its invisibility cloak fully activated, Jason pressed the button that noiselessly slid open the hard metal cover over the vessel's wraparound window. Instantly, there was revealed a starry night sky, reaching down, in the distance, to thick, leafy treetops, looking in the night, like dark, irregular mounds of feathers. He felt a flutter of anxiety deep in his stomach, but he was relieved to see that no crowd of curious onlookers peered in at him from outside of his ship. His landing had attracted no attention from the local population. He knew that Aphorian defense systems were not sophisticated enough to have tracked his descent. The Falstinians, being more technologically sophisticated, had ample tracking capability, but he also knew that here on Talus they did not use it, for the simple reason that their enemy, the Aphorians, possessed no air or space vehicles other than small, insect-like, single-passenger solar powered craft, which they used for individual travel.

He picked up the bag of supplies, which he would need for his extra-vehicular mission, supplies which had stood ready for his departure from the craft since the day he had climbed aboard. It was a small backpack. He needed to carry very little with him. Both Talus and its sister planet, Noruna had breathable atmospheres and flora that were edible for someone of Jason's race. He wore light but sturdy, walking shoes, as he had brought no type of vehicle along with him on the voyage. His bag contained mostly antibiotics to protect him against any unforeseen infectious agents, although he had been inoculated against every disease the physicians on his planet had been aware might be found on either Talus or Noruna. Shouldering his backpack, he clamored down the landing craft's ladder and placed one tentative foot onto the ground. He felt the thrill of being on strange soil. The feeling was immediately replaced by a sense of panic as he realized that he was alone, light years away from anyone or anything familiar to him. He looked up at the sky, knowing that the effort to see his home planet, or even the distant star around which it orbited, was futile. The distance was too great. And high above him, in the center of the night sky, looking like a gigantic presence gazing down at him, was the pale blue sphere of Noruna, Talus' sister planet, its orbit only one and a half million miles from that of Talus, shining with the ghostly illumination of the reflected sun around which both of them spun. Although Jason had never viewed the present scene before, he sensed the eerie similarity of the view of Noruna in the night sky to that of his own planet's moon, the luminescent orb in the evening sky toward which he had gazed through all of the years of his young life.

He turned around for a final look at his spacecraft, the one token of his home planet that existed here on Talus. But once he had left contact with the craft, it was no longer visible, even to him. He carried a small device to remove the craft's cloaking mechanism so that he could find it when he returned, as well as a sensor, sewn beneath the skin of his forearm, to detect the ship's locating beacon, so he wouldn't lose contact with the craft altogether, no matter what distance he strayed from it. With some effort, he resisted pushing the button to remove the ship's cloaking mechanism, if only for a moment, telling himself that the sense of security he would derive from seeing this last reminder of home would be too fleeting and would only be an illusion. He was here on Talus and he was alone.

He felt a moment of disorientation. Where was the murmur of other voices, the sea of faces that had populated his entire life? Jason had always been surrounded by people – either his parents or his fellow students – all of whom were highly trained empaths just as he was. Their communication with one another was intuitive and instantaneous, often requiring no spoken words. Since the earliest time that he could remember, his own thoughts had been inextricably intertwined with those of the people around him, a virtual cacophony of ideas and feelings, through which he had had to learn to sift, like searching through static on a radio, in order to distinguish his own voice, his own thoughts. On his spacecraft, during his waking hours he had been wired into the communication system of the flight team back on his planet, which had guided his mission. But since he had landed, he had disengaged himself from that last link to the familiar voices of his home planet. And now, his own voice was all that he was left with. He was, for the first time in his life, completely alone.

He shivered, not from cold, but from a feeling of apprehension, which he knew was unreasonable and, if he dwelled upon it, would become loneliness, a feeling he had never experienced, but had somehow sensed as a possibility, like a mysterious creature waiting to accost him at some unknown moment. Loneliness had been impossible where he came from. But here, alone on a strange planet, it lurked, ready to descend upon him, in the back of his mind. There was nothing for him to do but to go forward.

The turf surrounding the craft was soft and spongy, like the floor of the gymnasium where he had worked out in preparation for his voyage. This region of Talus was one of the planet's rainiest, being in the foothills of a major mountain chain, and the hilltop on which his craft had landed was one of the few places in the area that was nearly barren of trees. Around him stretched a dense forest, like an impenetrable curtain of green, for hundreds of miles in all directions. It wasn't the most hospitable spot on the planet, but it was near an ancient and important Aphorian village and, just as crucially, within walking distance of the Falstinian settlement.

But it was the Aphorians with whom he was determined to establish his first contact.

At the bottom of the prominence on which his invisible craft now rested, a smooth, paved road wound its way around the base of the hill and headed into the jungle in the approximate direction of the Aphorian village. In the several minutes that had elapsed since his landing, no vehicles had passed on the road, so it was presumably not a main avenue of transportation, which was fine as far as Jason was concerned. He knew that he would attract attention, once he was seen, and he hoped that he could be as near to the village as possible when that happened.

Although the Aphorians were completely unaware of the existence of either Jason or his race, he knew a great deal about them. He looked much as they did, except for his darker complexion and brown hair. The Aphorians were, as a race, light skinned and blonde haired. The Falstinians, the race which had recently founded the first of what they planned to be a long string of settlements on Talus after more than a millennium of absence from the planet, were darker than Jason and had straight black hair, although they were not as dark as the Tontors, the third race of the two planets, who were very dark skinned with tightly curled black hair. Jason's complexion and his hair color and texture, though they resembled all of the three groups, were similar enough to each to make his appearance palatable to all of the local races, but also different enough to set him apart as not belonging to any one of them

Jason's appearance was no accident, since all of the sentient races discovered so far in the Galaxy shared basic physiognomic characteristics, although what small, mostly inconsequential differences that could be found had served as the basis for hostility, suspicion and deeply ingrained prejudices among the various peoples, often becoming the basis for vicious and destructive genocidal wars, which sometimes lasted for centuries. There were some among the great thinkers he had studied who believed that all of the higher life forms across the galaxy had originated from one race on a single planet, spreading, over eons, across the galaxy during long forgotten voyages of colonization. Others believed that a natural event, such as a collision between a planet and a large meteor may have spewed DNA containing material from the original planet into space, and eventually to other planets throughout the galaxy. Following such an event, the environmental conditions necessary to support life, which had restricted the development of higher life forms to a mere 100 out of the more than 10,000,000 potentially habitable planets within the galaxy, had also constrained the evolutionary options within an extremely narrow range, yielding similar species regardless of the planet on which they developed.

What set Jason apart from others, both the members of his race and of any other, was his trait of highly sensitive empathy. Jason was a *Peacemaker*, one of the select few of his race, the race which, from behind the shadows of vague myth and superstition, sensed by other inhabitants of the galaxy only as mysterious, perhaps supernatural beings, watched over those myriad worlds and insured the ongoing tranquility of interplanetary relations. There existed no pan-galactic government to settle disputes; the majority of the inhabited worlds did not even know of each other's existence. But some planets, such as Talus and Noruna, had achieved interplanetary travel and with that travel came the racial wars, similar to those that had occurred within the confines of nearly every populated world, but this time among planets, threatening the peace of the entire galaxy. This was where the Peacemakers came in. Without revealing their own origins, the Peacemakers extinguished the fires of interplanetary conflict by bringing the truculent parties together to engage in peace.

Jason knew that, when he was still an baby, he had been selected by the mysterious *Leaders* from his race, because of his profile on the neuroimaging tests administered to all of the infants of his planet. These tests had showed that Jason was one of the very few children whose developing brain contained that rare configuration of highly sensitive mirror neurons, the cerebral cells which allowed his brain to generate an internal replica of the reactions of others, and intricately developed connections of those neurons to the medial and orbital prefrontal, frontal, temporal-parietal, and somatosensory cortices, all of which, as he grew, would contribute to his extremely sensitive recognition of and response to others' feelings. Most importantly, these circuits showed rich connections to his cingulate cortex and his amygdala, the emotional bedrocks of his brain, causing him to sense such feelings almost as if he were having them himself. Jason's brain physiognomy was uniquely suited to the task of sensing what was going on in the minds of other beings. But in addition to the neurological prerequisites, he had not only passed, but scored in the top 0.01% of his race on complicated tests simulating social interactions. Such tests had showed that, even as an infant, he had reacted with his own distress to the distress of others and with his own joy to their signs of happiness – the signs of a true empath.

Because of these qualities, he had been raised, separately from the rest of his race's population, by surrogate parents, themselves chosen for their empathic abilities. In fact, because of his isolated upbringing within the *Psychae Academy*, where he had spent all of his growing years, other than his adoptive parents, Jason had never met any members of his race except his fellow students and teachers and the occasional *Leaders* or members of the *Council*, who paid their periodic visits to the academy - those and the team of scientists who had prepared him for this voyage.

The years before he reached puberty, years of which Jason possessed only a sketchy memory, were ones in which every child in the Psychae Academy received the same training. At puberty the students were divided into two groups, depending upon the one overriding characteristic of whether his or her empathy, the signature genetic trait that set all Academy students apart from everyone else of their race, was inclined toward generosity or suspicion. Those students, such as Jason, whose empathy was combined with generosity, would go on to *Amity*, the upper school where they would be taught to be Peacemakers, while those students who were more inclined toward suspiciousness would attend *Animus,* the upper school in which they would be taught to be interplanetary *spies*. These latter students, after they graduated, would be sent to other planets to collect and send back data on those planets' races, creating a comprehensive and detailed profile of every race that inhabited the galaxy.

What was Jason's home planet like? No matter how many times he had ruminated on that question, Jason had no answer. It was a question that was forbidden to be asked aloud within the Psychae Academy. Of course the students constantly whispered their queries to each other and secretly discussed their speculations among themselves, but their teachers refused to answer, instead always responding that, "we," that is, theirs and the students' race, "just are." Every student grew up knowing more about every other civilization in the galaxy than about his own. At least Jason's education had not been restricted to those planets to which he eventually would be sent. He had been told that this was because it was never clear where his talents might be needed, since any planet in the galaxy could, at least theoretically, interact with any other.

As Jason stepped onto the road leading to the Aphorian village – Betlem, he recalled was its name – he felt another momentary rush of disorientation, realizing that the pavement beneath his feet had been laid by another civilization, not his own. Despite all of his education regarding the various races of the galaxy, this was his first tangible evidence that someone other than his own people existed.

He thought about what he knew about the Aphorians. He knew them very well indeed. Although he had received a broad education in all of the civilizations of the galaxy he had spent his last two years studying the inhabitants of Talus and Noruna – that and honing his empathic skills until they were completely second nature to him. No matter how well he knew the details of the histories and cultures of the peoples he was about to meet, he knew that his knowledge of any individual within those cultures would depend upon his understanding how that person experienced his own world. Jason's task – the reason he was here – was to bring that level of understanding of each other to the Aphorians, the Falstinians and the Tontors. Jason's whole education, his raison d'être, and the entire philosophy of the Amity School was predicated on the premise that the only way to bring peace and avoid interplanetary war was to cause the warring parties to be able to view their worlds from each other's perspective. That was the lesson he had spent his life, up to this time, learning. Making peace was the purpose for which his life had been designed.

As he journeyed along the narrow road, barely wider than a paved footpath as it wound its way through the forest, Jason encountered no motorized vehicles, nor had he expected to. The Aphorians confined themselves to the use of bicycles and tiny solar-powered one- and two-person land and air vehicles for most of their personal transportation, although walking was the preferred mode of travel. Larger groups who needed to go some distance traveled in horse-drawn carts or occasionally in solar-powered mini-buses. Public transportation consisted of wind-driven ships and boats on the seas and waterways of the planet as well as larger solar-powered buses, which traveled on broader paved highways connecting the major cities. Jason knew that Betlem was historically important to the Aphorians, being the first of their settlements in the great inland reaches of the planet's main continent after their coastal communities had been inundated by the rising waters caused by global warming more than a thousand years ago. It was within an area, originally inhabited by Tontors and Falstinians, which had been abandoned by those races when they had fled to Noruna from the environmental catastrophe that had been destroying the planet. Despite its historical importance, because of its diminutive size, Betlem was not connected to any of the major public highways but only to small roads and walking and biking paths which fanned out like spokes on a bicycle wheel into the vast forest surrounding the town.

The complete lack of motorized vehicles powered by fossil-fuel-burning engines was characteristic of the Aphorian culture. The Aphorians had always co-existed symbiotically with nature – at least in their own regions of Talus. Their concentration upon harvesting plants grown in their natural environment, upon hunting only when they required food, these had been a part of their cultural and religious tradition from the most ancient times that anyone on the planet could remember, although during the latter years of the Tontor domination of the planet, they had been forced to adopt that race's more technological style of life. Even then, however, they had eschewed building large cities or ravaging forests or savannahs for the sake of building human structures. For all of these reasons they had always been regarded as backward by both the Tontors and the Falstinians. Moreover, such attitudes toward the Aphorians had led to their enslavement prior to the *Great Migration*. The Tontors had built great cities, but it was the Aphorians who had supplied the labor – slave labor.

The Tontors were conquerors. They had conquered the almost defenseless Aphorians and put them to work doing the manual labor that Tontor people felt was beneath them as the superior race of the planet. But the Tontors did not stop with their conquest of the Aphorians. They had also subdued the peaceful and thoughtful Falstinians, the race that had valued learning and science, but which had a tradition of not waging war. The Falstinians too had been enslaved by the Tontors, not to do manual labor but to serve as teachers, tutors, and scientific advisors on Tontor projects to extend the control of the conquering race over the land and seas of Talus.

Two thousand years ago, Talusian civilization had thrived, at least by Tontorian standards. Cities had replaced the majestic virgin forests; sprawling housing developments, extending like vast children's toy constructions for miles without interruption, had replaced the great plains of the planet. The fossil fuels buried beneath the planet's surface had been mined on land, beneath the mountains and at the greatest depths of the oceans. Those fossil fuels had supplied the energy for transportation and power to keep the vast technological civilization churning. Every Tontor had possessed a vehicle and many Tontors had possessed several of them. Transportation had included land, air and sea vehicles, all powered by fossil fuels. Eventually, the Tontorian technology, built upon Falstinian science, succeeded in developing the means to leave the planet, which had allowed the founding of settlements and mining operations on the nearest neighboring planet, Noruna, slightly smaller and unpopulated, but similar to Talus in terms of suitability for habitation.

Unfortunately, there had been costs associated with Tontorian progress. Thousands of species of both plants and animals native to Talus had become extinct or nearly so. Air quality across the planet had degenerated to the point that lung diseases became a major cause of death and disability. The Tontors had tried to protect themselves and their Falstinian thinkers by building gigantic structures over their cities, bubble-like enclosures, which allowed in light and air but discharged pollution to the environment outside – the environment in which the Aphorians, even their Aphorian slaves, still lived.

When greenhouse gases shifted the balance of CO_2 and oxygen in the atmosphere and the planet began to warm, melting polar icecaps, raising ocean levels – oceans that had become so polluted that half of the species of fish and other sea life which had inhabited them had disappeared – and flooding great expanses of low-lying, inhabited land, the Tontors knew that it was time to leave Talus. The Falstinians agreed.

Using Falstinian science, Tontorian technological skills and Aphorian labor, the inhabitants of Talus built the means to export the entire population of Talus to Noruna. Only the Aphorians, valuing their freedom more than their safety, had stayed behind, no longer slaves to any other race on a planet abandoned by everyone but themselves.

Agreeing that the scientific-technological world they were importing to Noruna was no longer as dependent upon manual labor as the civilizing of Talus had been, the Tontors and Falstinians had been content to leave behind the bulk of the Aphorian population, adrift like castaways, on their dying world. They brought to Noruna only sufficient Aphorian slaves to serve them as household servants and to do the menial labor that had not yet been eliminated from such tasks as mining and farming.

Jason remembered his history lessons about the divergent pathways the civilizations on the two planets had taken after the *Great Migration*, which was now more than a thousand years in the past. The Tontors had learned few lessons from their near destruction of Talus. They were destroying the environment of Noruna at a slower pace, but destroying it they still were, because of the continued reverence of their culture for technological progress and building. Slavery had been done away with, although the Tontors still regarded themselves as the superior race. But segments within their own population, convinced by Falstinian arguments and the inexorable inclusion of Falstinians into greater and greater participation in their society, believed that slavery of one race by another was an unethical practice and had succeeded in having it prohibited nearly two centuries ago. The Falstinians were the first to be freed from their Tontor masters, and within another 100 years, the relinquishment of slaves was extended to the small population of Aphorians living on Noruna.

Prejudice and discrimination toward both Falstinians and Aphorians were still evident in cultural practices such as the discouragement of interracial marriage, exclusion of anyone but Tontors from the highest levels of government office, and proscriptions against including Falstinians and Aphorians in some social organizations. While Falstinians were overrepresented in the universities and academies because of their overriding penchant for scholarship and study, Aphorians were markedly underrepresented, a result of the inferior schools they were forced to attend in the poor ghettos where most of them lived, a fact which Tontors and Falstinians ignored when they pointed to the lack of Aphorian scholars as evidence of their limited capabilities.

Jason reminded himself of all of these facts as he walked along the narrow road. He looked to either side at the dense semi-tropical forest through which the road meandered and thought about Talus. The planet had not been destroyed, although it had come dangerously close to becoming uninhabitable. The Aphorians had now spread across the planet, having been forced to leave their original centers of habitation along the coasts of one of the planet's largest continents- coasts that had become permanently flooded when the oceans rose and remained at their higher levels, creating massive shallow bays and inlets where farmlands and villages had once existed. They now occupied portions of the grassy and forested areas in the interiors of all of the continents - lands that had been deforested or turned into near deserts by the Tontors and Falstinians and had been nursed back into fertility by careful Aphorian husbandry.

Talus had recovered from the ecological disaster that had caused the Great Migration. The Aphorians who had remained on the planet had learned the lessons from the practices of those who had left. They had learned that they must live within the constraints of the planet's ecological limits, not violate those boundaries. That is why they eschewed any use of fossil fuels, relying exclusively on solar, wind, and water power. They had few factories and conducted most of their manufacturing on a small, local scale. They had continued farming, but without the use of herbicides or pesticides or artificial fertilizers, relying, in place of the latter, upon extensive use of recycled animal and even human waste. Perhaps because they associated the building of vast cities and enormous structures with the destructive practices of the Tontors, the Aphorians continued their practice of living in relatively small communities, residing in houses built from natural materials such as wood and stone, no larger than what was required to be functional.

Because of its lack of large cities and manufacturing centers, the Aphorian civilization that had remained on Talus and witnessed its ecological rebirth, was regarded by the Tontors and Falstinians on Noruna as hopelessly primitive and a confirmation of their belief that the Aphorians, as a race, were backward. But the inhabitants of Noruna were ignorant of the Aphorian educational system, which stressed knowledge of nature, of animal behavior, of chemistry, of the biology of Talusian plant life, and of the their own racial instincts, which had to be either cultivated or mastered in order to live peacefully in their world. The Aphorians had not turned their back on science; they had simply emphasized the natural and biological sciences. Higher education was restricted to the brightest of the Aphorian youth, who received training at the planet's Eco-University, where they engaged in intense study of the science and technology necessary for their people to continue to live within the natural environment of Talus without destroying it as the Tontors had done. The rest of the population was composed of farmers, herdsmen and highly skilled artisans and craftsmen. The Aphorian society was a confederation of small communities, which only came together twice a year to discuss and agree upon how to interact with each other and how to live together on their planet. No one community or group had authority over another. All voices were heard at these semi-annual meetings. The only laws that were honored by everyone were those promulgated by the Faculty Senate of the Eco-University – laws that had been designed by the intellectual elite of their race and were designed to insure the survival of the planet's environment.

Jason continued his solitary nocturnal trek along the narrow roadway as it wound its way through the forest. Around him could be heard the sounds of night animals, small skitterings, sudden crashing sounds, occasional squeals and once, the unmistakable growl of a large predatory cat, no doubt prowling the deep jungle looking for food. He was unarmed and he hoped that his quiet progress along the road would not attract the attention of any dangerous, carnivorous creatures. There was a natural wildness about the Talusian forest, even in an area near to human habitation as this was, which Jason found both exhilarating and frightening. His surroundings, when he had been growing up, had been entirely civilized and shaped by the hand of men.

He savored the sweet smell of summer flowers in the warm night air. The gentle breeze brushing his skin intensified his sense of being alone at the mercy of the elements of a foreign planet. Jason had never felt himself this close to nature. The Aphorians had done everything in their power to bring back the planet's endangered species, both animal and vegetable, and to foster their growth, leaving most of the species' natural habitats alone except when it was necessary to hunt for food; and even then, their hunting was restricted to only fully replenished and viable species. The difference between the habitations of men and those of the rest of the creatures of the planet was less marked on Talus than anything Jason had ever experienced in his life.

The sound of something approaching along the roadway behind him alerted Jason…

About the Author

Following along and distinguished career as a research and clinical psychologist, a university professor and dean, and many years of with service in the field of public mental health, Casey Dorman turned to the field of literature. He is the Editor-in-Chief of Lost Coast Review, a quarterly journal of short stories, poetry, book and film review and opinion. He is also the author of the mystery, "Pink Carnation," and the Nyles Monahan mystery series, which includes "I, Carlos" and "Chasing Tales," as well as the Brian O'Reilly, Cruise Ship Mystery series, which includes "Appointment in Mykonos" He is also the author of "Unquity," a literary romance novel and the historical thriller, "Prisoner's Dilemma: The Deadliest Game. He lives with his wife Lai in Newport Beach, California.